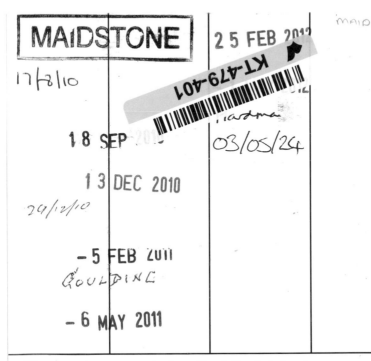

A KIKI LOWENSTEIN SCRAP-N-CRAFT
MYSTERY

# CUT, CROP & DIE

## JOANNA CAMPBELL SLAN

**WHEELER
CHIVERS**

This Large Print edition is published by Wheeler Publishing, Waterville, Maine, USA and by BBC Audiobooks Ltd, Bath, England.
Wheeler Publishing, a part of Gale, Cengage Learning.
Copyright © 2009 by Joanna Campbell Slan.
The moral right of the author has been asserted.

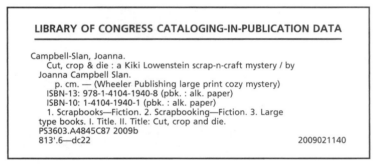

LIBRARY OF CONGRESS CATALOGING-IN-PUBLICATION DATA

Campbell-Slan, Joanna.
    Cut, crop & die : a Kiki Lowenstein scrap-n-craft mystery / by Joanna Campbell Slan.
        p. cm. — (Wheeler Publishing large print cozy mystery)
    ISBN-13: 978-1-4104-1940-8 (pbk. : alk. paper)
    ISBN-10: 1-4104-1940-1 (pbk. : alk. paper)
    1. Scrapbooks—Fiction. 2. Scrapbooking—Fiction. 3. Large type books. I. Title. II. Title: Cut, crop and die.
    PS3603.A4845C87 2009b
    813'.6—dc22                                                    2009021140

BRITISH LIBRARY CATALOGUING-IN-PUBLICATION DATA AVAILABLE

Published in 2009 in the U.S. by arrangement with Midnight Ink, an imprint of Llewellyn Publications, Woodbury, MN 55125-2989 USA.
Published in 2010 in the U.K. by arrangement with Llewellyn Worldwide Ltd.

U.K. Hardcover: 978 1 408 45752 8 (Chivers Large Print)
U.K. Softcover: 978 1 408 45753 5 (Camden Large Print)

Printed in the United States of America
1 2 3 4 5 6 7 13 12 11 10 09

For my gorgeous and talented son, Michael Harrison Slan. I'm going to miss you, sweetheart, while you're off at college. Please call me! Love, Mom.

# ONE

"All we're missing is a corpse." I hadn't realized I was thinking out loud until Mert Chambers, my best friend, stopped in her tracks. She turned and nearly crashed into me. We were both carrying heavy cardboard boxes of supplies, so our inept maneuver had a Keystone Kop clumsiness.

"Why, Kiki Lowenstein, I can't believe you said that! I think all these flowers are beautiful," said Mert, as we continued our trek down the short flight of stairs into a church basement. She smiled at the big pots of day lilies we'd purchased to give away as door prizes.

"It's the smell," I explained. "When my eyes are closed, all I see are caskets and corpses. Plus, I haven't been in a church since my father died." The slightly dank basement brought back horrible memories.

That said, I had to admit we'd been lucky Mert was able to find us a place so close to the Missouri Botanical Garden and willing to let us hold a crop — a scrapbooking event — in their basement for a small donation.

Our boss, Dodie Goldfader, wagged a finger at me. "Knock it off with the morbid talk. We can't risk customers hearing you."

Dodie owns Time in a Bottle, nicknamed TinaB by those in the know. At six feet tall, she towers over Mert and me and walks like that cartoon version of the Abominable Snowman.

After shushing me, Dodie glanced pointedly over her shoulder. Women were filing in, towing their picnic coolers and Cropper Hoppers, rolling suitcases full of papercrafting materials. "The shuttle bus from the Botanical Garden has arrived!" Dodie sang out with delight. "Ladies, did you enjoy your tours?"

Women nodded and chattered happily. They staked out places at long tables covered with white butcher paper to create a clean surface. Some opened their supplies and started to work on pages immediately. Others shared the photos they'd just taken by handing around their digital cameras. Many of our guests had never seen the Jenkins Daylily Garden in full flower. The women were chatting happily about the glorious sight of all 1,350 different varieties of Hemerocallis (Greek for "beauty for a day") spreading their luxe petals toward the sun.

Nicknamed "Shaw's Garden" after Henry Shaw, the Englishman who in 1859 opened his personal place of refuge to the public, the Missouri Botanical Garden is considered one of the three great gardens of the world. It's the oldest continuously operating display conservatory in the United States. Part of my prep for this outing was spending an entire day roaming the grounds last week. I familiarized myself with what was blooming, taking photos to help me design page layouts, some of the best work I'd ever done.

I should have been in a great mood, but I wasn't.

Dodie pulled me aside and whispered, "This is a prime moneymaking event for us. Don't you dare spoil it! I've worked all year to be included in the Crop Around Missouri Program. When these scrappers think special events, I want Time in a Bottle to be the first name that pops into their heads."

"I know, I know. Sorry." I grumbled. I'd had a rough morning with my pre-teen daughter. Lately I couldn't do anything right. Her hormones must be going bonkers because Anya had become increasingly moody. I was trying to stay calm, but geez, she was wearing me down.

And yes, I was sleep-deprived. Everyone associated with TinaB — Mert, Dodie, our new hire Bama, and I — had baked dozens of goodies for this gathering. I personally had contributed three dozen Snicker-doodles. We'd all delivered our treats to Mert's house the night before. Because she's such an early riser and because she had room in her truck, Mert offered to bring over our food, pick up more groceries, and with the help of her son, set up tables before the rest of us showed up.

That freed Dodie and me to concentrate on paper, supplies, and tools. Bama was in charge of working with the caterer. Scrap-bookers are a hungry group, so relying on the caterer for the more complicated food items such as breakfast sandwiches, quiches, and crepes, would keep our costs down. In an effort to be "green," we'd also arranged to rent glasses and plates rather than produce more paper waste.

Mert had seen Dodie corner me. She figured I'd been chastised. She came over and worked beside me. In a cheery voice she preached, "You know, they call it the present 'cause every day is a gift."

"Thank you, Dr. Phil-lis." She was right — but then, isn't she always? It's a quality

10

both endearing and exasperating.

Despite the hormonal harpy living in my house, life was good, and so was business. Since coming to work at TinaB, I'd "grown" a small but dedicated following of customers. If things went well, this outing would bring more scrappers into the fold. My notepad listed the names of nearly fifty patrons — many new to our business. I'd designed papercraft kits — "make and takes" — for each of our guests to turn into dazzling pages.

That's my job — I'm a professional scrapbooker. Ever since my husband, George, was killed last fall, my former hobby has supported me and my eleven-year-old daughter, Anya. Although we don't live in the style to which we had been accustomed, we are getting by. Before George died, I used to be Dodie Goldfader's best customer. And until recently, I used to be her best employee. That was another reason I was grouchy. She'd gone and hired Bama Vess without consulting me. Okay. So TinaB was a sole proprietorship, and Dodie was the owner. It still rankled. To add insult to injury, Bama didn't seem to want to be friends. She simply did her work and went home.

That hurt.

Thank goodness for Mert.

Before my personal series of unfortunate events, I had employed Mert as my house-cleaner. Now I work part-time in her dogsitting business. I'm comfortable with the change of roles. Mert's a thick and thin friend, the type who stands by you no matter what. She was working the crop because Dodie needed the extra help.

As Mert flitted around, she garnered plenty of admiring glances. She likes to "display the merchandise." Her halter top was florid orange with red, tangerine, and pink bangles around the neckline. Her shiny chintz Capri pants were of a matching colorful print.

My attire sure could be more daring. I wore a pair of khaki slacks from Target with a shirred cream short-sleeved blouse I'd rescued from Goodwill. I looked okay . . . but a safe okay, just this side of drab.

Not that my employer cares. From behind, it's tough to tell whether Dodie is animal, vegetable, or mineral. She's hairy, lumpy and shaped like a rock formation. But she's also a great person to work for and despite her terse manner, she's a sweetheart.

Dodie asked, "Where's Bama?"

Scrapbookers were flooding in and setting up their supplies. But Bama was nowhere to be found. That suited me down to the ground.

"Shoot," Mert said when we had talked the day before. "You're jealous. You liked being the one and only star at the store. You've got your panties in a wad because you have to share the limelight!"

"Not so. I'm being protective of my employer. There's something not right about that woman. Bama never looks me in the eye. I swear, what is she hiding? And she weaves like a drunk."

That was my public complaint. My private beef was Bama had an art degree and I had . . . bupkis. Everything I'd learned about scrapbooking came from trial and error, studying magazines, and educating myself about products and techniques. Seemed to me, in a twisted sort of way, Bama earned her stripes too easily. Even so, I knew I wasn't being fair.

Mert had it right: I was jealous. I admit. I'm insecure. I was scared I'd lose my job. I've only ever been good at two things in life: scrapbooking and getting pregnant. For the first time in my thirty-three years, I was gainfully employed, responsible for my own welfare, and getting compliments. If I was overly protective of my new life, I had reason to be.

Dodie interrupted my thoughts. "I told Bama to be here no later than ten. The tours of the Botanical Garden should have ended. The last shuttle bus is due any minute. Where is she? These women are going to want to eat quickly and start on our special projects!"

She was right. I'd seen them eying the food on the serving table. They were being polite and waiting for us to give them the "go ahead," but we needed to get this show on the road. Bama was running late with the more substantial hot offerings.

Right on cue, Bama's dramatic voice echoed down the hall. "Set up warming trays along the far table." She waved a chart at workers who followed. A phalanx of young people with polo shirts bearing the name "The Catering Company" filed in carrying oversized metal pans. Our final shuttle bus must have arrived at the same time as the caterers because a handful of our guests had been pressed into service. Scrapbookers were balancing aluminum tins of food on the tops of their Cropper Hoppers and carrying coolers marked with The Catering Company's logo.

I'll give her this: Bama sure knew how to make an entrance. She also knew how to dress. Today pencil-thin black jeans scrunched over the top of pointy-toed boots. A sparkling brooch of jet-black beads gathered the simple neckline on her T-shirt into an asymmetrical shape, forming a sort of jaunty, impromptu V-neck. She couldn't have projected an artistic image better if she'd slapped a black beret on the crown of her head and spoken with a French accent.

As Bama directed food placement, she steadied herself by keeping one hand on the edge of the tables or against the wall. What was it? Drugs? Booze? A part of me was dying to know while another part was ashamed of my mean-spiritedness.

The noise and activity level rose along with the sensuous aroma of bacon and cheese. The caterers finished lighting the Sterno and headed out of the building. I felt a rush of happy excitement. My efforts were about to pay off. I'm not bragging when I say that I had a bit of a reputation around town. My work has been published in all the big scrapbook magazines. The page kits I'd created for this outing represented my best efforts. Dodie had lobbied hard for membership in the Crop Around Missouri Program (CAMP), a coalition of area independent retailers. Since independents don't have the buying power or ad budget of big chains, we have to find other ways to keep our customers happy. So the store owners created CAMP to pool their resources. They all put aside their differences . . . all of them, that is, except Ellen Harmon, owner of Memories First. Ellen seemed determined to cause dissension and trouble. Worse yet, Dodie and I had noticed whatever classes we offered, Ellen copied immediately — at a lower price.

Standing up and waving for attention, Ellen started the crop five minutes early. "Welcome everyone! Let me talk, then you can eat!" The women fell silent watching her expectantly. Dodie and I exchanged shocked glances. This was our crop. It was customary for the hosting store to start the festivities. Ellen had just robbed Dodie of the privilege of greeting the crowd.

Everyone's eyes were on Ellen as she announced, "As all of you know, the most prestigious contest in scrapbooking is the Scrapbook Stars competition held by *Saving Memories* magazine. Thousands of scrapbookers enter each year." Ellen paused to give her words full effect. "We are delighted to announce that one of our Memories First Design Team members has been named a Scrapbook Star! Let's hear it for . . . Yvonne Gaynor!"

A cheer erupted from the crowd, and

16

Yvonne stood to acknowledge the applause.

Ellen hadn't finished. "Yvonne's winning pages are on the magazine website. She'll be teaching exclusively for my store, Memories First. Class space is available on a first-come, first-serve basis." Here Ellen paused to stare directly at me. "Yvonne is a unique talent in an industry full of copycats."

I bit my tongue as I felt my face turn red. Boy, that was rich. Calling me a copycat? What colossal nerve!

Shake it off, I warned myself. You don't want these women to know how upset you are!

Ellen gestured at the serving tables. "Now . . . we have lots of yummy food and fun pages for you. Yvonne, why don't you lead the way to *our* brunch?"

There we stood, Dodie, Mert, Bama, and I, feeling like uninvited kids sneaking peeks at a popular girl's birthday party. We'd organized this whole event — and for what? For Ellen Harmon to take over? For her to call me a copycat and slip in an advertisement for her store? None of us spoke up because — how could we? Anything we'd say would make us come off like poor sports.

Bama, Mert and I shuffled off to one side. Fortunately, Dodie knew how to handle this. Our boss tinkled a spoon against a glass and shushed the crowd. "All of us at Time in a Bottle want to add our congratulations. Let's hear it for Yvonne! Hip-hip-hooray!"

Mert and I followed her lead and raised our water glasses high. Bama hesitated before chiming in, plastering a painful grin on her face.

Now Ellen's expression turned sour. She knew exactly what we were doing. When giving credit, the rule is: The person giving credit has more stature than the person receiving. Time in a Bottle had regained the high ground.

"Please, help yourself to the food! Eat up!" Dodie motioned to the tables. "Kiki Lowenstein will explain our first project as soon as you all have food."

"Nice save," I muttered to my boss as women streamed past with plates in hand. At the front of the line was Yvonne, scooping up an obscene number of scones and cookies.

Her best pals, Nettie Klasser and Rena Rimmel, walked in the new star's wake. Rena piled her plate high but Nettie was more selective, picking only a few items and pausing to wipe her nose.

Dodie whispered in my ear, "I don't care what contest she won; I'm glad I fired

Yvonne as a customer."

I remembered the day Dodie told Yvonne her business was no longer welcome. Her vow never to buy from us again came as a relief. We were even more pleased when Yvonne's friends made it clear they didn't intend to leave with her.

"Hey, we know her faults," said Rena as she signed up for a crop. "We're her friends, but we aren't clueless."

"That's right. She's not a very nice person." Nettie was a shy scrapper who liked to stop by early mornings when our store was practically empty.

Now it was my turn to save face. Walking over to the new celebrity, I managed a warm smile. "Yvonne, that's great news about the contest. Congratulations again." Yvonne barely nodded to me and didn't stop eating.

But I was determined to be gracious. "Did you all drive over together?" They nodded. "How fun. Rena, is that the new stapler you can use anywhere on your page? I've been meaning to try that," I lied. Heck, I'd been using one for ages. "Hey, Nettie, good to see you. What are you working on today?"

"I'm sorting photos." Nettie removed her white cotton gloves so she could blow her nose. Dedicated hobbyists wear white cotton gloves to protect the surfaces of our

19

photos from oil and dirt on our skin. Nettie sniffled and reached for a Mountain Dew. "Sorry. With all the rain we've had, the mold count is unbelievable."

"Why don't I take your empty plates so you can go back for more? Are you finished?" I was going to be helpful if it killed me.

Nettie nodded. Rena pointed to a stack of cookies and shook her head no. Yvonne was still cramming her mouth. She spread a hand over her orange scone to warn me away.

I had taken two steps toward the dirty dish cart when I heard a glass hit the floor behind me.

I whirled around to see Yvonne's hands moving across the table, searching blindly, knocking her plate and utensils to the floor in ineffective sweeps. I tossed the dirty plate at the cart and ran to her side. A wheezing sound rumbled deep inside her.

"Get help! Call 911!" I yelled to Dodie.

"Are you choking?" I asked Yvonne.

She answered by shaking her head, banging the table with her hands and whimpering. "Urs! Urs!" Nettie offered her friend a glass of water.

That flew all over us and the floor. Yvonne slammed against the back of her seat, legs moving wildly. Finally she grabbed her purse from under her chair. I watched her dump the contents of her handbag. Yvonne's fingers raced through the mess, discarding this and that. Tissues, lipstick, wallet, cell phone, pencil, notebook, checkbook all went flying by. Time seemed to slow down.

Yvonne pulled a yellow box from the clutter. Her skin was a dusky shade; her lips were trembling. She unscrewed a cap. A tube fell apart in her hands, exposing a syringe. Holding the implement like a hammer, she swung her arm wide and jammed the needle through her slacks into her leg. Her eyes were wide with fright.

With a clatter, the needle dropped from her hand and rolled across the floor.

Yvonne slumped to one side and slid toward the floor. Her friends and I grabbed at her, trying to soften her impact. She wheezed, bucked, and wheezed some more. I tried to raise her head, in the hope it would help her breathe.

The Emergency Medical Service crew arrived. They pushed us aside, stepping forward to work on her, asking questions, examining one of those silver Medical Alert bracelets on her wrist, checking her vitals, and moving in a synchronized blur.

I stepped away, shaking my head in horror. Mert took me by the arm. "This don't look good," she said. "Not at all."

# TWO

"What on earth happened at your crop?" asked Sheila Lowenstein. Dressed in tailored pants and a white sleeveless silk blouse, my mother-in-law knelt on a foam pad in the middle of her lawn, a box of moth balls within easy reach and a trowel in her hand. "I'm sick of these moles making a mess of my yard," she offered by way of explanation.

My daughter was nowhere in sight. Anya probably didn't appreciate her grandmother's efforts to scare off the intruders taking over her pristine lawn. My kid was a budding animal rights activist. She was rooting for the critters.

Sheila said, "It's been all over the news. There couldn't possibly have been two large scrapbook meetings over by the Botanical Garden."

Every local station buzzed with reports of a woman dying at a scrapbook event. I finally gave up punching buttons and turned off the car radio rather than listen to more speculation about Yvonne Gaynor.

"Our guest went into allergic shock. Anaphylaxis. It happened so quickly." I watched Sheila jabbing her trowel into a clump of grass. "Can I help?"

She bashed the green leaves with her tool. "Drat, drat, and double drat. I hate these moles. Mr. Sanchez would know what to do, but he's in Mexico for his granddaughter's Quinceañera."

Sounded like a great escape plan to me. Sheila could be notoriously hard to please. I retrieved a screwdriver from my car, used a stack of old newspapers headed for recycling as a kneeling pad, and knelt down beside her. My tool formed a hole in the soil. I shoved mothballs down the dirt tube. Finally, I pressed the parted grass together to lock in the aromatic critter chaser.

"That's right. Mothballs every foot or so ought to stink these nasty varmints out of house and home." Sheila paused to wipe her brow with an embroidered linen handkerchief. "And that woman didn't have one of those pens with her? The kind where you give yourself a shot? If she didn't, she was a fool."

"She did, but it was empty." I turned my

face to hide any wry twist of my mouth. Good old Sheila. She certainly didn't bother to censor herself or think twice about sounding cruel. Despite the color all around us — or perhaps to counterbalance it — Sheila's world was black and white. Fortunately, these days I was on her good side. I'd been on the other end of her sliding scale, and believe me, it wasn't much fun.

"How stupid! People with severe allergies generally know what to avoid. For an anaphylactic reaction to occur, you must have been exposed in the past to the substance that causes the reaction, the antigen. The process is called sensitization."

I didn't know she was so knowledgeable about severe allergic reactions. In many ways, Sheila and I were just getting acquainted with each other even though I'd been married to her only child, George, for nearly twelve years before he died. "Right. That's what the medic said. Yvonne carried a kit with a premeasured dose of epinephrine, to rapidly reverse the most serious symptoms — but the syringe was empty. She reached for it while she was flailing around. Managed to grab the Epi-Pen and inject herself, too, but it was empty. By the time help arrived, it was . . . too late."

Sheila shook her head and waved away

25

any compassion lingering in the air, "What an idiot. She was asking for it. What sort of extremely allergic dope would run around with an empty Epi kit?"

I sighed. I do that a lot. "Beats me." I winced, "All I can say is . . . her death sure put a damper on our special event. It was awful. And afterward, we were questioned by the police —"

"The police!" Sheila punctuated her statement with a stomp, mashing down the hillock the moles had formed.

"It's procedure. After all, the death was unexpected. The officers were pretty nice about the whole thing, really. You know, the cops weren't much of a problem. The real crisis came as the scrapbookers realized their day had been ruined. Ellen Harmon made sure to complain long and loud. Not only had she lost her 'star' scrapbooker, but to hear her tell it, we were to blame for Yvonne's death."

Again Sheila waved away the problem. "That's ridiculous. How could you be responsible for a woman dying unexpectedly? Honestly, some people don't have the brains God gave a flea." She paused to study me. "You can't concern yourself about this. For goodness sake, even if one trouble-maker whines about this . . . this inconvenience . . . how could it possibly reflect poorly on you? Or on Dodie Goldfader?"

Inconvenience? Again, I turned away and counted mothballs. This time I bit my lip hard. A person going into spasms as she fought for oxygen was much more than . . . inconvenient.

"Kiki?" Sheila demanded an answer. "How could this reflect poorly on you?"

"It shouldn't. You are right; we weren't to blame. It's just that the whole thing happened on our watch, at our event. It's kind of like shooting the messenger," I said. "The fact that these potential new customers will link our name with Yvonne's death is . . . unfortunate. It's exactly the opposite of what we'd planned to have happen. We wanted them to think of Time in a Bottle and remember what a great experience they'd had. Now . . . well, now I worry that our name will conjure up . . . uh . . . horrible images."

Sheila's turn to sigh. "People can be so petty."

Oh golly. Coming from her, that was almost too much to take. Given her past behavior, Sheila was a great one to talk. Other people had prayer lists; Sheila had a grudge list.

But we were getting along now, I reminded

myself. Now was all we had, wasn't it? Like Mert said, "This is a present." Being able to chat with Sheila was a new source of pleasure in my life, even if we didn't agree, and even if she didn't see herself the way I saw her, I was happy we were being cordial. While I often didn't like what she said, I found her thought-provoking and interesting. Each time we conversed, I walked away a little smarter, a bit more educated, and much more worldly.

Still, I couldn't let her remark go unchallenged. "I know what you mean about their attitude being petty, but Sheila, if you'd have seen it . . . it was really upsetting . . . I guess when we're helpless, we want to blame someone. And in this case, Dodie, Bama, Mert, and I were in charge."

I couldn't even describe to Sheila the pandemonium that took place as the EMTs loaded Yvonne onto a stretcher. The technicians were working valiantly to bring her back, but the light faded from her eyes as if on a dimmer switch. A small, calm voice inside me decided, "She's gone." Even as I prayed for a miracle en route to the hospital, I didn't hold out much hope.

Several police officers showed up quickly and took cursory statements.

"For heaven's sake," fumed Sheila. "We're

not talking about murder, after all."

"Of course not. But the cops had to respond to the 911 call and whenever someone dies unexpectedly, they have to poke around a bit."

Sheila considered this. "What do they think caused her reaction?"

"Hmm, maybe a bee or bug stung her and she didn't notice. Who knows? Until the authorities talk to her doctor, they can't generate an accurate list of possibilities. Or totally rule out foul play. You know they say in forensics, better to have and not need than to need and not have. So they took a videotape of the room, asked a few questions, took names, collected samples of the food and so on."

The police worked quickly, but our group was understandably shook up. Not only had they missed out on the good time they'd been promised, but they'd had a ringside seat at the ugly death of a colleague. Thank goodness all of the women except our staff had chowed down before Yvonne died or we would have had a near riot of hungry, angry, and scared women.

"Yvonne's death ruined our event." Even as I said it, I cringed at how heartless I sounded. "We handwrote 'rain check' notes and passed them out. Most of the women were too shocked to do much besides tuck the notes in their Cropper Hoppers. Some of the ladies started crying. It was a real mess. It couldn't get any worse."

"Yes, it could," says Sheila. "Things can always get worse."

Yeah, I wiped my hands on my pants. She was right about that.

# THREE

Before I left, Sheila pressed a flat of flowers and a bag of potting soil on me. "Take these pots, too. I've changed my color scheme. Your front door could use a seasonal display to brighten it up."

The large faux limestone pots were gorgeous and exactly the right size to fit on my stoop. I thanked her profusely, touching the hot pink striped petunias, blue salvia, and marigolds with one finger. Not a lily in the bunch! I was delighted. "And there's a box of coral geraniums and vinca in the garage," she said. "I'll help you carry them to the car. I don't know what possessed me to buy so many plants." We both knew she hadn't done any such thing. Sheila was allowing me to save face. Anya must have told her I'd been longing for flowers to brighten up our front walkway. My budget simply wouldn't stretch to cover such frivolous extras. Now Sheila had given me exactly the plants I'd been coveting, and I was grateful for her thoughtfulness.

Anya and I drove straight home to let out Gracie, our harlequin Great Dane. She had all four paws crossed by the time she raced past us and into our fenced-in yard. Anya disappeared into her bedroom to chat on her cell phone with friends. My head was pounding from stress. The clothes I'd worn to the crop were soaked with nervous perspiration. All I wanted was to take a cool shower and go lie down. I stood under the meager stream of water and sniffed my lavender body wash for a long time. After I toweled off, I changed into a pair of loose drawstring gym shorts and an oversized T-shirt.

I was towel-drying my hair when the doorbell rang. Standing there was Chad Detweiler, the Ladue detective whom I'd met last fall when my husband died. Detweiler had become more than just a "friend." He inhabited my fantasies, and he showed up at my doorstep on a pretty regular basis, usually with a cheese pizza in hand.

I kept waiting for him to kiss me, but he hadn't. Mert and Dodie thought we'd moved along in our relationship, but I was too private a person to tell them he hadn't even tried to get to first base. I kept coming up with all sorts of excuses — at first I was a suspect, and of course, he had to maintain a professional detachment. Then I was injured by the killer, and maybe he thought he'd be taking advantage of my post-injury trauma. Now five weeks had gone by, and I was starting to worry. Did I have a bad case of dreaded halitosis?

I had tried licking my forearm and sniffing it. (I'd read somewhere it was a surefire test, but all I got was a mouthful of body lotion.) Was he not attracted to me physically? His pupils widened as he stared at me — I took that as a sign he was attracted. And occasionally when he thought I wasn't looking, I noticed him looking. So what was his problem? Was he worried about taking on a woman with a child? If so, why did he testify on my behalf at family court so I could regain custody of Anya?

I was both frustrated and stumped. Had I more courage, I would have simply asked him.

Here he stood, pizza in hand and goofy grin on his handsome face. If he didn't like me, he certainly was a glutton for punishment. Or maybe my house was the only BYOP (Bring Your Own Pizza) place he knew.

"What is it with you?" he asked. "Did the grim reaper hire you as a personal assistant?"

I couldn't help it. I laughed — and felt guilty afterward. "Gee, and after that, I'm supposed to let you in?"

"Only if you want a piece of pizza. Otherwise I'll stand on this side of your screen door, and we can talk through the wire mesh."

"Hmm. Pizza or put-downs. Okay, you win." How could I resist those gorgeous eyes?

"Huh. The mozzarella and tomato sauce wins. I'm just along for the ride." His long legs stepped over the threshold. The cologne he wore — and wore lightly, he didn't soak himself the way some men did — gave off a clean, spicy scent that smelled even better than the pizza.

No doubt about it. I was falling for him — hard. I was just too old-fashioned to make the first move. But if we kept up this physical détente much longer, I was going to give in and do something rash. Not that I knew what that would be. I just wasn't sure how much longer I could stand the racing heart, sweaty palms, and onslaught of hormones that bombarded me each time he was around.

"Where's Anya?"

I nodded toward my daughter's bedroom. He took off down the hall and rapped sharply on her door. His voice floated back as he asked her, "Want a piece of pizza?" He returned with Anya in tow. I poured iced tea for all of us and added a tossed salad to our feast. Okay, I tried to wipe the big smile from my face, but I couldn't. The easy way Detweiler rounded out our family made me glow with pleasure.

Even when Anya wasn't interested in my company, she'd surface from her hidey hole to come out and say "Hi" to Detweiler. They chatted about the Cardinals, worried together over Albert Pujols' pulled groin muscle, and made fun of Cubs fans. Anya still missed her father, but she seemed to accept Detweiler like she would a favorite teacher or older brother. Since her grandfather Harry, Sheila's husband, died before she was born, and I had no brothers or living male relatives, I was glad for her to have an adult man as a role model. Detweiler shared her love of baseball, critters, sports cars, and music. Hearing the two of them go back and forth about whether *American Idol* contestant Taylor Hicks or Elliott Yamin had a better voice, filled me with a sense of wholeness.

Sure, I could — and would — raise my daughter myself, but having other people who cared about her couldn't help but bolster her security and self-esteem. I never wanted her to feel awkward around men as I had.

On the other hand, if I'd known a little more about men and how they thought, she might not be here. Had I been smarter, had I understood how frat parties worked, if I'd known what went into Purple Passion, I might not have tumbled into bed with her father — the first man I'd made love with — and she might not have been born.

In the big scheme of life, who knows how things will turn out? What seems to be a disaster at the time can bring you joy you never dreamed of. What seems like the wrong road could be the right one. There are no right decisions, only decisions that seem to go more smoothly than others. There are no wrong turns, only unexpected potholes in the road. And at the end of the day, all you can do is keep moving forward even when it's only an inch at a time.

At this moment, I was happy. I loved my tiny bungalow, my oversized dog, my turning-into-a-teen daughter, and I was beginning to feel all warm and mushy about the man who sat across from me at my kitchen table.

Anya left to watch TV, and Detweiler got down to business. "Tell me what happened this afternoon."

"How about you help me plant flowers?" I gave a jerk of my head toward Anya's room. "That way we can talk privately."

I told him everything. He poked around in my memory as adeptly as he handled a shovel, asking a question, changing the subject, going back to the original question, and pausing to make notes. Since he'd questioned me when George died, I was familiar with his technique. Still, I marveled at Detweiler's ability to pull minute details from the detritus of my mind, details I was positive I'd forgotten or didn't exist. The process was gentle, unhurried. It felt like we were simply having an intense rehash of the disaster . . . until suddenly I realized he was too interested, too painstaking in his questioning.

"Are you here on official business?" A sharp edge of anger began to form in my solar plexus. "This isn't just professional curiosity, is it? Are you investigating Yvonne's death? Am I a suspect? Because I was there and tried to be a Good Samaritan? What gives?"

He frowned, turning over the last of the

dirt in a path parallel to my short sidewalk. "Right now there is no investigation. The autopsy is scheduled for tomorrow. I'm trying to get a feel for the background, that's all."

"That's all?" An ugly feeling of distrust swept through me. "Are you being straight with me?"

"Yes, I am. But . . ." His voice trailed off.

"Spit it out, buddy." I tucked the last petunia into its new home. "Are you hankering for another stint on the Major Case Squad?" Since 1965, the squad has brought together specially trained, highly motivated law enforcement officials from around the six counties in Missouri and the four counties in Illinois. It was an honor to be asked to serve; their 80 percent clearance rate spoke to the competency of personnel involved.

He grinned at me and shook his head. "It's just a feeling. I don't know. I guess my gut's telling me something's hinky." He paused, "You can't breathe a word of this, Kiki. Her allergist says she was highly allergic to only one thing: aspirin."

"So?" A familiar feeling of worry started in my mid-section.

"The paramedics say she died from an anaphylactic episode."

"I know! I was there. And she must have known what was happening because she grabbed her Epi-Pen and tried to use it."

"That's what doesn't make sense," he squatted next to me, speaking softly in case his voice carried. "Think about it, Kiki. You don't happen across aspirin. It's not like fructose or sodium that they dump into everything these days. How did she wind up with a dose of it? Where did she get it? And why was the Epi-Pen in her purse empty at the exact time when she had a reaction?"

His green eyes darkened and his face closed down. I'd seen this version of Detweiler before. This was his "I'm on the case" expression.

"You think it was done on purpose. Oh, my word! You think this was murder, don't you?" I couldn't bear his gaze. I focused on his hands, clenched and tight around the wooden handle of the shovel.

"Yes," he said quietly. "Yes, I do."

We moved the big pots into place on each side of my front door, covering the drainage holes with rocks and adding potting soil. I arranged geraniums and vinca to suit me. Detweiler lifted the heavy bag of dirt so I could fill in around the flowers. Since he'd been raised on a farm in Southern Illinois, he wasn't shy about directing my efforts. Once I'd patted down the fresh soil, I turned on the garden hose and gave all my new friends a thorough dousing.

After putting away the gardening tools, I let Gracie out back to do her duty and to love up Detweiler. He massaged her behind her ears and under her neck while the big girl — Gracie weighs more than I do — leaned against him with her eyes half-closed in a state of bliss. While they enjoyed each other's company, I lit two citronella candles and poured us each a tall glass of iced tea, turning the area outside my back door into a "livable" space.

In St. Louis, if the heat and humidity don't get you, the 'skitoes surely will. A small personal fan with a cord trailing from my slightly open kitchen window added a refreshing, if limited, breeze for us. Detweiler sat down in a wrought iron chair, pulled from his back pocket a list of all the scrappers who had been in attendance at our ill-fated CAMP, and set it between us on the matching wrought iron table.

"What can you tell me about each of these women?"

I scanned the list of names. A few of the women were friendly with Yvonne, and I mentioned them. Of course, he already knew Dodie and Mert. Bama was largely an unknown quantity to me, but I shared how I felt about her.

"And you think she's on drugs?" he asked.

The baldfaced accusation made me squirm.

"Uh, I can't say that. She's just . . . weird." I went on to describe her physical behaviors. "See? She sure seems like she could be drunk or high, but I have no way of knowing. And even if she is, why would she want to harm Yvonne? Anything that hurts our business isn't good for Bama. Dodie hired her with the clear understanding that she would work when the store was too busy for the two of us to handle. Any problem at CAMP would hurt — not help — our business and her cause."

Detweiler tapped the pencil against his leg. "Maybe not. Maybe she underestimated how quickly Mrs. Gaynor would react to the aspirin. Or maybe the job was a cover for killing Mrs. Gaynor. Remember, what's logical to us is rarely logical to a criminal. That's why we're on opposite sides of the law."

I chewed on an ice cube. "Back up, partner. We're taking giant steps here. First you're assuming Yvonne Gaynor was killed. That's a big leap. And now we're looking

41

for suspects? This is crazy. And although I don't like Bama, well, this is a stretch."

Didn't like Bama? Okay, it was an understatement. I started looking for reasons to hate Bama the first day Dodie said she was coming on board. The woman was a threat to my job. The fact she hadn't bothered to treat me with any deference — and I'd been at Time in a Bottle longer than she — ticked me off. I mean, couldn't she at least have acknowledged I'd been working at the store longer than she had? What was so tough about giving me a little respect? So, yeah, suspecting Bama was a stretch. But it was one I could go along with reluctantly.

Feeling unkind toward Bama didn't display the best part of my personality, but . . . what can I say? This job represented the first time in my life when I was given attention and praise for my talents. I'd gone from being an ignored wife, a dutiful colorless mother, and an undesirable daughter-in-law to a person of worth, all thanks to my job at Time in a Bottle.

Was I protective of it?

You bet.

Even so, I tried to be fair. Not real hard, but I did try. "I don't know if Bama and Yvonne had ever laid eyes on each other until today. How would Bama know if

Yvonne had allergies? Besides, what if Yvonne wasn't the intended target?"

The detective's handsome profile was silhouetted by the sun disappearing behind the trees. I liked looking at Detweiler. The stark planes of his features were so masculine. His kind eyes and gentle hands were the perfect balance to his more rugged features and build.

"Right," he said reluctantly. "She could have taken an aspirin by mistake. Maybe she thought it was something else."

I nodded. I carried painkillers in a miniature recycled jam bottle in my purse. The pills were generic. I paid scant attention to whether I refilled my supply with Tylenol, ibuprofen, or aspirin.

Detweiler continued, "Someone else could have been a target. Maybe another one of your guests had allergies to aspirin. Or this could have been a simple case of food tampering."

"Food tampering?"

"Sure. Fingers in chili, razor blades in apples, that sort of thing. Even so, this is a pretty unusual allergy. Aspirin doesn't usually kill. Plus, there's the issue of timing. Mrs. Gaynor didn't have a reaction until after she was eating. That leads us to believe something was in the food you served."

I shuddered. This was getting worse by the minute. I thought of all the work we'd put into the crop. I thought of Dodie and the store and how I loved my job. I couldn't go there. And I didn't want Detweiler to, either. "You're really getting ahead of yourself. Maybe Yvonne had other allergies that hadn't been diagnosed. They don't test for everything, you know. I'm allergic to horsehair, and no one regularly tests for that. What if Yvonne's reaction was to a chemical on a plant? It might have taken awhile for her to react."

"Granted, we might be grasping at straws." He cocked his head and gave me the smile of a nonbeliever. "Okay, so Mrs. Gaynor got a bug bite and didn't notice. Or brushed up against something in the garden. Or she was distracted and took the wrong pill by mistake. Then her Epi-Pen didn't work. Come on, Kiki. You have to admit the circumstances are pretty coincidental."

When he investigated my husband's death, Detweiler told me he didn't believe in coincidence. Much as I was loath to consider it, I had to agree: The timing of Yvonne's allergy attack did seem pretty weird. "Yeah. That empty Epi-Pen doesn't make sense," I said. "How bizarre. Yvonne must have thought it was functional because she

44

jabbed herself with it. This whole thing is such a shame. Right when she was in her glory."

"Explain."

I told him about the Scrapbook Star award. "It made Yvonne a highly desirable commodity. To some people at least. See, she could be a real stinker. She had this amazing ability to walk into a place and leave ten minutes and four new enemies later."

"Give me an example."

"Couple of times she spilled drinks on other scrappers' work. We ask customers not to bring liquids anywhere near the crop tables in our store. But Yvonne would sneak stuff past us. She accused us of price-gouging. When the price was printed on the item! One time she demanded Dodie give her a refund for a pad of papers — after she ripped out the designs she wanted." I was on a roll now. I shook my head remembering all her antics. "Once Yvonne insisted that I match all the papers in a magazine layout for her. Even brought along a magnifying glass to check my work."

Detweiler asked, "So? What's wrong with that?" At the querulous sound in his voice, Gracie rose from her pre-bedtime nap. Resting her head on his thigh, she rotated Tootsie Roll eyes upwards at her main man. Much as she loved Anya and me, she'd have ditched us in a heartbeat to take off with the detective. I hoped it never came to a showdown at OK Corral, or we'd be minus a dog.

"Magazine photos are notoriously inaccurate with color. Even in the pickiest of publications, color can get altered during the printing process."

"What you're telling me is . . ." Detweiler stopped. He waited for my answer.

"The woman was a real pain in the tushy. If this was murder, you should have no shortage of suspects."

# FOUR

I was sure Detweiler was going to kiss me goodbye. We stood in my doorway as I thanked him again for the pizza and the help with my plants. Reaching for my shoulder, he pulled me close. I tilted my face and shut my eyes. I could feel his breath on my lashes. After what seemed like ages, I opened them in time to watch him pull away with a tortured expression on his face. My stomach dropped to my feet, and a flush of embarrassment spread through my body.

"Uh, good night," he stammered.

If he hadn't moved quickly toward his car, I would have slugged him. What the heck was going on? Now I definitely needed to ask Mert if I had bad breath. What was it about me that turned this guy off?

Gracie hopped on my bed as I slipped my feet under the covers. Usually I shoo her away. Once when we slept together, she rolled over on my legs during the night. I woke up paralyzed and panicked that I'd had a stroke. This evening, after coming so close to being kissed and feeling totally rejected, I relished my pooch's unconditional love. I threw my arm around the dog's neck and stroked her velvety ears.

"At least you think I'm wonderful. Probably because I feed you," I tried to joke. But I was too frustrated to feel jovial. Sleep was a long time coming and with it came bad dreams, unformed events where I sat in a corner alone while George walked by me, my mother made fun of me, and Mert didn't seem to hear my cries for help. At some point, I must have whimpered out loud because Gracie pushed her head under my hand and licked my fingers until I woke up.

In the morning, my eyes were blotchy. My throat felt scratchy and sore. Even so, we had a tradition to uphold. Sundays were all about special breakfasts and parks. I pulled on undies, shorts, a bra and a tee, and scrubbed my teeth, blowing on the mirror and trying to catch a whiff of my breath. All I smelled was cinnamon from a Snickerdoodle I'd grabbed on the way to bed. A quick swipe of the brush through my hair, and I was ready to face the day.

I opened Anya's door and said, "Good

morning, sweetie."

She raised a bleary head and said, "Leave me alone."

Okay, she's a slow waker-upper.

I fixed myself a cup of coffee before trying again to get her out of bed. The small transistor radio was on the shelf with the instant hazelnut brew. The announcer rattled off national news before telling all of St. Louis that "a scrapbooker died yesterday at an event hosted by a local retail store. Yvonne Gaynor went into anaphylactic shock . . ." I snapped off the set.

So far, the day was off to a yucky start.

I trooped back in, coffee mug in hand, to rouse Anya. The lumpish group of covers that was my child had moved to the far side of the bed. I sat on the edge nearest the door and stared at the waterfall of platinum hair spread across her pillow.

"Anya? Anya, honey. Wake up."

"Leave me alone."

"Which park do you want to visit? Shall we take Gracie for a quick walk and then bring her back home? Maybe go someplace we haven't been in a while, like the Art Museum?" A long drag on the hot caffeine helped me act neutrally rather than let her bad mood infect mine.

Anya sat up halfway. Her eyes narrowed

into small slits of blue, and she said, "Why don't you get a life? Huh? Why don't you find a boyfriend or a pal and go do things with people your own age? What's wrong with you?"

She might as well have slapped me across the face. My gums were flapping as I struggled to form an appropriate response. Translation: I was stifling the urge to grab her and shake her . . . hard. As I stared at her sullen little countenance, it came to me that any day now she might have her first period.

In a month she'd be twelve, but that wasn't too early to become a teenager. The angry face that glared at me was not the angelic façade of my baby girl. It was clearly a hormone-infused, self-centered tableau of features belonging to a quarrelsome, nasty teen. She'd always been cross when tired, and now her changing body was demanding more rest than her developing mind wanted. A quick glance at her bedside table confirmed my worries — her cell phone was sitting on top of a short stack of books. She'd been using it when I'd thought her asleep.

"All right, in the future I'll make other plans," I managed through gritted teeth. "But today I expect us to do something together. What will it be?"

She tossed back her hair and gave me the evil eye. What a rude little minx! "If you must know, I'm busy. I'm going to the mall with my friends. People my age. They're picking me up at noon." And with that she sank back into her pillows, arm across her forehead, exuding all the world-weary mien of Sarah Bernhardt. What a card! The kid had a budding future on stage. Next up, she'd be asking me to peel her a grape.

"Uh, my dear darling child. You are going nowhere with no one unless I say so. Who's picking you up? You need to clear all flight plans with me, got it?" I stopped before reminding her that her father's killer was on the loose. Authorities had bulletins out, but so far, there'd been no arrest. My goal wasn't to frighten her, but to remind her who was boss.

She sniffed. "Nicci Moore's mom is driving us. If you want to talk to her, you go call her yourself."

"Don't worry, kiddo. I plan to do exactly that." I paused in her doorway. "But here's a word to the wise. You will speak to me in a civil tone with courtesy, or you will spend the rest of your natural life inside these four walls. Got it?"

■ ■ ■ ■

Jennifer Moore assured me she'd keep an eye on the girls. "Are you still worried about that horrible murderer? The one you escaped from?"

I explained about the threatening letters that showed up periodically in my mailbox.

An hour later, I watched my daughter ride off with mixed feelings. It was important that she have friends, and Nicci seemed like a nice enough child, er, pre-teen. Jennifer was a bit overindulgent, but then, who wasn't these days? My being overprotective might backfire by making Anya too eager to shed my influence. Being unconcerned could also be dangerous. She needed to know I had her back. That I was watching out for her. I had to find a middle ground.

And what exactly was a middle ground? Where did that phrase come from and what did it mean? Jennifer's white Mercedes pulled out of my driveway as I pondered the question. At some time, in some distant place, had there truly been a geographic middle ground? Or had this always referred to a mythical spot? A fantasy locale like Camelot? Surely in real life, middle ground was every bit as elusive as the kingdom of

King Arthur.

Yes, I'd eluded a killer who was now on the lam. Two postcards and three letters had been mailed to me bearing the handscrawled message, "I'll get even." Each was postmarked in a different part of the country. Duh . . . of course, this criminal was too smart to come back to St. Louis. But what was it Detweiler had said about a criminal's logic being different from our logic? Revenge was, as I had the scar to prove, a strong motivator. Maybe even stronger than self-preservation.

I walked back into my house as my cell phone started ringing. Mert wanted to drop off a dog for me to babysit. I was glad to have both a reason to visit with my best friend and an opportunity to make extra money.

"This here's Guy, and he's a nutcase," she explained an hour later, handing me a brown, black, and white Jack Russell terrier. Mert put a bag of dog food and a leash on my kitchen counter. The small dog regarded me warily while I gave him a similar once over. Evidently I either passed muster or wasn't worth the effort because a big yawn overtook Guy. His little pink tongue lolled in the most comical way. Gracie sat next to me, examining my burden, head cocked and curious. I lowered Guy to the floor. The two sniffed each other's nether regions and wagged their tails. It was a stretch for the terrier to browse Gracie's behind. I think she's thirty-four inches at the withers, but I've never dropped a tape measure from under her tail. Anything a dog can do, you can watch, but it isn't smart to push your luck.

"Ethel Frick's daughter's boyfriend bought him for the girl when she was in college. She's since graduated and found a job and can't have a dog in her new apartment, so Ethel inherited Guy. He's named after that British dude who tried to blow up them Houses of Parliament. Guy Fawkes? This little squirt is more terrorist than terrier. By the way, you get combat pay for watching this monster. He comes with special instructions." Mert pulled a sheet of paper from the pocket of her short-shorts. "Do not under any circumstances let him watch *Sesame Street.*"

"Huh?"

"You heard me. He can watch anything else on TV, but no *Sesame Street,* see? It's written right here in big block letters." A frosted pink fingernail traced words underlined four times in bold marker: NO SESAME STREET! "Otherwise, he likes to run around and play a lot. I haven't had him as a guest, but Ethel assures me he's a lover, not a fighter."

We put up the gate to keep Guy in my kitchen and sat down to yak. I didn't go into everything Detweiler said — I'd promised him to stay mum, after all — but I intimated he was concerned about the circumstances around Yvonne's death. Mert gobbled down two Snickerdoodles. With her heavy schedule of house and office cleaning she burns calories like Lance Armstrong ascending a mountain with a pack of French bikers in his downdraft. I, on the other hand, have the metabolism of a garden slug on Valium.

"I used to clean for Yvonne. We had ourselves what you might call a falling out," Mert said. To my surprise, an expression of sheer hatred took over my friend's face. I pulled back in shock. I'd never seen Mert like this. Never.

She continued, "That woman's a pis-tol, heavy on the pissy part of the toll. Once she tried to return a pair of dirty panties to Victoria's Secret. Got all huffy when they wouldn't take them back. Liked to brag about what she'd got for free by conniving folks. She was one to eat halfway through a meal and set a hair on the plate, then call over the waiter. Once got some poor server fired over some ruckus she made. Didn't make no secrets 'bout her tricks neither. Don't know how a person can live with herself doing all that. It isn't right — and mark my words, it always comes back and bites you in the rear end."

"Wow. I knew she was awful at the store, but I didn't realize her behavior was so . . . global." Every time I closed my eyes, I saw Yvonne thrashing about.

"Dodie mentioned she'd fired Yvonne as a customer," Mert said. "I wish I'd'a had the good sense to do just that."

"What happened?" I asked.

Mert waved my question away and turned her head so I couldn't see her eyes. "It was years and years ago. Don't matter. Don't bear repeating or remembering. I should've seen it coming. She wasn't right in the head. But at the time, I thought I needed the money. Since then, I've learned there's money and there's money, and some money costs too much to get. You got any idea what happened at the store to make Dodie kiss Yvonne's business goodbye?"

I filled Mert in on a few of Yvonne's more notable antics.

"Ho boy. But Ellen sure acted pleased as punch to have Yvonne as a design team

56

member over at Memories First."

"Of course she is. That's a prestigious award. Remember, Ellen said the magazine had Yvonne's work on their website. I bet she'll have other pages in one of those big spreads in an upcoming issue. Some of their winners have even created their own lines of paper products. They get hired to demonstrate supplies at shows and on QVC. Plus, manufacturers send them the latest products free. Ellen's going to get a lot of mileage from being Yvonne's retail home base. Maybe Yvonne behaved herself at Ellen's store. Whatever."

I was tired of talking about Yvonne.

Instead, I wanted Mert's opinion on how to handle Anya. I needed a sounding board. Mert has raised three kids, so her input was always valuable. I told her what my daughter had said earlier that day.

"Hello, Miss Sassy Mouth! Buckle down the hatches, a teenage storm is appearing out there on the horizon," Mert's laughter was more sympathetic than her words.

"What the heck do I do about it?"

"Pray a lot." She smiled a wry grin, her eyes crinkled in amusement. "I been through all this with mine." Her nineteen-going-on-twenty-year-old son Roger was Anya's secret crush, a sweet boy who often helped me with odd jobs like moving things I couldn't budge.

A funny sound caused us both to look down. Guy had started to hump the table leg.

Mert snorted with laughter. "Go for it, buddy. You get splinters, don't expect me to dig 'em out." Her expression turned thoughtful. "Anya's right. You can't build your life around her no more. She's not a baby, Kiki. And even if she was, you need to move on. You need a social life. Tell me what's up with that hunky detective. No way he showed up just to cuss and discuss ole dead Yvonne."

"He shows up about twice a week 'to check on us,' because of those weird post-cards and all. We go to lunch every week or so . . . but he's never asked me out to dinner. He's never made a move on me, and heaven knows, I've been patient. It's not like Anya is here all the time. She's at Sheila's three nights a week at least. In fact, I'm so frustrated I picked up this book at the library — *He's Just Not That Into You.*"

Mert gathered her purse and said, "Like some smug couple in New York City can straighten out your love life. Man, I sure do wish there was a magic formula. For menfolk and kids. But there ain't. It may be time to move on. That Detweiler's a real dream-boat, but he's gotta poop or get off the pot. In fact, I see him, I'm going to tell him so."

"Don't you dare!"

"Phooey. Tell you what. I'm having a barbecue at the house next Sunday. Why don't you come? I'd like you to meet my baby brother, Johnny. Remember? I told you about him moving back in the area after be-ing . . . away."

What, I wondered, was "away"? Mert wasn't one to be coy. I didn't recall ever hearing her say much about Johnny. "Aw, I don't know. Wouldn't that complicate our friendship? What if he hates me? Worse. What if he likes me?"

Mert snorted. "It don't matter neither way. I love you, and your little dog, Toto, too," and she gave Gracie a pat. "Besides, we're going to have ourselves a good time. After a couple of beers, the whole world looks better, and that's a fact. Iff'n it weren't for Budweiser, I'd'a been wiser." Her phone rang. "It's my sister over in Indiana wanting to talk about what to get our daddy for his birthday. I'll tell you more about my baby brother later. Got to run."

"Um, one last question."

"Shoot. But make it quick-like."

"Do I have bad breath?"

"Not that I ever noticed. But don't you dare plant a big French smooch on me so I can find out."

"Remember, no *Sesame Street*," I cautioned Anya as I finished making our dinner. The chicken drumettes in my crock pot were cooking in honey-mustard sauce, and the homemade cole slaw chilled in the refrigerator. I stirred a half gallon pitcher of water until the brown peach tea powder dissolved. A bowl of cut-up cantaloupe sat in the middle of the table. For dessert we had frozen bananas dipped in chocolate in the freezer. It might not be gourmet fare, but it was wholesome and economical.

"I'm not hungry," my daughter stopped protesting when she saw the look on my face. Anya was underweight. The school nurse had been worried enough to call me and query about her eating habits right before the academic year ended. Since then, my child and I had had a talk about taking good care of our health. As a result, Anya had promised to eat — or at least to try to eat — something at every meal.

Now she avoided my glare of reproach by watching Guy bounce around the kitchen like one of those superballs you buy for a quarter from a gumball machine. He was literally running up the walls and turning flips. Guy landed on Anya's feet, springing up at her like a kid on a pogo stick. Obviously, he'd discovered the girl of his dreams.

"I think I'll take him for a walk." At the mall, she'd used her money from Sheila to buy a new pair of flip-flops. They were cute, with sequins and big silk flowers in shades of blue and green. I suspected she wanted to practice walking in them so she didn't embarrass herself.

I hesitated. I didn't like the thought of her being out alone.

Anya read my mind. "Mo-om. I'll be right out in front of the house. Geez. Give me a break. I'm practically a prisoner in my own home! And look, see? Here's my cell phone, all charged and everything!" With that she flounced out, slamming the front door behind her.

Gracie turned doleful eyes on me. I knew exactly how she felt. Her floppy ears drooped, and she set her big blocky head on her paws, watching the front door as though it were a living thing.

"Hey, girl, I guess we better get used to this, huh? Our baby is growing up."

# FIVE

That darling daughter of mine woke up the next morning loaded for bear. Anya snarled every half-mile of our journey to the Science Center. "This place is for babies. Everyone else in my school is going to camp in Wisconsin or hanging at the mall. I hate this! Hate it! I don't want to make clay models of the solar system and electric toys using batteries. It's stooo-pid. And you're mean to make me go."

Gripping the steering wheel hard so I wouldn't be tempted to smack her, I said softly, "As long as that killer is loose, you aren't like everyone else and neither am I."

"Huh, you just use that as an excuse."

I didn't respond. She might be onto something. Hey, a crazed serial killer had a lot more elephants than "I don't want you to go away for the summer because I'll miss you" or "You can't hang around the mall because you might get into mischief," right?

Wasn't I within my parental rights to drum up whatever excuse I thought I could get away with?

At least I didn't stoop to say, "Because I'm the MOM." But I thought about it.

When I didn't take the bait, Anya turned her face away from me and stared out the window. Her jaw was set, her lower lip poked out. A few minutes passed. Then, in the sweetest voice imaginable, she asked, "Can we stop at McDonald's?"

I couldn't decide whether to laugh or cry. That mood swing took all of a few deep breaths. Oh, boy. And this was a preview of coming events?

We pulled into the drive-up, and Anya leaned over me to yell into the squawk box, "A sausage egg McMuffin, two hash browns, and a large orange juice." This was the kid who seemed on the path to anorexia last month? The cashier named an amount that shocked me.

I dug around in my purse, but Anya tapped my arm. "I've got it, Mom. Nana gave me money for kicking around. Want anything?"

I ordered a breakfast burrito and a large coffee.

Anya seemed rather pleased with herself as she counted out the money for the cashier. Yet another sign — my baby was growing up.

After we finished our breakfast in the fast food parking lot, I dropped her off and let myself into the store. Gracie followed docilely on her lead while Guy wrapped his leash around both of us as he did laps. Taking hobbled baby steps, I moved toward the stockroom. I unhooked Gracie and plopped Guy into a doggie play pen before calling my mother-in-law to thank her again for the flowers.

Sheila brushed away my words of gratitude. "Anya's eyes were red and crusty last time she spent the night. Cottonwood is in full bloom."

"Yes, several of our customers are sneezing and wheezing."

"I made an appointment for her with Andersoll, Weaver, and Sealander, the best allergy partners in town. Ralphie Andersoll and I go way back. I can't wait for him to see my gorgeous grandbaby. God knows, I've been clucking over photos of his motley brood for decades. What do scrapbookers do when they have ugly kids?"

No way was I going to touch that comment.

She continued, "Unfortunately, I'm scheduled to play in a foursome for a charity match at the club the day of Anya's appointment. You'll have to take her to their office after science camp on Thursday," Sheila said.

I hesitated. If these docs were the best, the office visit alone would be formidable. On the other hand, I was fortunate Sheila could wrangle a spot on their schedule for my child. I swallowed hard. "Thanks so much for making the appointment. I'll be glad to take her."

As if sensing my concern, she added, "They'll send me the bill. The paperwork's already filled out."

A huge wave of relief swept through me. "Sheila . . . I can't thank you enough."

"If my son had been alive, or hadn't been so dumb about whom he trusted, you wouldn't have to worry about this." She stopped herself.

I understood why. Neither Sheila nor I wanted to think about the financial shenanigans that ruined my late husband's business. The auditors were still sifting through the wreckage and trying to track down hidden accounts in the Cayman Islands.

I hung up the phone and stared thoughtfully at the dogs. In one way, she was right. George's bad judgment set in motion a string of life-changing events. But I am a grown woman, and it rankled I couldn't provide for my daughter. I take that back — I could only provide the barest of necessities. I gritted my teeth and vowed to work harder at bringing additional business to the store.

Dodie struggled through the back door with a box of supplies left over from the ill-fated CAMP crop. She brushed aside my offer to help. The plum-colored crescents under her eyes and her brusque manner underscored her bad mood. The woman I'd always considered a pillar of strength crumbled before my eyes. Her voice was flat as she spoke. "I've had a dozen calls at home from women who want their money back. Despite the rain checks. Plus, the other stores want to meet with me to discuss what we need to do next. That's code for 'how to toss us out of the program,' sunshine. This was all because of Yvonne Gaynor."

Then Dodie mumbled something in Yiddish.

"Pardon?"

"From a fool one has grief," she translated.

Now I knew exactly how upset she was. Dodie trotted out her pithy "old country" sayings when she was stressed.

I shook my head. "They can't blame us."

"They keep repeating the same thing over and over. Word for word. They say they were traumatized. They don't want rain checks. They say that to try again would be disrespectful to Yvonne's memory." She lifted her shoulders and let them fall expressively. "How can they blame me?"

"Us," I said in a moment of solidarity. If folks were parroting the same script, I'd wager someone was coaching them. And I bet I knew who — but blaming Ellen Harmon wouldn't solve our problems.

I decided not to tell my boss about my discussion with Detweiler. Maybe, I prayed, word would come from the authorities that Yvonne reacted to a substance she hadn't been aware she was allergic to. Surely, considering the size and acreage of the Botanical Garden, the woman could have brushed or touched a lethal plant. And certainly, with all those flowers in bloom, there had to have been a lot of bees. I prayed for something — anything — but a delivery system suggesting a deliberate desire to do her harm. And if any angels were listening, I asked them to make it abundantly clear none of us at Time in a Bottle had anything to do with Yvonne's abrupt departure from this earth.

"More supplies still in your car?" I asked as Dodie shoved the box she'd toted in along the floor.

My boss sank into her office chair. She appeared not to have heard me. Her face was hidden in her hands; her body slumped over her desktop. Built like a Valkyrie, Dodie seemed invincible — not only because she could make two of me, but because she had a warrior's spirit. She was not a Pollyanna or a Suzy Sunshine, but an Unsinkable Molly Brown who rolled up her sleeves and made the best of tough situations. When George died, she was the one who forced me to take charge of my life — reminding me Anya's welfare depended on it. Through thick and thin, chipboard and vellum, Dodie stood by me. She refused to let me wallow in my misery. Once I learned she'd been through her own personal hell — the accidental death of her teenage son — I never questioned her right to tell me to "buck up."

That strong, invincible woman was difficult to reconcile with the haggard ghost sitting in front of me. Crumpled over her workspace, she seemed eerily small and defeated.

"Dodie? I asked if you have more boxes in your car. I'll go get them if you give me the keys."

She turned blurry eyes to me. Their washed-out gray was as flat as a piece of Bazzill Basics cardstock. "Huh?"

I opened the mini-frig near her desk and grabbed a Diet Dr Pepper, the official store remedy for nearly all of life's crises. "Drink this. You need caffeine. It's going to be okay. Yeah, the women will complain, but they'll get over it. So give them their money back. Big deal. It's not that much, and we'll make it up some other way."

A meaty hand reached for the cola. Her flesh was puffy around the wedding band that cut a deep groove in her finger. "Maybe. I haven't even checked the answering machine here at the store. Didn't feel like it."

"I'll do it." This felt odd. Usually, Dodie oriented my emotional compass due north, zero degrees past nonsense. She ran the store like a well-drilled military operation. The ding-ding-ding of an internal alarm sounded inside my head.

There was more to this than Yvonne's death.

I pulled up a chair.

"What's going on?"

She turned her face away.

"Hey," I tapped her downy forearm. "I know I'm just a lowly employee. But we've known each other for years. You've had my back every step of the way. It's my turn to return the favor. What's wrong, Dodie?"

The words poured out. A week ago Monday, her husband Horace's boss called him into the executive's office and let him go from his job at RCC, a local telecommunications company. Since he was six months from retirement — and had never had a performance review below superlative — the Goldfaders were caught totally off-guard. All their benefits disappeared when the boss told Horace: "We're letting you go."

"Is that legal?" I asked. I did a quick calculation. This all happened before our horrible CAMP outing. I knew from experience that events tend to gang up on you. It's not one straw that breaks the camel's back — it's the cumulative straws piling up and weighing you down.

"I doubt it," Dodie said. "But in the meantime, we're without health insurance."

"How's Horace taking this?"

"He's in shock. He has all these papers but he hasn't looked at them. Couldn't even bring himself to open the Yellow Pages and find a lawyer. I had to do it for him. That's not like Horace. Usually, he's . . . he's very protective of our family," whispered Dodie.

Her voice broke as she added, "He sits in a chair all day long and stares out the window. Doesn't even move. He devoted most of his life to that company. Knew the president and worked beside him when they started. He feels betrayed."

She spread her fingers and examined her wedding band carefully. "You see, Horace was a company man. When they said, 'Jump,' he said, 'How high?' He gave up a lot. Time with our son, Nathan, and our daughter, Rebekkah. But he thought he'd made a good trade — security for togetherness. Now . . . he's doubting everything."

I knew how that felt. You thought you'd been making good decisions. Then, suddenly, your life is turned upside down and you question everything. "Give him time," I said. "He'll get over it. Horace is a good man." He only came up to Dodie's shoulder, but he exuded a happy masculinity that expressed itself in a can-do attitude. Horace made no secret of the fact he adored Dodie and supported her in every way possible. The few times I'd seen them together he watched his wife with misty eyes, his face bearing a nearly religious expression of approbation.

Guy broke the tension by yapping. I grabbed a hollow dog toy and dabbed a half a teaspoon of peanut butter inside. Sniffing the air cautiously, his rocket of a tail moved back and forth at the speed of light. I smeared a second toy with a lighter coat of peanut butter, in deference to Gracie's touchy tummy, and offered her a similar distraction.

"New guest," I said, gesturing to the Jack Russell. "His name's Guy. He's a wild man."

The freedom to bring pets to work with me is a big perk of my job. Dogsitting money covers the cost of feeding Gracie and adds enough padding in my budget for Anya and me to see a movie once a month. Typically Dodie loves to give my guests a cuddle. Even though she claims no interest in owning a dog, she has a real soft spot for my charges. It's not unusual to find her sitting in front of her computer with a canine companion on her copious lap. Today, she wasn't one bit interested in the perky dude with the black patch around his eye. She took in my boarder with a dismissive glance.

"How do things stand now? With the lawyer that is."

Their attorney was confident RCC would pony up a settlement. Even as Dodie shared this good news, her mouth was slack, and her expression dull. Some part of her was beaten, whipped, defeated. I opened a Diet Dr Pepper for myself and considered the situation. Maybe, I reasoned, she was genuinely worried about our store. I didn't know how well-capitalized Time in a Bottle was. We'd never discussed it. It wasn't really any of my business.

Maybe she was just overwhelmed. She'd grown up dirt poor. Perhaps the one-two punch of the miserable CAMP event and Horace's firing overwhelmed her, sent her back into the memory of a childhood of poverty, and stripped her of hard-won adult responses to a financial challenge.

Something similar happened to me last fall when I was told George died owing his business partner a half a million dollars. Every step toward resolution of the problem had been a struggle, fighting my childhood demons and facing new adult tests of my mettle.

If Dodie was worried about the business, I needed to be also. When I sold my fancy house and most of our possessions, I'd banked a meager amount of savings. This job kept a roof over my head and food on our table. I asked, "How can I help?" and meant it sincerely.

Her eyes turned to me curiously. For a moment, she said nothing. Then Dodie spoke slowly. "Summer is the doldrums for scrappers. Put on your thinking cap. We need an exciting program that'll get them in the store and make them open their wallets."

The rest of the morning went better than expected. None of the women who left messages were home when I returned their calls. I was spared hearing them complain or ask for money back. I restocked the CAMP merchandise. The "make and take" pages were untouched, so I labeled their box and shelved it in the back. That kept me busy until lunch, a peanut butter and jelly sandwich washed down with copious amounts of ice tea.

I walked the dogs. Avoiding entanglement with Guy's lead kept me hopping. He was a busy boy, sniffing, peeing, and racing about, zigzagging wildly as he caught a scent or saw something interesting. His tail moved as quickly as a hummingbird's wings. Unsure about Guy's sanity and his flight path, Gracie stayed close to me. As we meandered up and down residential blocks behind our store, I contemplated replacing the income the store had lost from CAMP.

My first priority would be setting the situation right. Most upsetting to most of our guests — besides Yvonne's death — was giving up their cameras. I made a mental note to call the police and ask when the cameras would be returned.

I put Guy back in his playpen. I was deeply engrossed in a milieu of ideas when the door minder buzzed loudly. Running to the front of the store, I nearly slammed into Roger, Mert's son.

"They've taken Mom in for questioning." His eyes were wet. He snuffled in an effort not to cry. "The cops. They came an hour ago. She was cleaning a house and they . . . they made her go with them. She called me."

"Questioning? About what?"

"About that woman who died on Saturday."

Dodie lurched out of her office. "What? Where'd they take her?"

"I . . . I don't know . . . I . . . she . . ." Roger was having a hard time talking.

"Okay, honey, calm down. It's going to be all right. When did this happen?" I opened my cell phone and hit the speed dial for Detweiler. His voice mail answered, and I left a message for him to call me.

"Should I call Bonnie Gossage?" I asked Dodie. Bonnie was a regular customer who'd temporarily suspended her legal career to give birth to her son Felix. (Someday I intended to ask Bonnie what on earth possessed her to give that poor child such a bizarre name.)

Roger interrupted. "Mom said . . . she said . . . not to do anything. She said just tell you what happened. She told me she'd call if she needed help."

Dodie's eyes blazed angrily and a flash of her old self came through loud and clear. "This is ridiculous. What are they doing with Mert? Yvonne's death was an accident! An allergic reaction!" She stopped. Her eyes widened as she suddenly understood. "They must think Yvonne was murdered!"

We gathered around the television in Dodie's office and watched a terminally blonde reporter explain Yvonne Gaynor had succumbed to a tainted orange scone. The newscaster held up a similar pastry for the camera. "Police say someone substituted icing mixed with orange-flavored baby aspirin for the original topping. Yvonne Gaynor was highly allergic to aspirin in all its forms. Of course, anyone who was sensitive to aspirin could have fallen victim to the contaminated food, but insiders are calling this murder because of one critical piece of evidence."

The yellow box of an anaphylaxis kit appeared on the screen. The reporter continued, "This is the type of Epi-Pen that highly sensitive people like Yvonne Gaynor should carry at all times. Police department sources tell us they now suspect someone traded Yvonne Gaynor's functional Epi-Pen for an empty one."

Dodie switched off the television. "And on my watch, too."

I needed to talk this through. "Someone iced a scone with the one substance toxic to Yvonne. The 'bad' scone or scones found their way onto our food table. Someone knew Yvonne liked pastries. That someone had exchanged her full Epi-Pen for an empty one and hoped Yvonne would have a fatal reaction."

"And not be able to save herself," finished Roger.

"But Mert didn't have access to Yvonne's purse and she never touched the food! She was nowhere near it," said Dodie.

"That's not true." I hated to say it, "But remember? She brought in everything we'd baked and what she'd picked up from the store. Roger helped her set up tables, but she was there alone when we arrived."

"But adding aspirin to icing! That's ridiculous. Mert had no reason to hurt Yvonne Gaynor."

I gently corrected my employer. "Uh, that's not exactly right. There was bad blood. Mert used to work for Yvonne and something happened."

Dodie and Roger both glared at me. Roger's lip trembled. "Whose side are you on?"

"I'm on your mom's side," I said firmly as I put an arm around the teenager I'd known for ten years. He might look like a man, but he was really just a very tall and hairy boy. "She's my dearest friend, and she couldn't possibly have done this. But we can't overlook the facts. If we do, we can't help her or prove her innocence because the police will use those facts to build a case against her. We need to work with the same information if we hope to solve this."

"You're planning on tracking down a killer?" Dodie could barely spit out the words. She stared at me.

"Maybe. It still might be an accident. The police could have it wrong." I shrugged. I was trying hard to remain cool and collected. I didn't want to upset Roger more by letting my emotions show. I was worried. Plenty worried. But that wouldn't help my best friend's son. Nor would it help her. "It's early days. Let's see what happens." I didn't turn away. She knew, as I did, that it was folly to depend on others. Others who were supposed to be fair and honest. Wasn't she the person who preached to me about being self-reliant? Didn't she know what happened when you put all your eggs in someone else's basket? Witness what had just happened with poor Horace.

Roger wiped the back of his hand across his eyes and blinked hard. He was on the verge of breaking down. I patted his arm. "I won't rest until we clear your mother's name. It's going to all be okay. I promise."

Now, how was I going to keep my word?

# Six

Roger left for class at Meramec Community College. Dodie and I walked around the store like two zombies. I finally sat down to work on an anniversary album commissioned by a customer, relieved that the work was far enough along it only required the mindless task of adhering mats to photos. My brain was numb. The store phone rang, and I answered it.

A woman demanded her money back. "I expected to have a great time at CAMP, and . . . and . . . instead my camera is gone and you . . . you stood by while Yvonne was murdered!"

I took a deep breath before responding, "We'll be happy to issue a refund. All of us at Time in a Bottle are devastated by Yvonne's death and shocked to hear it might have been intentional. It's awful, isn't it?"

As the Bible says, "A soft answer turneth

away wrath." Mollified that I agreed with her, the caller became downright chatty. "Who do you think did it?"

"I wish I knew. We are cooperating fully with the police. Unfortunately, a lot of people had access to the food. Do you have any idea who might have held a grudge against Yvonne?"

The customer thought for a second. "Yvonne could be a real pill. She never bothered me, but she upset several of my friends." She paused, "I'm sorry if I came on too strong earlier. I'm . . . I'm just upset."

"We all are. As for Yvonne, well, none of us are perfect. I've certainly ticked off more than my share of people. Now, what should I do about that refund?" By the time we hung up, the caller decided she'd rather take a rain check for the next CAMP event. "Goodness knows," I said, "it can't possibly be as eventful as this one. And you probably still have pages you want to get done. I have a call in to the police to find out when the cameras will be released."

That was the first of many conversations with our CAMPers. In the end, only one woman demanded a refund. Clearly, as distressed as the customers were, more than anything they wanted to be reassured and comforted.

Later I opened my cell phone to Mert's ragged voice. "Did Roger come on by? They done questioned me, but I can't get a'hold of him. I figgered he'd probably run to you, Kiki."

I took that as a compliment. My best friend and her son were family by choice, not by blood. "Are you okay?"

"They was just asking questions. It weren't really bad. Wanted to know what I'd done, if I'd touched the food, and whether I hated Yvonne or not. The cops are taking heat from some of them women who was at CAMP. You know how it goes."

"Yes, unfortunately I do. What did they ask?"

"I can't go into it now." Mert cut the conversation short. She'd left in the middle of a cleaning job and needed to get back. What she didn't say, and I knew from her voice, was how the whole ordeal had exhausted her. I promised to check on her later. "I'll tell you about it then." She sounded strong, but I knew her well enough to hear the edge in her voice.

Detweiler called immediately after Mert. I explained about Roger's visit and that she'd since been released. He told me that he had been tapped for the Major Case Squad. "I might need your help. We're constructing a timeline, identifying where everyone was in relationship to the food. The goal is to establish opportunity."

"Huh, that's like trying to figure out which ant in an anthill had the chance to steal a bread crumb." I was being truthful and I was also stalling. Why should I volunteer information? He and his friends were already breathing down the neck of my best friend. I debated about whether to tell him to buzz off. As I hesitated, Dodie ambled by. One glance at her miserable face and I decided I wanted Yvonne Gaynor's murderer brought to justice — pronto.

"I'll help you if I can, but honestly, anyone could have tampered with the food. We bought groceries, baked things at home, hired a caterer, and scrapbookers also brought their own goodies."

"Huh?"

"It's a tradition. Women like to share their favorite recipes. Sure, we were responsible for providing brunch, but that didn't preclude folks from bringing their own treats."

"I was afraid you might say that. We're busy with interviews. Officers are taking statements from the caterers. We're going through the trash cans on the off-chance we'll find evidence. I also need more background on Mrs. Gaynor. We're making a list of people who wanted the woman dead."

"Mert didn't do it."

Detweiler replied cautiously. "I can't rule out anyone at this juncture. Anyone."

I fumed. Could he be including me? What a jerk! "That sounded like a threat."

"No, but it is a warning. Don't get too emotionally involved in this, Kiki. You don't have the training or experience to rule out suspects. Especially when one of them is your friend."

"We're talking Mert! I'd trust her with my life! She's helped me raise Anya, she held my hand when George died, and all I need to do is call, and she's there for me. What more do I need to know, huh? I judge people by their actions, not their education or their clothes or their status."

"Everyone has a breaking point. What do you know about her past? I'm warning you, Kiki, stay out of this or you'll find yourself in jail for obstructing an investigation."

"That's your idea of encouraging co-operation? A threat like that?" I was steaming mad. How dare he? "By the way, pal, when are our customers getting their cameras back? Or do we need to call a lawyer about your search and seizure?"

"This was a murder, Kiki. A woman — a wife and mother — is dead. The fact your scrapbook friends have to wait to see their photos, well . . . that's not my problem. Their cameras should be released tomorrow afternoon, but in the meantime, we have other priorities. As much as I ca—" and he stopped himself before he said "care." "As much as I think of you personally, I have a job to do."

Hello! Didn't he realize how important the cameras were to our customers? The longer he withheld them, the angrier the CAMP attendees would be with us. And that quick avoidance of saying he "cared." What was with that? I was sick and tired of not knowing where I stood. He gave off signals like he was interested and then he'd pull back. There was a name for women who did that! Was there an equivalent term for men? I raged inwardly, not daring to open my mouth. I was too near to saying something I'd regret.

He cleared his throat. "We are investigating a murder. Cameras have to wait. I realize you have a stake in this, and your friends may or may not be involved, but I have a job to do. Do you understand? Are we clear here? Because I can repeat myself if necessary."

That last phrase sent me over the top. He was belittling the people and the craft I held dear as well as treating me like an imbecile. "I'm *so* glad to hear you are on the job. That's good news. We can all sleep easy at night. If you recall, last time you were on the job I had to solve the murder for you, bucko."

"Solve the murder? Ha! You bumbled your way into a dangerous situation."

I mouthed air. I was speechless. "You jerk!" I popped my hand over my mouth. I couldn't believe I said that.

"Stay out of this, Kiki. Like that cat you're named for, you've already used up one of your nine lives!"

"Right! No thanks to you, pal. You want to talk to me? Fine. You can come by the store and talk in front of witnesses. Got it?" I snapped my phone shut and stood in the middle of the empty sales floor and screamed.

Fifteen minutes later, Detweiler stormed in. His Heineken-bottle-green eyes with those dancing gold flecks were dark with fury. I clamped my jaw shut and didn't greet him. I didn't even get up. I ignored him while I continued to work on the anniversary album. This book of memories paid homage to sixty-five years of love and trust between two people. Not all of us could focus on

86

death and destruction! Some of us had to applaud the living!

I could feel the heat of Detweiler's body as he stepped behind me, nearly hanging over my chair. Suddenly, I started sticking down photos on an angle. I peeled one up and tore the background paper. That just capped it.

"Kiki."

I ignored him, keeping my gaze on the work. Trying to figure out how to fix what I'd ruined. "If you are here on official business, my name is Mrs. Lowenstein. I'm busy with work right now, so you'll have to wait."

Next thing I knew, he pulled my chair away from the desk. It felt like that obligatory scene in an earthquake movie where the furniture hops around. I grabbed the edge of the table, but Detweiler slipped between me and my work. I stared at him in shock. Both of us glared at each other.

To my horror, a nearly irrepressible urge to laugh bubbled up inside me.

Then I remembered he'd made it clear he didn't care for me. He'd gone out of his way to avoid saying I mattered. My lower lip trembled. A lump formed in my throat and my heart hurt. Against my will, tears threatened and my mouth trembled.

"Oh, honey," he said. "What am I going

to do with you?" His expression softened as he searched my face. Those eyes! Those gorgeous eyes. I got lost in them. He reached for me.

Before I could catch my breath, we were kissing.

The noise of Dodie walking out of the back room startled us into breaking apart. Detweiler and I quickly put distance between us.

"Kiki?" Dodie called over the racks of paper. "Another unhappy scrapbooker on the phone! I took a message. Call her back!"

I ran to the back room, woozy with desire. I stumbled into the bathroom, put down the toilet lid and sat there for a while. When I regained control of my body, I splashed my face with ice cold water. For good measure, I grabbed a Diet Dr Pepper and chugged it.

I dialed the number on the paper, but no one answered.

When I returned, Detweiler and Dodie were talking about the CAMP set up, the placement of tables, food, and so on. Dodie studied the list of attendees, offering whatever she knew about each of them. My face still burned. My legs wobbled like cranberry jelly. I felt as though I'd been ravished —

and all of me was aglow with the tingling, prickling sensation of arousal.

"I'm trying to put together a timeline," Detweiler turned to me. His tone was affable, almost conversational. "Here's what we've got."

He handed his notebook and a chart to me. I struggled to concentrate. When I glanced up to speak, he colored slightly. "This is right. At least as far as I can remember. And it matches the rough schedule I planned." I got up, retrieved my CAMP folder, and showed him and Dodie my notes.

Examining the timetable again, I realized something: The potted plants had been delivered some time that morning. Was it before or after Mert arrived? Dodie had purchased them. She pulled up at the same time I did, but it could have been her second trip.

Should I tell Detweiler? I couldn't decide. I was afraid if I did, the blame would shift to Dodie. That didn't make sense because she had the most to lose by killing Yvonne at her own event. Witness the fallout we were already taking! I opted to keep my mouth shut.

Dodie stared at the chart. "Wait a minute. Something's not right." She disappeared, returning with a dot matrix sheet in hand. "Here's the caterer's order form. We didn't order scones. Here's the grocery receipt from Mert. There aren't any scones listed there either."

"Any of the scrapbookers could have brought along the scones. Or the caterer might have thrown the scones in," I said. "Maybe they were a substitution. In which case, they could have been tainted before or after arriving at the church basement. But after would have been harder."

"Who worked with the caterers?" asked Detweiler.

Dodie flipped to the last page. At the bottom was Bama's signature. "But that doesn't mean anything," she added. "So Bama ordered the food and signed the form. Big deal. Did you check all the containers for traces of the icing and for prints? The trash cans? The plates?" She also handed over the list of goodies that each of us had contributed. What she didn't say, but all of us realized, was that he'd need to interview every one of our fifty-plus CAMPers to find out what each of them carried into the crop. The sheer magnitude of tracking down who brought tainted scones overwhelmed me.

I'd forgotten Dodie was a fan of police procedurals and true-crime novels. She watched every forensic show on television.

"The lab is going over everything we found. Of course at the time, we didn't think it was a murder so we might have missed something. But the caterer has been very accommodating. Both the chefs and servers have volunteered to take polygraphs. Probably at their employer's urging. As you can imagine, they're eager to prove this didn't happen in their kitchen."

"And the Epi-Pen?" I tried not to look directly at Detweiler. It felt too intimate. "How about it? Any fingerprints?"

"None besides Mrs. Gaynor's. Not even a partial," Detweiler admitted. "We got all excited when we found some empty syringes in the trash. But it looks like there's glue in them."

"That's right," said Dodie, "Using a syringe keeps the adhesive off your fingers and helps get glue into tight areas. I prefer using a toothpick, but each to her own. Since a tube is nearly airtight, the adhesive won't dry out like in a bottle."

"The empty syringes are being tested," Detweiler chuckled. "That was a new one on me. Son of a gun."

The door minder rang and Mert walked in. Her face was pale under her sun-bed tan, but otherwise she seemed fine. Dressed in her work uniform of white-collared knit shirt, black pants and black Reeboks, she approached with a subdued walk. I met her halfway with a big hug. Her shoulder muscles were hard as rocks, but she quickly relaxed under the warmth of my affection. I pulled back and gave both her hands a squeeze of encouragement.

"Don't trust him, Kiki," Mert stared at Detweiler. "I done thought he was different, but he ain't. He's a sleezeball like all the rest."

Detweiler turned away. But before he did, I noticed his face was bright red.

Since I had to pick up Anya at my mother-in-law's house, I couldn't stick around. I wasn't sure I wanted to either. When I left, Mert and Detweiler were glaring at each other. Dodie stood hands on hips and stared off into space. Time in a Bottle had always been my escape. A place I could go and forget my troubles. Where I could get lost in creative activity.

But that had changed.

Even so, I touched my lips with my finger-tips as I drove. He kissed me. He kissed me. I kept repeating that over and over in my head, dumbstruck with wonder and amazement. As much as I'd hated the scene with

Mert, I couldn't help myself. I was blissed out. And I wanted more.

Sheila was out in her front yard, pouring a green liquid into mole tunnels. Yellowish stains and blotches of mud splashed the hem of her ivory linen slacks. The ground was littered with empty jars that said "Kosher Dills" on the label.

Really, I was afraid to ask what she was doing.

"Pickle juice," she said. "Two new tunnels popped up overnight. One website said this will scare these suckers off. I saved the leftover dills for you because Anya likes them."

I surveyed the containers scattered across what had once been greens fit for a golf course. What on earth would I do with all those pickles? I considered helping, but there didn't seem to be anything left to do.

Sheila wore an expression of triumph as she waved a hand over the mess. "I got them this time. Fixed their little wagons good. Did you know moles have three to five pups a litter? And they don't really dig? They sort of swim through the dirt? Their front paws scrape at the soil. The back legs push it like a back-stroker moves water. Once the animal loosens enough soil, he turns a flip and from his back pushes the dislodged stuff upwards, creating the mole hill."

In my best imitation of Butterfly Mc-Queen, I said, "Golly, Miss Sheila, I don't know nuttin' about birthin' no moles, and that's the truth."

Sheila gave me a sidelong look. "I'm surprised at you, Kiki. You love animals."

"Animals, yes. Rodents, no. Not real fond of most reptiles, either."

"Moles are insectivores, not rodents." Sheila pointed to the nearly dry pickle bottles. "You can take all those home."

Right. We needed twelve bottles of pickles like I needed a fresh set of stretch marks across my stomach. Just to keep Sheila happy, I twisted lids on empty bottles. She shoved a cardboard box with dividers under my nose. Six bottles fit into the spaces. Sheila duplicated my efforts with the other half dozen jars. Without preamble my mother-in-law said, "I want you to come with me to the annual Opera Theatre Dinner this Saturday. It's black tie."

Super. Those were the operative words: "I want you to." Well, I had a perfect excuse. "I don't own a black tie. Black's not my color."

She gave me a scathing look.

I continued, "In fact, I don't own any evening clothes. I have nothing to wear." I'd lost weight after George died, and my old gowns hung on me. I happily donated them to a shop providing prom dresses to low-income girls.

If you live long enough, life displays a circular quality. I grew up as one of those impoverished girls, and now was back where I'd started. From poverty, I'd won a scholarship to opportunity, in the guise of college. From opportunity, I'd lost my chance at education to unplanned pregnancy. From unplanned pregnancy, I'd received the greatest gift life could offer — my child. Weighed on cosmic scales, I was infinitely rich, although my bank account might not concur with spiritual accounting practices.

Sheila lifted the box of pickle jars. "I'll take care of that. Anya and I will go shopping tomorrow to buy you a suitable gown, accessories, and shoes. I booked you into Spa La Femme, that new spa in Defiance, for various beauty treatments."

Sheila never bothered to ask. She simply assumed acquiescence. I gritted my teeth. If I kept it up, I could take a pass on beauty treatments and go directly to one of those "Dentures in One Day — $99" places advertised on billboards all over rural Missouri.

Two could play this game.

I trotted out my all-purpose excuse. "I have to work."

"Not this Saturday. Dodie scheduled that other woman. Florida? New Mexico?"

"Bama," I mumbled. "Like Alabama."

We loaded jars into my trunk while Guy hopped up and down barking furiously in the back seat.

"Good Lord, are you babysitting rats these days? You said you didn't like rodents."

I grimaced, stifling the urge to defend Guy's reputation. He might be a brat, but he wasn't a rat. As I mustered a comeback, Guy hurled himself toward Sheila, hitting the half-open passenger window, bouncing back and landing on Gracie's slumbering head. Aroused, my Great Dane lifted her blocky countenance to gaze at me sadly. Guy's short legs dangled around Gracie's ears like flaps on a hunting cap. My dog tilted her head to stare at me, dumping the terrier with a thump onto the car floor. Gracie lifted an eyebrow at me.

The message in those gentle brown eyes was clear: You just can't fight stupid.

Sheila dusted her hands. "I'll take Anya shopping in downtown Ladue after science camp tomorrow."

"Okay," I called to Sheila's back as she headed toward her front door. "I'll go with you to Opera Theatre. And I'll spend the day Saturday getting a manicure. Pedicure. Whatever."

Sheila continued walking, her hand fluttering like a queen bored with an impertinent courtier. She'd commanded, and I'd given in. What else was new?

Maybe I could make up the lost weekend hours by working on a freelance project. First I'd have to scrounge up a freelance project. I'd finished the anniversary album and the happy recipients had been in to pick it up. But they'd quickly started asking questions about "that woman who died while scrapbooking." When I didn't have much to say, they'd paid their bill and toddled off into the sunset.

Fat chance of getting more freelance business while people were blaming us for Yvonne Gaynor's death. I leaned my head against the fabric roof of my old convertible. Why was life so complicated?

Sheila disappeared inside her impressive home. I felt too spent, too tired, and too grubby to follow. Minutes later she returned carrying a tray. With an imperious gesture, she bade me to come join her. As we settled in her wicker chairs, she poured ice tea. I asked nervously, "When will Anya be ready?"

Sheila waved off my concern. "It's shady and cool where you parked under that tree. I think your dogs can handle another five minutes. That's all I gave her. She's on the computer Instant Messaging her friends. I expect she gave you an earful complaining about science camp. Don't pay any attention. That's to be expected. She's growing up. This will be like the terrible two's all over again. Including, but not limited to, rejection of everything, whether she really means it or not."

"Did you go through this with George?" We'd never talked much about her relationship with her son while he was alive. Now it seemed the most natural thing in the world. Sharing made us less alone in our grief. My marriage to her son hadn't been perfect, nor was it a match made in heaven. But he'd been a wonderful friend and a committed partner in raising our child.

Maybe romantic love is overrated.

I remembered Detweiler's kiss.

Not a chance.

A gentle breeze ruffled Sheila's hair. Until Harry's death, she'd been a brunette, but shortly thereafter, white hairs crowded out their darker neighbors. When her son died, she let her stylist color her hair a stunning shade of frosty white. As she considered my question, I noticed the features she'd passed through her son to my daughter: those lovely denim blue eyes, a high forehead, and a determined set of her jaw.

"Yes . . . in fact, George was absolutely hateful to me. And everyone else. Nearly got expelled from high school for his snotty attitude. When the teen years strike, the closer children are to their parents, the tougher it is for them to act independent in a respectful manner. Instead, they use the people they love as a battering ram. Once they've destroyed our figures, our hearts, our egos, our bank accounts, and our self-esteem, it's on to our jugular veins. That's one reason we work hard to get them into a good college. It's good for us — and for them — to move away. While they're under our roofs, they make us miserable with their in-your-face presence, and when they're off at school, they make us so lonely we could cry. It's a no-win situation. But before you get to the point of losing it with Anya, call me and I'll pick her up." Her eyes twinkled over the sprig of mint in her tea. "It's harder for her to break my heart than to break yours. Mine's been around the block a couple of times."

At home, Anya insisted on taking Guy for a

walk. Watching her wrap the leash around one hand and maneuver her cell phone in the other, I could tell this wasn't about exercising the dog. It was a thinly veiled excuse for privacy. The dynamic duo were gone about five minutes. Upon returning, Anya plopped down on the sofa, still chatting into her cell phone. While he'd been nosing around at Anya's feet, Guy discovered a rubber ball in the box of dog toys we keep for our guests.

Next thing I knew, Anya was tossing it for the little fellow. Airborne Guy appeared in snapshots, leaping past the kitchen door to snatch the toy mid-flight. I put down the hamburger I was forming into patties, washed my hands, and stepped into the living room to issue a caution. Now Guy was running up the side of the walls and turning flips. Anya paused her conversation long enough to look on in shock.

"Stop that, honey. He'll break something." I walked over to Guy and patted him, running my hands along his body to encourage him to settle down. He wriggled with joy, but I shushed him until he grew calmer.

"All you do is gripe at me," said my daughter. "I hate living in this tiny box of a house. If we had more room, I could play. And if I could play games on our computer like all my friends do, I wouldn't be so bored."

"Let's not discuss this right now," I countered reasonably. "I'm tired and hungry and —"

"And another thing. There's no privacy," Anya continued. "I can't even have a conversation without you listening in. If I had text messaging, I could —"

"Anya, not now. Not tonight. We'll discuss this some other time." Her angry eyes bored holes in my back as I turned toward the kitchen. I called over my shoulder. "In a few minutes, you need to set the table." I heard her mimicking my voice, but I ignored the invitation to a quarrel.

It had been a long, rotten day. I looked forward to a relaxing shower. Maybe under the stimulus of running water, I could come up with a plan for finding Yvonne's killer. And figure out what Mert meant when she warned me not to trust Detweiler — or was she saying I shouldn't trust cops in general? I hadn't had the chance to pin her down.

Probably her comment was a reaction to the grilling by the police. I knew she liked Detweiler and thought him a good man.

Yeah, that had to be it.

I leaned against the shower wall and opened my hands to the cascade of water.

The prickling of droplets on my palms always soothes me. Rubbing the fingers of one hand against the palm of the other stimulates a stress-reducing acupressure site. In the shower, you might as well let the water work on both hands at once. A long sigh released the last of my tension. Wrought-up energy leaked from my body and flowed down the drain.

Detweiler's face came unbidden. He always soothed me. Well, nearly always. His presence made me feel safe and . . . And what? Loved? Dare I think that? The memory of our kiss intruded on all other thoughts, even though I tried to put it aside. The warm and luscious feelings I'd locked away were dangerously close to breaking down my carefully constructed protective barriers.

I hadn't given my whole heart to George, but he'd had enough of it to hurt me deeply. My fingers touched my lips, re-igniting the passionate kiss Detweiler and I shared. I wasn't ready to love another man. Or was I?

## WHY YOU NEED DIFFERENT GLUES FOR DIFFERENT JOBS

Check out any crafter's supplies and you'll see a plethora of adhesives. The reason? Different sticky stuff works best for different jobs. Here's a rundown:

1. Photo splits — The most common way of adhering photos to paper. These are double-sided tape squares. To adhere them, first remove the ribbon of splits from the box. (Yes, they say you can use the box as an applicator, but don't believe it!) Next, peel off the waxy blue tab to reveal the sticky square. Now, press the square to the photo and lightly burnish it. This makes the square stick to the photo. Finally, lift off the ribbon.
2. Foam squares or dots — These raise your item off the surface. You peel off the backing almost like you do with photo splits. By the way, don't ignore the extra foam "frame" around the dots and squares. You can use that too!
3. Clear glue — Okay, they lie. A lot of these so-called "clear" glues aren't. So first test them on an

inconspicuous piece of paper. The best way to apply these is by using a toothpick or a coffee stirrer. Dip the toothpick or stirrer into the glue, wipe off the excess and apply.

4. Glue sticks — We love UHU Stic Glue Stick. This is perfect for adhering paper to altered items like chipboard.

5. Double-sided tape — Not so much. It can be difficult to peel off the backing. If there's no backing, it's just plain difficult. It is good for sticking a pocket to a page.

6. Tape — Make sure what you get is archivally safe, as the packaging can be unclear. This is great for reinforcing holes, for securing the ends of paper or ribbon, and so on.

7. Crafter's Pick "The Ultimate!" — A high-performance adhesive that will stick metal, plastic, and glass to other surfaces. Great stuff.

8. Xyron — This is a machine that allows you to create your own stickers by putting adhesive on the back of things. Works well for small pieces and for vellum.

9. HERMA Dotto Removable — Best bet for beginners because it's repo-

sitional. Use it when you want to try out an arrangement on your page, but you're not ready to commit.

# SEVEN

I dropped Anya off at camp with a reminder: "Your grandmother will pick you up to go clothes shopping, and I'll come get you tomorrow afternoon at her house."

"Goody, goody," she said sarcastically.

Gone for sure was the biddable sweet child of six months ago. Hello, hellion!

Actually I should thank the good Lord I worked forty-plus hours a week. If she'd been like this when I was a stay-at-home mom, it would have done me in completely. Now I needed to get her snarling tone out of my head. Other people depended on me. My mood needed a pick-me-up. I couldn't walk into Time in a Bottle wearing a grumpy expression. Especially not when we had a reputation to repair.

I pulled into Kaldi's for a treat. As I got out of my car, another patron walked by. Guy slammed himself into the back of my seat, barking like a Doberman on crack.

I ignored him and followed my nose to the origin of the scent of coffee. Then I ordered my current favorite: A toasted chestnut brew.

When I returned to the car, I opened my glove box and extracted two dog yummies while I savored my drink. Gracie sniffed the air and cranked up her big tail, thump, thump, thump. She had taken over the passenger seat when Anya left the car. My faithful co-pilot perked up her ears and kept her rheumy eyes fixed on the treats in my hand. A young woman was walking past, and Guy again hurled himself at the triangular backseat window which I'd left cracked.

"Hey!" she said, "Is that Guy? Hi, boy! How's life? Huh? How's the widdle Guy-boy doggers, huh?" She reached in and petted the small dog.

Guy pranced excitedly while yodeling. I asked, "You know this fellow? I'm just dogsitting."

"Yeah, I went to college with Karen. Heard she got a job and her new apartment doesn't allow pets. Lucky thing. About the job, I mean." This sweet-looking girl had more holes in her face than a colander. I wondered, wasn't all that painful? Who signed up for more misery in life? Only the young, I guessed.

She withdrew her hand from the window, but Guy wanted more. He jumped from the back on top of Gracie. Now he was dangling from my passenger side window. I had him by his back legs as he accepted the girl's affection with glee. His pink tongue slathered her hand, and his front paws pinned her forearm as effectively as a pair of handcuffs.

I carefully retrieved the half of Guy that was sticking out, lifting him up and over Gracie, depositing him onto the back seat, and praying the coffee between my thighs would not get knocked over in the process. A sad howl erupted as the girl started to walk away. She'd only gone a few steps when she turned, a finger to her mouth thoughtfully, and came back.

"Whatever you do, don't let him watch *Sesame Street.* Especially Elmo. Wow. Not Elmo. Ever."

After I got the dogs settled in the back room, I took out the trash and set the recycling crates by the curb. Seeing neatly stacked newspapers reminded me of the ones I'd used as padding under my knees when helping Sheila. Here was my chance to trade those papers, with their dirt and damp, for a new set. I pulled the society section from the clean recycling and started toward my BMW.

That's how it came to me. I was staring down at the wedding photos when I realized most of the portraits were taken by professional photographers. Those photogs must have pretty stiff competition. Wouldn't custom albums give them an edge? And who better to offer them than TinaB? All it would take was a few phone calls, and I'd know whether this idea was a keeper. I hurried into the store and flipped open the phone book to make a list of commercial photographers mentioning "Wedding" in their ads.

Since the listings covered a page and a half, my sheet filled up quickly. A few of the ads contained only names and phone numbers. Those I wrote on a second sheet. Maybe some did weddings, but some probably didn't, so a phone call would sort what was what. Midway through my second list, the back door opened, and Dodie straggled in. Her hair stuck out from her head like a bad pincushion, and her clothes sported wrinkles as though she'd slept in them.

She tossed a newspaper onto the desk in front of me, scattering my work. Her lack of concern about what I was doing irritated me, and I nearly said so — until my eyes focused on the banner across the front page:

"Tainted Scone Kills Scrapbooker."

According to *Post-Dispatch* sources speaking on the basis of anonymity, "noted local scrapbook celebrity" Yvonne Gaynor died from a severe allergic reaction to baby aspirin mixed with icing on an orange scone. Yvonne's photo appeared alongside a picture of our storefront. The cutline announced, "The scrapbooking event hosted by this business turned deadly when contaminated food was served." St. Louis Police Chief Robbie Holmes said, "The killer knew the victim was highly sensitive to aspirin. It's a rare allergy. The Major Case Squad is vigorously pursuing several leads."

Jumping inside, the story continued with remarks by Ellen Harmon, owner of the area's "premier" scrapbook store. "Yvonne Gaynor was the sweetest woman, well-liked by everyone. One of her dreams came true when she was chosen as a Scrapbook Star winner." Ellen explained this award made Yvonne a target. "It certainly is interesting that her death would occur at an event hosted by one of our competitors."

My coffee almost made a repeat performance. I swallowed hard to keep from upchucking.

A photo of Yvonne's grieving husband and children ran beside a sidebar explaining that

Memories First would host a memorial program and display of Yvonne's work sometime next week. "We hope to raise money for Yvonne's children," said Ellen.

Dodie hung over my shoulder reading along with me, her eternally clogged sinuses rustling as she breathed warm air on my bare arms. When I closed the paper, she murmured, "I think I'm going to be sick," before heading for the john. All I could do was bury my head in my hands. This was a lot worse than I'd expected. Ellen insinuated we were responsible for Yvonne's death while finding a way to draw a crowd to her store and make money.

I didn't resent the fact Yvonne's family would benefit from the memorial program. Not at all. But I took exception to the light we were cast in. Clearly the finger of responsibility was pointed at us — and we were innocent! With a feeling of dread, I checked our messages. The queue was full. Reluctantly, I pressed the replay button and started listening.

One caller condemned us as murderers and thieves. Two women wanted refunds. I couldn't blame them. Obviously, the news had spurred them to action. A lot of our scrappers are on a tight budget, and who knew when we'd offer a new CAMP session? For that matter, who could be certain we wouldn't get kicked out of CAMP? Or go under completely? One strident voice suggested we close our doors and leave town — or else. Didn't sound like a scrapbooker to me. Most people who scrap are nice. That sounded more like a hatemongerer.

Even so, I was shaking, I was that upset, when I recognized the warm voice of one of our regulars, Vanessa Johnson, on the phone.

No, no, not Vanessa too, I prayed. She was one of our scrapbooking stalwarts. I closed my eyes and listened.

"Dodie, Kiki, and Bama? I've been thinking of you. Those of us who know you realize this isn't your fault." I silently blessed the woman. She continued, "Most of us will be coming to the Friday crop. 'Til then, please know you are in our prayers. Keep your chins up."

For the summer, we'd moved our regular Monday crop to coincide with our Newbie-Do-Be-Do, our beginners' crop held every Friday. Learning our regulars hadn't deserted us ignited a small flare of hope in my heart. What was it they said about the public having a short memory? Maybe by the weekend, this would blow over. I thought if we were really lucky, some other calamity would take our place on the front page! Then I immediately chided myself for being so callous. How could I hope for tragedy to strike someone else? How selfish was that?

Well, selfish or not. I crossed my fingers. I loved this place. I loved the women who trusted us with their photos. I loved being creative. I couldn't stand to see what I loved — and needed — disappear.

The sixth call was a tinny, metallic voice. "We're going to get you. Just you wait. You think you can kill a good Christian and get away with it? You'll die, you monsters." I instinctively recoiled from the phone, pushing away and staring at the machine as though it were alive. The message ended and I sat frozen in place. I gathered my senses and decided not to share what I'd heard with Dodie. She'd left the bathroom and walked past me on her way to open the front door for the day's business — her shoulders heavy with worry; her gait slow and shuffling. The sight of her saddened me.

I didn't erase the message. I sat quietly staring at the answering machine and running my hands up and down my arms to warm away the chill. Two more communications were from hesitant customers who left their names and requested a return call. Yet another message began in the same tinny voice and suggested God's warriors would avenge Yvonne's death. The voice described in hideous detail how we would be . . . molested.

That did it. I hit the call back code and discovered both threatening messages were blocked. No surprise. I dialed Detweiler, and he picked up right away. I asked if we could meet for lunch. He suggested Alandale's, a brewing company a few blocks south and east of the store. Making an executive decision, I disconnected the answering machine and put it in the oversized bag I use for transporting my crafts. Anyone who wanted us personally had our cell numbers. Customers would have to wait until business hours anyway. With the machine gone, there could be no sly and threatening messages.

This way I could share the message without involving Dodie. This crisis — taken with Horace's bad news — demoralized her. I couldn't fix the problem, but I could spare her more pain.

The Churovich brothers opened Alandale Brewing Company in a former furniture warehouse on a corner in Kirkwood. Detweiler was sitting in a large booth in the back and nursing a beer.

"I'm off duty," he said.

He ordered a Cuban sandwich of ham, roast pork, Swiss and Monterey jack cheese and other toppings, with house-made potato chips. I chose the fish and chips because I hadn't had fish in a month or so.

Daren, the Churovich brother who is brewmaster, came by and asked Detweiler how he liked his blackberry seasonal beer. "Is it hard to brew beer?" I asked. Daren, tall and blonde and shy, smiled. "Nah. It's mainly watching. We hold classes on Tuesdays if you want to learn more."

My meal was fantastic. The batter light and fluffy and the fish firm and flaky. I thought I was full until Dana, Daren's wife and a Jazzercise instructor, happened by and suggested dessert.

Detweiler and I decided to split Dutch apple bread pudding with pecan streusel. I told myself that I was eating fancy Granny Smith apples, which was true. While we shared the food, he passed me a copy of his tentative timeline. He was right about most of the morning, but I clarified, "People were in and out for a good half hour hauling in their scrapbook gear and food."

"But the event was catered." Detweiler's fork paused with a chunk of apple midway to his mouth. Instead of splitting the piece into two, we'd companionably taken turns dipping our forks into the dessert.

"It was, but scrapbookers are big eaters. A lot of the women bring homebaked goodies or their favorite munchies. One woman is this big Fresca freak. She drags her own cooler to every crop."

"How much Fresca can one woman drink?"

"I've seen her plow through a twelve-pack in a three-hour crop. Of course, she doesn't do as much pasting as peeing, but point being, lots of folks had access to the food and the room."

"Did you leave anyone alone at any time?"

I hesitated. I'd asked Dodie about her recollection of the crop before I headed out. She'd admitted she'd made two trips to the church. One before Mert arrived. "But that doesn't mean anything."

He gave me a disgusted grunt. "You didn't tell me this earlier."

I shrugged.

He leaned in close. "Mrs. Goldfader and I talked last night. She told me about delivering the plants. When are you going to learn to trust me?"

The answer was probably never. Not with my track record with men. And now I realized, he'd tricked me. He'd known she'd been there alone.

I gave a small, "Huh." Clearly, neither of us was honest with the other. How sad was that?

Detweiler crumpled his paper napkin and finished his beer. "That brings us to Mrs. Chambers. I know she's your friend, but she has a reason to hate Mrs. Gaynor."

"Maybe so, but that was years ago."

Detweiler pushed aside our dirty utensils. "So give me another suspect. Mrs. Harmon says the four of you were jealous. According to her, you copy every program she offers and fob it off as your own."

"That's a lie! In fact, it's the exact opposite. Whatever we do, she copies! She's . . . she's . . . such a creep! And I don't know why she's singled us out when there are three other stores in direct competition with her!" A big swig of ice water cooled me down. "Let me ask around, okay? Scrapbookers get to know each other. Maybe one of our customers can suggest someone in particular who wanted Yvonne dead."

He slammed a palm on the tabletop. "Whoa. It's one thing for you to tell me who you suspect. It's another for you to play detective. Stay out of it, Kiki. This isn't your job. Don't put yourself in harm's way. If you won't protect yourself, think of Anya."

"If our business doesn't rebound, I won't have a job. That's going to hurt my child *and* my friends. I have a stake in this, and I'm already at risk." I told him about the threatening phone calls, handing over the answering machine. "It's already out of control."

Detweiler shook his head. "This qualifies as a hate crime. I'll alert the Richmond Heights P.D. They can have a patrol car watch the store."

"Have you investigated Bama Vess?" I asked casually. "She was fired from her job at the Art Supply Superstore." This I knew from overhearing two customers as they picked out paper. I hadn't confirmed it, but the two who were talking were women not prone to idle gossip. I went a step further. "I bet I can find out why. Something's not right about her. Maybe she has a criminal history, hmm?"

He leaned close to me, so we were nearly nose to nose. "Don't you dare." I had a sudden impulse to kiss him. But of course I didn't. I did hope he'd notice the posters advertising live music at Alandale's and ask me on a real date.

He continued, "You better not interfere with our investigation. Do you realize you might tip off the killer? Or be next in line?

Kiki, this is dangerous stuff! I would've thought being chased by a gun-toting murderer this spring would have slowed you down, but I was wrong! Your escape gave you a skewed sense of invulnerability. Quit thinking of ways to get yourself in hot water." He huffed and puffed and settled down. "Tell me about this contest Mrs. Gaynor won."

A bright spark at *Saving Memories* magazine had devised a contest to round up cutting-edge work from new, undiscovered talent. The prize was publication and its attendant recognition. I explained, "But the powers that be at the magazine stumbled onto a gold mine. Soon advertisers jumped on the bandwagon, sponsoring the contest and donating sample products as prizes. Now winning means an endless supply of free merchandise from a variety of manufacturers and guest appearances as teachers for conventions."

"Back up. How come the winners get freebies in addition to the initial prizes?" Detweiler asked.

"The magazine posts designs on their website. Then they print a few winning layouts in each monthly issue, and more layouts appear in a special book. A list of products is printed along with each page design. Since scrapbookers hanker after the newest, brightest, best, most interesting supplies, having your product in one of these pages sells merchandise. Lots and lots of merchandise. Sending winners your good stuff functions like a product placement deal, see?"

He nodded. He ran his index finger around the curve created by my thumb and first finger. I felt a warming trend south of my equator. He was getting to me . . . again. My lips started to burn. Was it the vinegar I'd sprinkled on my chips or the memory of our kiss?

The restaurant was nearly empty. Detweiler didn't seem concerned about the time. "I still don't get it. Why would manufacturers send these women free supplies?"

I smiled. "Having designers use your products on pages is the least expensive and most rewarding way of promotion."

"How expensive can paper be?"

I laughed. "It's not just paper. It's printers, photo developers, scanners, machines that laser cut designs, and on and on." I marveled at how little he knew. "Scrapbooking is at least a three billion — with a B — dollar industry. That probably doesn't take in stuff like computers, printers, copiers, and travel to conferences."

His jaw dropped. "Three billion?"

I nodded.

"Are the prizes the only reason women enter?"

"Oh, heck no. After they win, the women can be asked to write articles for the magazine. Some go on to design their own merchandise lines. A few get paid to teach or demonstrate products at conventions. Or at local stores."

"You're telling me Mrs. Gaynor became a player."

I laughed. "Well, that's a streetwise way of putting it, but yes. She was a real rising star."

"And two days later, she's dead."

I nodded soberly. "That's right. She had two whole days to enjoy her fame. It doesn't seem fair, does it?"

"Murder never is."

The store was eerily quiet when I returned. Dodie sat in her office, staring at a computer screen. I took Guy and Gracie for a quick trip around the block. Our store sat in the midst of a residential area, mostly inhabited by senior citizens. As our neighbors died or moved to nursing homes, new owners converted the houses to apartments or duplexes.

I felt a wave of sadness as I walked along

with the dogs. Without the steadying influence of its senior citizens, the whole tenor of this area would change.

After I settled Gracie and Guy in their playpen, I brainstormed new ways to bring business to Time in a Bottle. But my vagabond thoughts returned to Yvonne's murder. The newspaper article called her a celebrity and tagged Memories First as the area's premier store. Huh. The magazine issue featuring the winners' work hadn't hit the newsstands yet. Yvonne's star status was not widely known. And those who did know her were finding this new attention difficult to credit. After all, her work hadn't garnered any accolades before.

Calling her a celebrity was a bit over-the-top. In fact, it was exaggeration with three Gs. And claiming that Memories First was the "premier" scrapbook store in the area?

Puh-leeze.

Memories First occupied a squat building with peeling siding north of St. Louis. The interior was plug-ugly institutional green with linoleum floors. Ellen Harmon filled the place with rickety wire racks full of the cheapest products she could buy. Even though she copied our classes, she was always a half-beat behind us. No way was her store the top of the food chain. She was barely dragging her one-celled body through the mud.

But I was media savvy enough to know that a lot of folks believe whatever they hear on radio and TV. If it's in print, they think it must be true. None of this media attention reflected well on my place of employment.

How could we regain the luster Time in a Bottle once enjoyed? Was that why Yvonne had been killed? To hurt our business? That was pretty drastic. Or had she died because of some unknown aspect of her personal life? Thinking back to the tangled situation surrounding my husband's death, this seemed most likely. What secret could Yvonne have taken to her grave? A marital problem? An old grudge? A vendetta?

Not for one minute did I believe my friend Mert had anything to do with Yvonne's death.

Could it have been an accident? Was the tainted food intended for someone else? Was Yvonne simply both incredibly unlucky and incredibly ill-prepared?

Who knew she had allergies? Her husband must have, of course. Had he planned her demise? He had access to her purse and the Epi-Pen. Was he involved with someone else? Did he have a life insurance policy on her? Detweiler hadn't mentioned whether the police were looking into her family life, but didn't they always?

Pushing my speculation aside, I concentrated on coming up with a new technique for the Friday Night Crop. I decided we would create a subtitle within a title. It's a clever but simple idea that can be used on pages or on cards.

Adding a cutting-edge learning experience and special projects to a crop was just one of our innovative ideas. Providing super classes, ongoing support in the store, the latest merchandise, an on-site computer and printer, well, those were some of the extras we offered our customers.

And Ellen Harmon said we copied her.

Huh! Not hardly.

# KIKI'S SUBTITLE-WITHIN-A-TITLE TECHNIQUE

(Inspired by a similar step-by-step created by Venessa Matthews and featured in the May 2006 issue of *ScrapBook inspirations* magazine.)

This idea gives your titles a cool, fresh, and funky look — plus it allows you to add extra information about your page or project.

You'll need letter stamps at least 2″ high, ink or acrylic paint, a pen, temporary adhesive, and a strip and a large piece of waste paper.

1. Choose a word to be the predominant portion of your title. (Example: let's use HOLIDAY)
2. Roughly stamp out your predominant word on your waste paper. This will be used as a pattern to help you figure out dimensions for Step 3.
3. Cut a strip of waste paper 3/8″ wide and 1″ longer than your predominant word. (For example, use your pattern of HOLIDAY to figure out how long to make your strip of waste paper.)
4. Figure out where you want your

title to go on your "good" paper. Adhere that strip with removable glue (HERMA Dotto is perfect) so it will run through the middle (top to bottom) of your predominant word — so the strip will run smack through the horizontal middle of HOLIDAY, almost like a lane stripe runs down the center of a road — through your desired background. The strip will run horizontally across the middle of your title.

5. Ink your letter stamps and stamp the predominant word (HOLIDAY in our case) right over the top of strip of waste paper. Remember to center the letters as you stamp them, so the strip runs through the middle, top to bottom, of the word.

6. Let the stamped word dry. Remove the strip of waste paper.

7. In the un-inked space — the blank, unstamped area between the top and bottom of your letters — you can now write a subtitle or a message with your pen. (Example: You would have printed out the word HOLIDAY, but in the middle of the word there's a blank space 3/8″ wide. There you could write the

words "family traditions.")

*Note: Of course, you could also use a stencil instead of a stamp for your letters. Follow the steps to #4. Instead of using the stamps, stencil in each letter by dabbing paint or ink through the negative space.*

# EIGHT

At five o'clock, Dodie and I went our separate ways in the parking lot. She hadn't left her desk all afternoon and barely said "goodbye" as we were leaving. I drove Guy and Gracie home, making a quick stop at the public library to pick up one of the current bestsellers they loaned out for seven days at a time. I grabbed two: the latest "Jack Daniels" book by J. A. Konrath and a new "Ophelia and Abby" book by Shirley Damsgaard. What I needed, I reasoned, was a way to "get lost" mentally. To leave all this turmoil about a real murder behind. To give my brain a breather from worrying about business.

And, yeah, I also wanted to quit thinking about Detweiler. We'd had such a nice lunch together. He'd followed me to my car for a repeat performance of his knee-buckling kiss. I could still feel the warm, liquid response of my body. But he hadn't asked

me to dinner or out on a date. This relationship — if indeed, it could be called that —
was moving at a glacial rate.

I fixed myself a huge bacon, lettuce, and
tomato salad using a lush homegrown
tomato from an "I trust you" produce stand
where an empty coffee can announced,
"One lb. for 25 cents." I dropped in a dime,
sniffing my singular fragrant prize with
delight. The sun-warmed fruit in my hand
smelled red. Unlike mushy tasteless veggies
bred to withstand coast to coast shipping, a
homegrown Big Boy or Better Girl has firm
fleshy chambers and a mouthwatering taste
coming from the jelly surrounding its seeds.
That first bite of my BLT salad transported
me to the days of growing up dirt poor. In
my little neighborhood, every family planted
at least a dozen "tomay-ter" plants in the
backyard.

Afterward, I took a hot bath and started
reading about Ophelia and her teenage
charge, Tink.

It should have been paradise: a great meal,
new books, and a relaxing bath.

But I couldn't stop worrying.

Was Dodie going to be okay? Who killed
Yvonne Gaynor? How would we rebuild our
business? Why didn't Detweiler pursue our
relationship? When did my daughter get so

sassy? And how could I get out of the fancy Opera Theatre dinner with Sheila?

Researchers have found there's a worry gene, a genetic component passed down through families.

It figured. One more problem people could blame on their mothers.

Of course we always worry about the wrong things.

I thought my list of concerns exhaustive, but I was in for a surprise the next morning when I pulled into the Time in a Bottle parking lot. A big red swastika dripped its way down the side of our store. Written in the frayed lettering of spray paint, the words, "Die Jews! Die!" were scrawled below the symbol. I staggered out of my car like I'd been punched in the gut. A wave of nausea roiled over me.

Thank goodness dogs can't read. They simply stood beside me, wagging their tails and wondering why we weren't going inside. I fumbled around in my bag and hit the speed dial for Detweiler, turning quickly to see Dodie drive her big black Expedition up the alley and park beside me. It wasn't until she climbed down from the driver's seat that she noticed the graffiti.

"It's okay," I stepped between her and the

ugly epithet. "I called Detweiler —"

She stuck out her neck to see around me, pushed me gently aside, and moaned. Her normally ruddy complexion turned ghastly pale before she ran for the bushes, making horrible retching noises.

I was stunned. My poor boss had been physically sickened by the paint smears on the building.

I tied the dogs' leashes to my car door and hurried to her aid. Puking preferences are highly individualistic. I always feel like I can't breathe and even though it embarrasses me, I like to have someone nearby. George used to lock himself in the bathroom, refusing all help or attention. Anya wants someone to hold her lightly around the waist so she doesn't tip into the toilet.

I had no way of knowing how to help Dodie, or if I should, so I stood a respectful distance — until she sagged like a marionette whose handler had dropped the strings. Kneeling beside her, I put my arm around her big shoulders to keep her steady and called Horace, her husband.

*"Oy vey,"* he moaned. "My poor, poor *far-mutshet* darling. My own *sheyna ponim!* Her parents, you know, they survived the Holocaust. My poor darling. Please say I am coming to her. You're a good friend to my

131

*kallehniu.*"

Only later did I learn he'd said Dodie was "exhausted," calling her by his pet nickname "pretty face," and thanking me for being a good friend to his "little bride." Horace's switch to Yiddish signaled the depth of his despair. With her family history, I could understand why the vandalism hit her so hard.

And on top of all her other problems? No wonder she had headed for the shrubs.

No matter how I tried to rationalize, her recent behavior was out of character. Meanwhile, I patted her back softly and told her Horace was on his way.

"It's just paint," I spoke to that big bush of gray hair. "Silly old paint. We'll get it off as soon as Detweiler checks it out."

The detective and Horace arrived simultaneously. They made an odd pair, Detweiler being well over six feet and Horace barely topping five. I relinquished my spot beside Dodie to her husband. The gentle way he slipped his arm around his wife reminded me how comforting it was to be married. Dodie rose tiredly and rested against the little man, the way Tiny Tim relied on a crutch.

I told her, "I'll take care of the store. Go on home, Dodie. Put your feet up and take a break, okay?"

Detweiler reached over to squeeze Dodie's shoulder. "Mrs. Goldfader, the crime scene people are on the way. They'll see what clues they can uncover. Have you had any threats at home? On your phone?"

Dodie shook her head. "No. None. Just here. I've been getting mail addressed to me with . . . images."

I was shocked. She'd never mentioned any problems to me. Turning bleary eyes toward the building, she added, "I suppose this is about Yvonne Gaynor, right? We had all those calls yesterday . . ."

I was glad I hadn't told her about the threats on the machine. "It wasn't as bad as we expected. Really, it wasn't. Vanessa Johnson even called to say she and our other regulars sent kind thoughts. Try not to stress out about this, Dodie. Sure, a few people have wanted refunds, but you know scrappers. They were just being practical."

Detweiler added, "A police department clerk called your customers yesterday and told them we'd finished looking over their cameras. We've made arrangements for them to be returned. The women acted pleased. None of them seemed rude or angry." He paused. "I realize this has been tough on you and your business. Try not to worry. We'll get to the bottom of this, Mrs. Goldfader."

Dodie's mouth quivered. "You even suspect me! You asked me to come to the station the night before last, after the store closed."

Shock number two. I mean, I should have known. Hadn't he said he wasn't ruling out anybody? Geez. And he'd told me they talked! Right. He fussed at me about keeping secrets when he'd omitted hauling my boss in for questioning.

"It's my job to investigate every possibility. You know that." He glanced my way. "Even Kiki is under suspicion."

Despite my irritation, I gave Dodie a little wave, a flutter of my fingers and a "yep, me too" nod of the head.

From under one of Dodie's tree limb-like arms, Horace's lively eyes studied the bigger man. An almost imperceptible movement of his eyebrows acknowledged his understanding of Detweiler's difficult position. He turned his wife toward his car. "Let's go home, my love. Don't worry about your car. I can drop you back at the store if you decide to return later."

"Horace, is there anything I can do to help?" I asked after he'd closed the passenger door with Dodie safely inside.

He turned to the heavens. "God gives troubles, and shoulders." He smiled a sad smile. "If I think of anything, I'll call you."

People could say what they wanted about how mismatched they were physically, but Dodie and Horace were *the* perfect couple. They depended on each other, turned to each other for consultation and comfort, and most of all, respected each other. That old fashioned word "helpmeet" came to mind. Dodie once told me, "I can't understand people being rude to their spouses. Your husband or wife should be the one person in the world you treat with loving patience. He or she chose you above all others — for a lifetime! And yet I see women who are nicer to their girlfriends, and men who are more thoughtful toward their employees. That's *meshuganeh.* Friends come and go. Employees move on. Your partner is there for the long haul. He deserves your best every day of your life."

It was a comment I took to heart. I only prayed that one day I would have another chance to put her advice into practice.

It was weird. I was fine while I concentrated on Dodie, but the minute I was alone in the store, I started to shake like a sapling in a tornado. Stop it, I told myself. I didn't have the luxury of going to pieces. Graffiti or no graffiti, I needed a fun project to go with the "subtitle within a title" technique for our regular crop.

I decided to experiment with paper bag albums. True, the bags aren't archivally safe, but they make a fun base for collecting memorabilia after a trip or special event. As a cheap project, they were unbeatable. I whipped up one or two in no time. While I stood back to critically assess my results, Nettie and Rena walked in. Luckily by then, the clean-up crew had removed all traces of the ugly message from our wall.

"I know, I know," Nettie said to me. "You've never seen me this late in the day. I'm usually such an early bird. But Rena wanted to stop by, and I needed more patterned paper."

"Actually, I'm glad to see both of you. I was thinking of sending you both a note. I am so sorry about Yvonne. My sympathy goes to you both, as well as her family. I know you three were close. I recall she rode with you to the crop. That must have been hard — going home without her."

Despite Detweiler's warning about meddling, or perhaps because of it, I was determined to move this investigation along. The fact he'd fingered both of my friends as suspects added to the urgency.

"That's right," said Rena. "I drove. Yvonne was so excited about the contest she chattered the whole way there. I was nearly deaf from all her jabbering. And Yvonne made Nettie sit in the back with our supplies because she's started smoking again. That's so gross. Stinks up everything."

Nettie shrugged off the aspersion and added, "She called us the day she got the news. Couldn't wait to brag about winning. Have you seen her pages on the website?"

No, I admitted I hadn't.

Nettie snorted.

I filed that away.

Both women stared at me expectantly. They'd lobbed the conversational badminton over the net and expected me to return it. But I was not on my game. "I'm sure I'll be surprised. To be frank, I hadn't realized Yvonne's skills were so . . . advanced."

Nettie's face twisted. "They weren't."

Rena cut in. "Her death is devastating to her family. Really. Why poor Perry, her husband, is going to need a lot of TLC to get through this."

Nettie snorted. "Pollen count is up. Sorry." She covered her nose and mouth with a grubby handkerchief and blew hard. A whiff of stale tobacco floated my way. I couldn't help but think that smoking and allergies were a bad combination.

Nettie was tall and large-boned with a disappointed and tired face. "So are we, but life goes on, right? Rena and I thought we'd make a memorial album for the family. Or we could do a group project. We figured you'd want to contribute."

"Of course. What did you have in mind?"

"We'd considered making pages for the kids to fill in as the years go on. Leaving blanks for birthdays and holidays and such. What do you think?" Rena asked.

"They're already making a tribute album covering Yvonne's life over at Memories First," Nettie said. A certain sourness colored her voice. "Excuse me, I need a ciggie. Do you have any more cola?"

I volunteered to get another couple of drinks from the back. "Don't mind her." Rena noted me watching the front door. She fiddled with a combination of ribbons and tags. "You do know about Nettie, right?"

"Um, know what?"

Rena leaned close to speak to me just under her breath. "She's suffering a psychological problem related to getting Lyme disease from a tick bite. It causes really big mood swings. She's had seizures and now brain lesions. Medication can keep it in

138

check, but still . . . she has her ups and downs." Rena shook her head and continued. "I guess Nettie hates how the drugs make her feel. Her husband left her. Once her kids were old enough, they all moved out of the area. She's lost contact with them."

"Wow." That hit me like a blow to the solar plexus. I'd almost lost Anya in a custody battle, and the memory felt raw as an open sore. My heart went out to Nettie. Suddenly, I put her sharp comments and her angry manner in another light: the woman was hurting.

"All she has is her scrapbooking," whispered Rena as we heard Nettie's footsteps. "It's her whole life."

Nettie was heading back toward us. Rena changed the subject and began to speak loudly. "Ellen is putting pages up on the store website as quickly as they come in. But they aren't doing it because they care about Yvonne. Ellen Harmon is a publicity hound, through and through. And under most circumstances, she wouldn't even let kids into her store. Now she wants to make the Gaynor kids the centerpiece of her event!"

"The carpet mishap right?"

Nettie nodded as she took her seat.

This was legend in our scrapbooking community. In a store newsletter Ellen published a close-up photo of saltine crackers ground into her rug. Underneath she put the headline: Vandalism! The article was a rant about how unsupervised children — indeed, all children — were no longer welcome in her store.

The article appeared right before Christmas. Dodie and I had read it in stunned silence. Here's the $64,000 question: Who did she think her customers were?

Duh. Women with kids?

Ding-ding-ding! You win the prize!

Rena nodded. "The carpet incident. After that, kids were *verboten.*"

Nettie said nothing. The part down the center of her dark hair served to emphasize her broad and freckled forehead. I thought about what Rena said. I'd often thought Nettie was distracted or shy. Now I knew better. Probably she was just heavily medicated.

Rena interrupted my reverie with, "Trust Ellen to capitalize on a tragedy. Her store's so full of customers, you can't walk around. I hate that she's benefited from Yvonne's death."

"I agree totally," said Nettie. "She should be shot."

I curbed my tongue. This was getting interesting. I wanted desperately to keep the women talking. "Look, why don't we make a list of special occasions you'd like layouts for? I'll photocopy them for you. We can coordinate papers — patterns and solids — and suggest folks use them so the album has a good flow. You can tell me more about Yvonne. I didn't know her very well." I cleared a workspace for the women and went to the back to grab a couple of colas.

The women were eager to chat. At one time, they had all been neighbors. When Yvonne's husband, Perry, was promoted to IT department manager at RXAid, Inc., a drug manufacturing company, the Gaynors traded up to a bigger house in a nicer neighborhood. The family enrolled their children in private schools and upgraded every portion of their lives. Soon Yvonne was bragging about their vacations to Los Cabos and Cancun. She joined Weight Watchers and lost forty pounds. Bit by bit, she also shed her old friends.

"But she still liked to hang around with us when she scrapbooked," said Rena. "Her hoity-toity pals didn't do crafty stuff."

Nettie shrugged. "She could show off to us, but she was bottom of the totem pole in their eyes. She wasn't as well-accepted as she'd hoped to be. And she started gaining back the weight."

"What was her marriage like?" I was striving for that oh-so-casual tone of voice.

The two women exchanged glances full of meaning. Rena cleared her throat and compared two identical pieces of cardstock for what seemed like forever. Nettie hummed and fingered a stack of patterned papers. Finally, she said, "Perry wasn't happy with her . . ."

"Weight," finished Rena. She put her cola can in our recycling container.

Ah, there it was. The scourge of my generation of American women. Too much food, too much fast food, and too many empty calories. We were victims of our success as a nation of food producers. We'd succeeded in stocking our pantries, overloading our refrigerators and dispensing food at every stopping point along our daily path. I mean, where could you go and NOT find food? Add surfeit to surplus and multiply it by the lack of physical effort in our electrically enhanced lifestyle, and you got . . . fat. And lots of it. Enough to fill Oprah's little red wagon a zillion times over.

"There was talk about him having an affair," Nettie added. "Someone said it's with his secretary. Such a cliché," and she waved a hand in the air. "But still . . . you know, he thinks she's different, and she will be until he marries her. Different evaporates somewhere between pursuit and capture, if you want my opinion. Of course, we shouldn't be sharing any of this. The other woman was only a rumor."

Rena shifted her body and turned away. Obviously, Nettie's disclosures made her uncomfortable. She picked up a package of Mrs. Grossman's Stickers and examined them carefully. "Nettie, all that's just a rumor. Perry's really a wonderful guy. Very caring. And romantic. You're being unfair. Why are you so crabby?"

Nettie sniffed. "I haven't been getting any sleep. They're changing my meds."

If the conversation lingered on the subject of marital infidelity too long, I'd surely seem to be prying. Which I was. Besides which, I'd had my own little marital experience with a lying, two-faced sack of cattle dung, and I wasn't eager to reminisce.

Best to move on.

But before I could change the topic, Nettie continued, "I can say for a fact Perry lost a lot of money at the riverboats. I know, because my brother-in-law was with him when he dropped a bundle. Perry told him it wasn't the first time. The cops should consider that a motive. I heard Perry had Yvonne insured for, well, an obscene amount." She held up two patterned papers and a stripe for my approval. "Gee, you don't suppose he . . . uh . . . needed the money and planned her . . . demise?"

We all shuddered at the thought. Riverboat gambling in Missouri had traveled down a slippery embankment and landed in hot water. At first, the state allowed gambling vessels to cruise down the Mississippi, in part as tribute to the historical steamboats of yore. After awhile, boat owners argued that the cruises were dangerous and inconvenient. A compromise was reached to permanently dock the boats. More time passed, and investors diverted a small trickle of water from the Missouri River into a shallow pool, called it a tributary, and opened a casino there. With a wink and a nod, these have been nicknamed "boats in moats." At this rate, legislators might settle for having boats sprinkled with river water to bless them.

Rena glared at Nettie. "So Perry likes to play Texas Hold 'Em. A lot of people do. It's fun to visit the boats. He can afford to lose the money because he makes a healthy income. Perry's really a very nice man. Kind. Thoughtful. A good father. He has the most sensual mouth." She colored. "Yvonne always said that."

"Who knew she had allergies?" I asked.

"Nobody," said Nettie.

"Everybody," said Rena quickly.

Nettie shrugged. "Yvonne was a drama queen. You did things her way or she made your life miserable. She was a taker, not a giver. And she took a lot."

Rena pushed a list of special occasions toward me. "How does that look?"

"Terrific. I'll offer participants a discount on supplies."

Nettie sneezed. "That darn mold." She blew her nose and dabbed her eyes before focusing on me. "So . . . are you investigating Yvonne's death?"

"No, why would I?"

"One of the other scrappers said you solved your husband's murder." Nettie gave me the once-over as if to determine whether I was up to the task.

"No, it wasn't like that," I explained. "I . . . uh . . . I didn't solve anything. I just got in the way of a very nasty person. That's how the whole mess unraveled."

I might talk big to Detweiler, but the last thing I wanted was for anyone to know I considered myself an amateur sleuth. (Even if, in my heart of hearts, I did. Didn't I read every one of the Nancy Drew books over the course of a junior high summer? You betcha. And since last summer, I was an even more avid reader of mysteries. I had a newfound empathy for the characters and the puzzles they solved.)

Time to move on. "How many copies should I make? Nettie, should we use your name as the person collecting and collating the pages?"

In pearls, pumps, and a St. John's suit, Sheila stood in her front yard, bashing mole tunnels with a shovel. Dirt flew past me and rained on her. Raising the tool again and again, she walloped mounds until they flattened. I stepped back quickly, realizing the only control Sheila had was in her upswing. Gravity took over on the down stroke.

This was going to play heck with her golf game.

"We didn't find anything appropriate for you to wear to the Opera Theatre dinner. Friday, after science camp, Anya and I will hit more stores." The word "hit" was emphasized with a bash of the shovel. "Don't forget her allergist appointment tomorrow at eleven. You'll need to pick her up early from camp." She paused to wrestle the heel of her leather pump out of a sink hole.

"Drat these stupid *hafarferot.*" She smacked a loose clod of dirt and scattered chunks across a two-foot area. A clump of soil the size of a quarter landed on her nose. She rubbed it, creating a dark smudge across her stunning cheekbones.

"Ferrets, huh? At least you don't have moles. Good news, right?"

"You ninny. *Hafarferot* is Hebrew for moles, plural. The word has a common root with the verb 'to dig.' And that's exactly what these rascals have done. Just look at my yard!"

From my vantage point, she'd made more of a mess than the critters had. Poor Mr. Sanchez. He would return from Mexico to find himself groundskeeper of a mudflat. Sheila had managed to mash, mutilate, or mangle every stinking blade of grass in her front lawn. I hoped she didn't get hold of a copy of *Caddyshack,* or Mr. Sanchez would be in charge of a nuclear waste site.

*"Hafarferot,"* I tested it on my tongue.

She heaved a mighty sigh. "No. That's a *'het'* at the beginning. It's a more guttural sound. You might be a *shiksa,* but you don't have to sound like one."

"Excuse me," I said, as my face colored. "I am a lot of things, but I am NOT an abomination."

Turning icy blue eyes on me, she gave me an expression of new respect. I guess she didn't think I knew what *shiksa* really meant. Well, I did. She didn't apologize, but I knew she wouldn't use that word again.

"Let me get my kid and I'm out of here." God forbid I should expose my sleezy Church of England roots. Time to collect my mixed-breed offspring and go home.

And to prove what a classy chick I was, I'd planned a dinner with international flair. The piéce de résistance was an Oriental salad made with Ramen noodles that I'd picked up at the dollar store. I headed toward the front door to fetch my daughter.

"By the way," Sheila called to my back. "She's in a nasty mood. Up and down like that roller coaster at Six Flags in Eureka."

I was lightly browning the Ramen noodles in margarine when I heard the cheerful question of the *Sesame Street* theme song, "Can you tell me how to get . . ."

"No! Not *Sesame Street*!" I raced into the living room. I heard, "Elmo likes —" and a brown, black and white fur ball flew past me, like a rocket launched toward our twenty-five-inch TV screen. Guy hit the glass hard, his body arching as he pummeled the image of the red puppet. He had not gone silently into that gentle air. No, he'd raged, raged against the fuzzy singing muppet. His yelping and snarling filled the air. He bounced like a basketball on a backboard and then fell to the floor, scrambling to his feet and beginning anew with a somersault. This time Guy boinked like a coiled spring, meeting me at eye level and intercepting my reach for the dial.

"Grab him!" I screamed.

Anya sat paralyzed on the sofa, her blue eyes open as wide as they would go.

"Anya! Help me!" This time I grabbed at the pooch and succeeded only in flailing empty air. I decided to focus on the stationary television. My finger stabbed the power button. The picture imploded, swirling red and orange as Elmo disintegrated. Not that Guy cared. He raced in tight circles, his tail in his mouth.

Anya lunged for him. He uncoiled, ran up her arm, down over her back and did a half-gainer, coming to land on the sofa. Bouncing up again, he knocked over the lamp and careened toward the floor.

He would have made it, too, but the electric cord wrapped his paws like a bola, bringing him to a skidding stop. The motion tangled his feet, flipped him over, and while on his back, he did a canine moonwalk. A pink tongue lolled past gooey pink gums. He was panting hard. I pulled him close and shushed him, nestling his heaving form to my chest before running tentative fingers over his frame. He was out of breath, certainly, but as far as I could tell, he was all right.

"Thank God," I said, and I meant it as a prayer. I couldn't have faced Mert or Ethel with the news that he was hurt.

"Mom," whimpered Anya as she slunk over to my side. She touched Guy gently. He responded by hopping onto her lap and shoving his tongue into her mouth. "Uuu-uck. I'm really, really sorry. I just wanted to see what would happen. I never expected this. It was an accident."

"Anya, it was not an accident. It was an on-purpose. What would we have done if he'd been hurt? Anya, he could have killed himself!"

"I know! Honest, Mom, I didn't think he'd go nuts! Please don't tell Mert! She'll kill me!"

Oh boy, I thought. Given my friend's recent visit with the police, that was a real bad turn of phrase.

# NINE

The next day as we flipped the OPEN sign, Dodie got a call from a CAMP representative. The other store owners wanted to meet at three. Dodie asked if I could watch the store from two until seven.

Of course, I could. I would do anything to help, anything at all.

After my "go ahead," Dodie retreated to her office, shutting the door firmly. Two inches of solid wood are a sure-fire conversation stopper. I desperately needed to know what was bothering her besides Horace's unemployment, the death of a customer, and the hateful graffiti.

Duh! Put that way, the list made substantive emotional baggage. But I'd seen her go through worse and keep ticking. The Dodie I knew was an Amazon, a Bodecia, a stalwart, stoical "kick it to the curb and spit on it" figure of a woman. Years ago she'd survived the accidental death of her beloved son, Nathan. Surely by comparison, this stuff was small potatoes. More was going on than the obvious. Maybe Horace could clue me in, but dare I call him?

That course of action seemed invasive and nosy. Even for me. Even under the banner of friendship.

Instead, I decided to bury myself in my work, dialing wedding photographers and floating my new idea. By the fourth call, I had my spiel down pat. Would they be interested in customized albums? I tallied one "bring one by and show us what you mean," a "let me talk with the boss," and two "You bet! Give us prices." Pleased with my success, I tapped on Dodie's office door.

She responded slowly, opening the door a crack. The woman who faced me had aged six years in the six days since CAMP. The skin under her eyes sagged and buckled, and her expression lacked vitality.

"Good news." I stood outside her office and shared the results of my phone campaign. Her face never changed.

"Fine." She hadn't invited me in, and now she was turning away.

"Hey!" I wedged the door open with my foot. "Wait a minute. I know you've had a bad couple of days, but geez, Dodie, what gives? You've got to snap out of it. Why don't you tell me about what's bothering you? Hmm? I'm a good listener."

Her hoary head turned away. I stared at a Brillo pad hairdo.

Not an inspiring view.

In fact, she was starting to tick me off.

"Whoa. When I had problems, you made me face up to them. So what's the deal? The rules are different for you? I have to handle my problems, but you get to lock yourself in your office and mope? That's not fair to me or to the store or our customers. And I don't know if you've noticed or not, but the business needs you. So do I! You've got to get a grip. You can't give up. If you do, Ellen Harmon wins!"

Her shoulders drooped and she turned to face me. A weak voice, an alien timbre said, "I just can't . . . I can't believe that horrid woman died. In front of everyone! And I'm upset with myself because I wanted her dead!"

I blinked fast and hard, trying to comprehend.

"You don't know how cruel she was to me. How she ridiculed me in front of customers," Dodie started. "I hated her. Despised the woman."

I lost my chance to learn more because the door minder sounded.

I left to wait on a customer.

But while I matched patterned papers and embellishments, I repeated her words in my head.

Was my boss the killer? She'd disliked Yvonne enough to tell her to take a hike. Still, I'd never seen Dodie get that frustrated with a customer. Never. Was there a history between them I didn't know? Could Dodie have hired someone to poison Yvonne? Had she worried Yvonne's new status could make it hard for us to compete? Had I let her down because I didn't enter any contests? Was her familial financial situation that bleak? Was her deep depression really remorse? Guilt? Fear?

What the hey was going on — and why wouldn't she tell me?

Shoot. This was bad. Really bad.

Anya was in a decent mood when I picked her up after camp. The top was down on my ancient candy-apple red BMW and the breeze in our hair felt great. No matter the passenger side front quarter panel was bashed in. Or that the car was so old it didn't have a cent of resale value. From the left, my car looked fine. And in our elcheapo sunglasses from Target, so did Anya and I. I smiled to myself when I caught my daughter preening in the sun flap mirror.

"So . . . how was camp?" My voice was light and neutral. All the better to tiptoe through the minefield of juvenile angst.

"Ummm. Okay." Anya's denim blues flitted from her reflection to the passing scenery. "Mom, I want to start wearing mascara. And colored lip gloss."

I braced myself. I wanted to scream, "But you are only eleven!" Didn't she think she was pushing it? Growing up too fast? While I stumbled over what to say, she moved on.

"Everybody else wears mascara. Foundation, too. If I wore eyeliner, like Nicci does, my eyes wouldn't look like little rat eyes."

"Little rat eyes?"

"Yeah. Missy Roland teased me about how my eyes are pink and my lashes are invisible. She says my eyes look just like the ones on lab rats."

"Gee, what an extraordinarily hurtful thing to say. Tell you what. Let me think about the makeup, okay? I'd like to talk it over with your grandmother."

She heaved a sigh to end all sighs. "Thank goodness. This isn't really a subject you're an expert in, you know? I mean, it's not like you care a lot about your appearance."

A direct hit to the gut. I didn't care a lot about my appearance? I choked back a response. Was that what she thought? Was that how I looked to the world at large? A warm flush burned my cheeks. I peeked at her. She didn't have an unpleasant expression on her face. It wasn't like Anya to be mean. Scratch that. It hadn't been like her in the past.

As we walked toward the tall building housing the allergists, I noticed myself in the reflective windows. My face was wavey and distorted, but even so, I wasn't wearing a stitch of makeup. My pants sagged in the butt, like a toddler with a full diaper. My hair stuck out every which way but loose. Was it possible that Detweiler hadn't followed up on his kiss because I wasn't taking pains to look like a woman? Maybe I didn't seem interested enough in the opposite sex?

In the waiting room of Andersoll, Weaver, and Sealander, a receptionist handed over a clipboard full of paperwork. Due to my heightened sensitivity on the subject, I noticed the woman behind the counter wore makeup that was subtle, but effective, giving her a sort of polished professionalism. Maybe my unadorned self was more "aw nuts" than "au naturel."

Anya and I sat across from a big sign — "Carry an Extra Epi-Pen!" I printed pertinent information about Anya's health. Since

I believe in including your handwriting in your scrapbooks, my script was delightfully consistent and cute. Sheila's details were listed in both the "who referred you?" area and the place asking who was financially responsible for my daughter's bills.

Anya grabbed a *Teen* magazine with a cover article, "How to Look Hot-Hot-Hot." A copy of the *Post-Dispatch* article about Yvonne Gaynor's death was pinned to the bulletin board.

The receptionist noticed my interest. "Isn't that awful? Mrs. Gaynor was one of our patients. You can imagine how upset we've all been. It could have been prevented. We tell every one of our highly sensitive patients to keep an Epi-Pen with them at all times. Every second counts in a life-threatening situation."

I said, "But she did have an Epi-Pen. I guess she forgot it was empty."

"Humph. That's ridiculous. She'd been in early that week. Doctor Sealander wrote a new prescription for pens. You don't forget using one. How could you? First of all, it takes a major attack for you to need one. And if you have a severe reaction, you're supposed to take the empty with you to the hospital. They'll give you another script there. Since the effects of the pen wear off after twenty minutes, you aren't likely to use one and go about your merry way. It's not like running out of sugar, you know!" With that, she slammed the window shut.

A practitioner clad in aqua scrubs with a pattern of tiny orange fish called Anya's name. I followed my daughter through the rabbit's warren of carrels, reflecting how times had changed for the better. The bright colors of the nurse's uniform were more cheerful and reassuring than stark white. The rest of our visit was routine — yes, Anya had allergies, and the doc thought antihistamines and nose spray were our best first line of defense.

After the exam, Dr. Andersoll showed us the photo gallery in his office. Each of his children and grandkids warranted an introduction and lengthy biographical information. Finally, he paused to ask, "Could you make me a scrapbook? One I could put in the waiting room?"

"Of course I could." And I handed him my business card. I wasn't sure his patients were as interested in his family as he was, but what the heck?

Sheila had been right: His grandkids weren't going to win any beauty prizes! Thank goodness love truly is blind, because, as my lovely daughter had so graciously pointed out to me, I was a few votes short of Miss Missouri myself.

I dropped Anya off at Sheila's, grabbed a SlimFast Optima bar from my purse, and checked my watch. Since I promised to cover the store from two to seven, Dodie had given me an extra-long lunch. There was time for a quick swing by Artist Supply, the place where Bama used to work.

You'd never guess from the neighborhood or from the outside that this was a chi-chi spot for the art-wardly mobile of St. Louis. Crumbling sidewalks, broken and boarded-up storefronts, faded neon signs, and billboards lined the north-south boulevard Art House called home. Under a ripped and torn awning, a heavy glass door streaked with layers of street dust marked the demarcation between the real world and the creative mind. One step inside, and your visual perception altered, in part because the sagging wooden floor was tip-tilted back to front. Racks of handmade paper formed a passageway. The sheets called to me. I lovingly fingered stitched mulberry paper, handmade paper, and screened prints from Japan. This place was heaven, absolute nirvana.

And totally out of my price range.

A haughty clerk with a stud under his lower lip sashayed over. Giving me the evil eye, he lisped, "The resale shop is two doors down."

I struggled with that. Oh-kay, I thought. I suppose my current style could best be categorized as early Episcopal Church rummage sale. Well, I couldn't let this deter me. "Um, I intended to come here. Uh, to Artist Supply."

His left eyebrow hesitated in its elevated position. He wrestled with this moue of disdain, before simpering. "Welcome, Dorothy Gale."

"Right. I'm not in Kansas anymore. My name is Kiki." I extended my hand.

"Ooo-oooh. My mother had a cat named Kiki." His fingers were long and cool.

"So did mine. Pretty pitiful, isn't it? All my sisters got real names, and she names me after her dead pet."

"Brings to mind Miss Pussy Galore of James Bond fame, doesn't it? At least you weren't named for an orthodontic nightmare." He fluttered a floppy hand at the name tag on his breast bone. It said "Bucky." He sighed. "Can you believe it? Pah-rents. What can I say?" His eyes (which I noticed were lightly rimmed with taupe eye pencil) twinkled as he asked, "What can

I do you for, Miss Kitty?"

"Actually I need information." I leaned toward his patchouli scented frame. The guy was built like an art easel. Did that come before or after working here? "Did you work with Bama Vess?"

Those taupe lined lids narrowed speculatively. "Why? What's it to you, Cat Woman?"

I thought fast. I needed a reason. A good one. Oh, heck, why not go with the truth? Maybe it would set me free. "We work together and . . . and . . . she's after my job." Okay, it was technically a lie, but it was something I worried about. That little umph of emotion gave my words an unexpected ring of veracity. "But I was wondering why she got let go. I wondered if it was . . . because of something recreational she did. See, some days she can't even walk straight. I mean, she can do whatever she wants on her own time, but . . . not at work."

Bucky studied me.

This wasn't looking good. I arranged my face in a downtrodden look. I didn't accuse her outright, after all. I just planted a seed. Bucky's response depended on his level of loyalty to Bama.

Which turned out to be nonexistent.

He clucked and nodded sympathetically. "Yeah, she pulled the same trick here. I

mean it's not like I don't toke up on week-
ends, but sheesh, you can't be hanging on
the display cases like a canvas drape, can
you?" His fingers spread wide across this
breast bone to emphasis the calamity.

"No kidding," I urged him on. "Okay, so
you tie one on after hours. No prob. But
that girl weaves like a cheap serape. Is that
what got her butt canned?"

"Um," Bucky hesitated. "Nah." He
straightened a row of acrylic paints. I
pitched in. Picking up after customers was
a never-ending and thankless job. Working
side by side, even briefly, creates a bizarre
emotional connection between people.
Okay, most people. Between Bama and me,
there was no camaraderie. Zip. Zilch. Nada.
None.

He cast an eye around the store before
fingering items on a lower shelf. His voice
dropped. "A customer complained. Duke,
he's the owner, he was cool with her 'til
then. That's when the ordure hit the fan, so
to speak."

Ordure. I'd have to look up that word in
the dictionary. But I got his drift. I prodded
gently, "Uh, any names? I mean, I wonder
who made a stink. See, uh, we've been
blamed for that woman's death. The one
who ate the tainted food? And . . . do you

think there's a connection?"

Bucky angled his body away from me. "Hey, you're talking murder, right?"

Suddenly I realized the gravity of what I was doing. And I felt ashamed. Really ashamed. In my zest to secure my job, fueled by my jealousy, I'd falsely accused another human being. My stomach knotted with a sinking sense of guilt. What was wrong with me? I covered my mouth with my hand lest any more awful comments flew out. I couldn't believe I'd stooped so low. Okay, I'm insecure, but never before have I acted so despicably.

Bucky stared at me. Hard.

"Uh, ouch. I can't believe I just said all that. Please . . . forget it. I'm not thinking straight. I'm scared. Really worried. This murder is ruining our business. People are blaming my employer. If we don't figure out who killed that woman, we'll go bust! And I have a child to support. Customers are complaining. The cops are grilling us. They hauled in my best friend for questioning. My boss acts like a zombie, and, and . . ." My voice thickened with tears. "We're getting death threats."

"Oooooohh. Really?" Now Bucky was interested. "Like, what do they say?"

I swallowed hard. "Stuff I can't even

repeat. It's that gruesome. I can't just hang around and do nothing! If this keeps up, I won't have a job! You'd try to get answers, too, wouldn't you? Or maybe not. Maybe you don't need this position. For all I know, your parents run with the St. Louis Country Club set."

"Whoa. Don't blame me for being a rich kid. That's not nice, lady."

"Sorry. I'm out of line. You see, Yvonne Gaynor died right in front of me. Practically in my arms. I've never seen anything so horrible. I guess it's all kind of getting to me." *That* was the truth. The events of the past few days were taking a toll. I hadn't realized how much I was bothered until I spilled my guts to Bucky. Suddenly, I realized I'd been running away from that scene in the church basement.

I'm not a bad person. Not really. At least, I hope not. But the way I'd just acted was inexcusable.

I faced him and said, "I'm sorry. Please forget everything I suggested. It was unworthy of me. And unfair to Bama."

Desperate to change the subject, I touched a tube of paint. "Cerulean is my favorite color. Did you know its name came from the Greek word for sky?"

He corrected me. "The Latin word for sky.

*Caelum.* The root word for 'ceiling.' This color was introduced by Hopfner in 1821, but wasn't widely used until reintroduced by George Romney in England in 1860. It's extremely stable."

"That is so cool. I mean, it's neat you know this stuff. Everything I've learned about art has been by observation, and trial and error — more error than trial. And from books. Most of this stuff," and I swooped my arms to include the vast contents of the store, "is foreign to me. I can't afford it and wouldn't know what to do with it. But I'm trying to educate myself. I challenge myself to master a new technique or use a new product each week."

A smile played at the corners of his lips. "Having rich parents does allow one the luxury of a good education. Especially in the arts. Tell you what. I'll ask around. Maybe I can find out why Bama left. And if anyone in particular was involved. I wouldn't ordinarily rat out a co-worker, but she really was a poseur, you know?"

I wrote my name and phone number on a slip of paper and thanked him. Before I left, he pressed a naked tube of acrylic paint into my hand. "This one's lost the label. Take it home and experiment."

The silver cylinder promised all sorts of

delights. I fingered it happily in my purse. On the way to my car, I caught my reflection in the shop windows and muttered, "Even Bucky's eye makeup is better than mine. I really do need to take more care with my appearance."

Dodie floundered around the store like a fish flopping around outside of an aquarium. Her eyes were big and bovine, and her gait was uncertain and panicked. After taking Guy and Gracie for a quick stroll, I set to work organizing the paper bag album class.

My hands sorted stacks of supplies and folded bags in half. My mind swirled with ideas for developing new business. Proposals to photographers for custom albums had gone out in the morning mail. I had suggested three levels of customization: (a.) imprinted album covers, (b.) imprinted album covers plus handmade but standardized page layouts, and (c.) imprinted album covers, plus handmade and customized page layouts. I'd also tried the idea on one of the photographers. He was cautiously enthusiastic and asked me to make a sample. I had ideas and knew which paper I wanted to use, but I hadn't had the time to go further.

Also, Dr. Andersoll's project was a go. He

promised to drop off photos next week. That was all good. But we needed more bright ideas, more incoming projects to offset the business we were losing.

One of those cartoon light bulbs went off in my head. In my mind, I saw the cover of Joan Rivers' *Bouncing Back,* written shortly after her husband's suicide, a $3 million business loss, and a cancelled talk show. The book wasn't your usual motivational fare. However, if anyone earned the right to discuss bouncing back, she did. The trick, she said, is to have so many balls in the air that something has to work out. Not only would the law of averages suggest at least one winner, but hopes for each new project would keep you going.

What we needed was more balls in the air. With Dodie under the weather emotionally, it was my job to start tossing.

I finished up with the paper bag albums and prepped for my favorite creativity booster, a synectics exercise, by tearing three shades of paper into small squares. On the pink, I put stages of life. On the green, I put as many places as I could think of. On the yellow, I added all the equipment I could brainstorm. My lists were eclectic and quickly scribbled. I shuffled each color group and pulled a slip of paper representing each topic. My first try yielded "childhood" (pink), "church" (green), and "hammer" (yellow). I wrote those down. I couldn't see any relationship to scrapbooking, but I firmly agree with Nietzsche, "One must still have chaos in oneself to be able to give birth to a dancing star." Right now the cards produced chaos. That didn't mean I was ready to give up. I tried again. This time I flipped over "grandparents," "home," and "carts." I copied those words down. I readied myself for round three when the door minder rang.

A woman of undetermined age planted herself in the center of the store, eying the paper racks nervously. This was a commonplace reaction. The awesome selection that attracts seasoned scrappers makes beginners throw up their scissors in despair.

"Hi, you look like you could use a little help."

She tucked her purse firmly under her armpit and continued to gaze about her aimlessly.

I followed her line of sight. "Pretty overwhelming, isn't it? My first visit to a scrapbook store I bought one sheet of paper, folded it, put it in my purse and walked out. The other customers doubled over with giggles."

Her body relaxed. "I'd heard this is easy. And fun. But how can that be when there's so much to choose from? Where does one begin?"

"Why not tell me about your project?"

Serena Jensen hoped to make an album for her mother. "She's in a home for people with dementia. She's stuck in the past. The caregivers, of course, don't know what a wonderful and exciting life she had before the Alzheimer's. I put a large photo of Mother in her youth on her apartment door. The nurse and the helpers responded so favorably that I thought I could do more along the same line. Maybe if there was an album about Mother's life, it would encourage providers to see her as the woman she was. Especially on those days when she is, uh, difficult."

"Wow. What a great idea," I said. Actually she wasn't the first customer who'd done this, but I'd totally forgotten about this strategy for improving the quality of life for the elderly. "And what a loving way to remind everyone to treat your mother with dignity."

Serena's lower lip trembled. "Do I have to do it all myself? I've never been handy with scissors. Mother gave up teaching me to sew! Even though I'm retired, my schedule is very busy. Between taking care of my husband, watching the grandkids, teaching Sunday School, playing golf, and volunteering at a thrift shop —" She stopped and blushed. "I hope I didn't imply my mother isn't important to me."

"Mrs. Jensen —"

"Call me Serena, please."

I introduced myself, and she interrupted with, "You must be Sheila's daughter-in-law! She's been telling all of us how talented you are. I should have thought to ask her where you worked. Imagine! Sheila swears you are a creative genius. A really sweet girl, too. And pretty. Which you are."

Well, blow me down, Popeye. Sheila said all that about me? What a pleasant surprise.

"That is so kind of you to say. Now why don't you have a seat? We can start by choosing an album style. As for the pages, you can do as much or as little as you wish. I can do the interior work, if you prefer. See? This will be easy. You just needed a little guidance."

Not only did Serena Jensen prove to be the bearer of compliments, she was also the midwife of a great idea. After she left, I contemplated how best to approach retirement homes and independent living communities. I jotted down ideas about teaching memory album making to residents and their families.

The growling of my stomach made me look at my watch. Mert should have been by an hour ago to pick up Guy. I dialed her number.

"I know," she answered without any greeting, "I'm coming. I jest spent another half-day being questioned by the police about Yvonne. I'll swing by a little later, if it's okay-dokey with you. With all this hassle from them cops, I'm running way behind."

Why, I wondered, did the police continue to be so interested in her?

# How to Use Synectics to Generate Creative Solutions

Developed by William Gordon, the name "synectics" means the fitting together of seemingly diverse elements. Creativity is, quite simply, combining old ideas in new ways. This is a simple version of the process.

1. Select at least three different colors of paper or index cards.
2. Select three topics from the list below.
   - Garden tools
   - Holidays
   - Foods
   - Relationships
   - Car parts
   - Nouns
   - Headings in the yellow pages
   - Headings in the classified section of a newspaper

Once you've selected your topics, write words associated with those topics. Do this as quickly as possible without pausing to think. Now put all the words associated with one topic on a particular color of cards or paper. (For example, all the car parts would be written or printed on blue index cards.) Do the same for two other topics.

Shuffle each color group. Pick one card from each color. Read the word out loud and write the trio down.

Ask yourself, "What analogies can I make between my problem and these words? How are these words different from my problem? Can any combination of these words be used to solve my problem?"

Go through the same procedure with another three cards.

If nothing comes to you, don't despair. Sometimes your subconscious needs a bit more time to sift through the cards and work out ideas!

# TEN

My busy social calendar fully occupied my thoughts as I drove to Sheila's. The barbecue at Mert's on Sunday afternoon would be fun. She was a terrific cook, and her son Roger was a sweetie who treated Anya like she was an equal, not a pesky kid. But Opera Theatre? Brrrr. I shuddered. Getting gussied up always makes me nervous. I feel like an imposter. I worry I'm making some mysterious fashion faux pas that's going to land me in *Glamour* magazine under the "Fashion Don'ts" heading.

Maybe I'd luck out, and Sheila wouldn't find a suitable dress.

In fact, when I pulled into her drive, you couldn't tell my mother-in-law had been shopping for formal wear at St. Louis' toniest stores. Her linen slacks were splattered to the knee with mud, and her crisp white blouse was polka-dotted with more of the same. Both hands clutched an active garden hose. She knelt to poke the nozzle into a mole tunnel. A geyser of mud, water, and grass shot out the other end of the tunnel. The yard was looking more and more like a construction site.

As I approached her, Sheila grunted at me! Grunted! Her war on nature was turning her into an animalistic predator. I stifled a giggle and said, "Any luck shopping?"

"I'll show you." She let go of the hose.

That was a mistake.

Evidently Sheila had never taken a hose management course. The metal nozzle rose like a cobra ready to strike. Before I could grab it, the healthy spray of water doused both of us, blasting Sheila squarely in the face.

The hose took off across the lawn, gyrating and spewing a strong stream of water.

Sheila followed it with weary eyes. She raised muck-covered hands to wipe her face and muttered, "Shoot."

I ran down the offending hose before twisting the sprayer shut. Dropping the hose in the mud, I walked to the faucet and turned off the flow. Squeaky, squishy sounds followed me as I picked my way back to where Sheila stood, pawing bits of leaves and dirt from her mouth.

"Shoot," she repeated. "That does it. Next

thing you know, I'll be cussing like a sailor."

"May I offer an idea? Try ordure. It's a new word I learned today."

"That's a heck of a lot more useful than anything I've learned today. Did you know a mole's fur grows straight up? That way he can go forward or backward in a tunnel and not get dirt in his hair." She stepped back to evaluate her experiment in drowning critters. "This is so *not* working. I need a new plan."

So *not* working? My daughter's pre-teen jargon was infiltrating my very proper mother-in-law's speech patterns.

A few minutes later, we were mostly toweled off. Sheila stripped to her lace undies in the center of her vast and elegant master bedroom and slid on a silk kimono. From her closet, she withdrew a gown worthy of Cinderella.

"So that's what you're wearing?" My voice dropped to a hush. The garment was breathtaking. A gold halter top extended into a beaded bodice. Below the waist tumbled a waterfall of chiffon over satin. A matching sheer shawl draped over the shoulders. Sheila reached into her closet and withdrew a pair of open-toed gold sandals.

"You'll look like a fairy princess," I said, turning to my mother-in-law and smiling.

"This is absolutely gorgeous, Sheila. A star could wear this to the Oscars."

"Don't be ridiculous," she said. "Gold isn't my color. I'm wearing turquoise. This is for you."

I backed away. "I couldn't, I mean, it's too grand, and I couldn't carry it off." Tears threatened to overwhelm me. My mother had never gone shopping with me or for me. In fact, no one but my late husband, George, had ever purchased any clothing for me. Correction: I now wondered if Sheila had been his wardrobe assistant all along. Running a tentative finger along the bodice, I mentally calculated the cost of this finery.

"This is too much," I stuttered. "I can't accept it. You spent too much money."

Anya gave a brisk knock and stuck her head around the door. "Hey, Mom, aren't you going to try that on? Isn't it too cool? Nana searched for days to get the right outfit for you. With a little sun, you'll look like a goddess."

I continued to step away as though the dress were a living thing. I shook my head. "I couldn't . . . I can't."

Sheila huffed. "Don't be silly. Let's see how it fits."

Conscious of my own tattered panties and

ratty bra, I did as I was told. Sheila sat next to Anya watching me. "You'll need the appropriate foundations. What size bra and panties do you wear?"

Anya made a disgusted sound. "Nana, I'm thinking Spanx."

I had no idea what she meant. I turned around slowly to view myself in the huge double-mirrors flanking Sheila's closet. My gaze swept from my feet upward. The woman who looked back at me wore an elegant, slender column of gold from shoulders to toes. I pushed back my damp hair and tried to imagine an appropriate style.

"Don't worry about your hair." Sheila studied me. "The dress is perfect, and the staff at Spa La Femme will make you . . . worthy."

"About that," I began, slowly unzipping the gown. "It won't take them long, will it? Dodie may need me in the store."

Sheila took my arm so I could step out of the dress. She slid the gown onto a padded hanger and into a plastic zip-up bag. "She and I have already talked. You're covered. A car will pick you up at eight a.m. When you're finished, my driver will bring you from Spa La Femme to my house, and we'll attend the function together. We should make quite an entrance. It's always easiest to walk in with someone you know. Besides, I want to enjoy all the admiring looks you're going to get. I've told my friends you are coming."

I mentioned meeting Serena Jensen.

"Serena and Bob will be there. She's a wonderful woman, and I'm not surprised she's figured out a way to help her mother."

"It was easy to talk to her in the store, because we had scrapbooking to discuss, but . . . what will I say to other people? People I don't know? I can't very well begin a conversation with, 'Hi, my name is Kiki and I'm a scrapaholic.' "

"Oh, Mom, honestly." Anya flounced out of the room. An odd odor followed her. Probably some sort of mole repellent, I reasoned. Surely she wasn't doing drugs? Just one more item to add to my worry-list. Placing my new shoes in their box, I braced myself for Sheila's response. She didn't have much patience with my lack of social confidence.

Instead of the pep talk or chastising that usually followed my whining, she handed me a brown paper package. "Open it."

Inside was the audio version of Barbara Walters' *How to Talk with Practically Anybody about Practically Anything*. "Making small talk is a skill, not a God-given talent. It's silly for you to be nervous. You need to conquer this and be a good role model for your daughter."

I must have looked dubious. I sure felt that way.

Taking the wrapping paper from me, Sheila spoke firmly. "You can and you will do this. No arguing." And to my surprise, she gave my shoulder a tiny squeeze. It wasn't much, but it counted as the first spontaneous affection she'd ever shown me.

A catch in my throat gave me trouble talking. Even five weeks ago, I would have never imagined this day. Sheila and I had come such a long way. Impulsively, I threw my arms around her. She stiffened. I turned her loose quickly.

"Thank you," I whispered. "Thank you." I pulled back to see doubt form in those clear blue eyes.

"Yes. Well. You'd better wait to thank me until after Opera Theatre." And she turned away.

# ELEVEN

Anya settled into the car and gave both Gracie and Guy some loving. "I think Grandma's lost her mind. All she thinks about is those moles. She asked me to go to the Internet and find ways to kill them. I think they're pretty cute, actually."

"Anya-Banana, what's that I smell on your clothing?"

My kid scrunched up her face. "Cocaine? Heroin? For goodness sake, Mom, I've been at a science lab all day except for hanging around with my grandmother. Hello? I have no idea what you're smelling on my clothes, but it's not dope if that's what you're think-ing."

We didn't have time to pursue the subject because Mert pulled up right behind us. The hefty slam of her truck door left no question about her mood. "Iffen I had more money, and a good lawyer, I'd sue all of them. Those no-good, eraser-brain St. Louis police! They'd be off my butt in a hot Missouri minute. As it is, they're bound and determined to bug the heck outta me, because they ain't got any other good ideas about who killed Yvonne."

Okay, she was ticked. I got it. Her rural roots were showing, big time. I led her into the house. Once she settled at the kitchen table, I poured her a tall, cool glass of tea. As I got one for myself, I asked, "But why you? There were a lot of folks around when Yvonne died."

Mert's eyelashes were typically clotted with mascara, but today more hairs than usual were stuck together — a sure clue she'd been crying earlier. A listless motion of her hand accompanied a weary voice, "It's complicated. How about you order us a pizza on my dime, and I'll 'splain it."

While we waited for the food to come, I gathered Guy's belongings. The comical fellow seemed to know his visit was over. He whined a lot.

Over a thin-crust veggie pizza, Mert told me what the late, great Paul Harvey dubbed "the rest of the story." Seems Yvonne did more than simply let Mert go. The woman accused my friend of stealing a diamond necklace. A few weeks into the investigation, the jewelry showed up in a pawn shop over in Illinois, a prime spot for Old St. Louis to hide financial problems. According to Yvonne, this proved Mert tried to sell the jewelry. The pawn shop owner shared his records with the police. A man's name and address were on the forms. The police could find no link between the mystery man and Mert.

Reluctantly, the Gaynors dropped charges. Even so, the woman trash-talked Mert to her entire neighborhood and beyond.

"She got me fired from a part-time cleaning job at Perry's company." Mert rubbed her face with her careworn hands. "Most all my income was gone. I had to start from scratch. And it was hard because people depend on your references."

When I hired Mert many years ago, I'd done the same, checking her references before giving her the run of my home. "But that happened, when?"

"Twelve years ago."

"Why would you wait until now to get even?"

Mert turned a ripe cherry red. Now I'd seen two things this day that I'd never expected: Sheila cussing and Mert blushing. I needed to write this in my diary!

Her white-frosted fingernails worried the seam of her black jeans. "All's I can figure is it's because Johnny is back. See, my brother was sent to Potosi for robbing a convenience store."

I forced myself not to show surprise.

"I guess the cops think now my little brother is out, he's encouraging me. Who knows?" She continued, "Maybe because Johnny's on parole, my whole family's on their radar. All I can say is, my brother was a young man who made a bad choice and paid dearly for it. Broke my parents' hearts. And, since his hearing and all, the law's been watching us close like. My whole family got tarred with the brush Johnny was carryin'. It about killed all of us. See, he promised to quit hanging around with this bad element. Then, one night when he'd had a couple of beers at a bar, a couple of his old friends — including a cop's son, mind you — asked if he wanted a ride home. He said yes, so's he could leave his car and not get a DUI. They swung by a convenience store, and next thing he knows, they got guns out and they're inside whooping and hollering.

"Johnny ran in after them, yelling, and he says they turned the guns on him and forced him back into the car. The cops got them afore they'd went two miles. Johnny told the police everything. But when it went to trial, the judge was up for re-election, and he didn't want to be called soft on crime. Said Johnny was to blame. Huh," she said and shook her head. "The cop's kid got off with a hand slap."

She turned her eyes away. "I been meaning to tell you. Especially before you and Anya come to my party. I'll understand if you don't want to come over on Sunday."

Before I could answer, she added. "Actually, I was meaning to tell you all about this so's you could make up your mind about being seen with me at all. I wasn't meaning to trick you. I'd never do that." Her eyes concentrated on a chipped fingernail. The tension in her body made her rigid.

"Mert, you are the most loyal friend I've ever had. I trust you implicitly. I'd love to meet your brother."

Well, that's what my lips said, but my gut cried, "No! No! No!" The truth was I felt conflicted. I love her, goodness knows I do. But I have a child to consider. Sure, she could say Johnny is harmless, but she's his sister. The man's a felon. I could just hear what Sheila would have to say about all this! She'd gone to court once to gain total custody of Anya. She said I was an unfit mother. What would she do with news I was palling around with a criminal? Oh, Lord.

My heart said, "Support your friend."

My brain said, "Are you nuts?"

I sidestepped the issue. "Come see my dress."

Mert's mouth fell open in wonder. "Glory be. You're going to look like one of them Disney princesses. I cain't wait to hear all about it on Sunday. Shoot. I suppose you're too high class to bring that there Hoosier Daddy Kidney Bean Salad to the shindig?"

I laughed. "Of course I can bring my salad. Kidney beans know no class barriers. A toot is a toot no matter who lets it fly."

# TWELVE

After Mert left with Guy, Anya fell asleep
on the sofa watching TV. My mind chattered like a squirrel being stalked by a cat. I
couldn't settle down. With the crop the next
evening, and how low Dodie'd been acting,
I thought a wee treat was in order. I baked
a special treat — a cookie-crust fresh fruit
pie. To cater to all spectrums of the diet
continuum, I also baked my bran banana
bread muffins.

I also had myself a good think. Who killed
Yvonne Gaynor? The sooner the police
discovered the culprit, the sooner they'd
leave my best buddy alone and our business
could return to normal. Detweiler was
focusing on who could have brought the
scones. That made sense, but he'd overlooked an important question: Who had access to the Epi-Pen? So many people
brought food — and came in and out of the
church basement — that tracking down the

person who supplied the scones was darn near impossible.

And the Epi-Pen? That exchange couldn't have been accidental — or intended for anyone other than Yvonne. First of all, it's a prescription drug and only a person with severe allergies would carry it. Second, the syringe was removed from the packaging and emptied — that took planning. And third, the kit had been replaced in Yvonne's purse so it was available on the very day she needed it! No way could you explain away that particular sequence of events. Oh, and also, the pen had been wiped clean of all fingerprints but Yvonne's!

Who, I wondered, had access to her medical history and her purse?

Her husband.

Why wasn't Detweiler focusing on him? Or was he?

Could Perry Gaynor have an accomplice? Could Bama have planted the tainted food? And swapped an empty Epi-Pen for a full one? A nasty little voice hoped so. Maybe she knew Yvonne's husband. Or maybe he'd tracked down the newest member of our store "family" and approached her with a bribe. Drugs maybe?

Either way, I needed to talk to Perry Gaynor.

The next morning Anya pitched a hissy fit about camp and refused to leave her room. She stood in her doorway and yelled, "I'm the only girl there who isn't wearing makeup. How come you treat me like a baby?"

I responded with charm and maturity. "Anya, get your rear end in the car or you'll be grounded for the rest of your natural life! You'll stay in that cotton-picking room until you're old enough to get an AARP card. Plus, you'll lose all communication privileges. Got it? No phone, no e-mail, no U.S. Postal Service, nada! When I get done with you, young lady, even Homeland Security won't be able to find you!" And I stomped off to load Gracie in the BMW.

I was still angry when I got to work. The flame under my emotional burner switched to high as I discovered Bama's car in my parking space. Her late-model hybrid sat crookedly across two places, leaving me a space on the far side of the lot. I'd no more than gotten Gracie and the baked goods into the storeroom and closed the door when the FedEx guy rang the back doorbell. He must have been right on my heels, and I hadn't even noticed. The man eyed the food hungrily until I explained the muffins were bran.

"Bran? No thanks. Hey, you hear the one about the old dude who goes to heaven with his wife? The man asks St. Peter, if since he's dead, can he have his favorite things to eat — steak, ice cream, bratwurst, beer? Yep, as much as he wants. Can he have sex? Yep, all he wants. Can he play golf? Yep, every day, all day. So the dead guy turns to his wife and says, 'Why all those bran muffins? I could have been here enjoying myself twenty years sooner!' "

I offered the delivery man a weak smile before hustling him outside. He was a real sweetie, but given the recent poisoning of our customer, jokes about the dead and dying were not well received. Dodie called Bama and me into her office to tell us the upshot of her meeting with the other CAMP store owners. The women were divided about whether Time in a Bottle should remain part of the group.

"Ellen Harmon is pressing them to dump us. Yvonne's death gave her a big bargaining chip. She's got all their sympathy. She told one owner she's needed therapy to sleep at night. She invited the other stores to participate in a memorial crop. Evidently, she's struck up a friendship with Wendy Smithers at Your Scrapbook Store. The two were acting cozy when I first arrived. Later, Wendy suggested that until the murder is solved, our name should be excluded from any CAMP ads or events."

"And how'd you respond?" I couldn't believe Dodie let them walk all over her. Shortly after Yvonne's death, my boss must have had a personality transplant. My whole world was turning upside down. Mert was teary eyed and upset. Dodie was unable to defend herself or her store. My sweet daughter was acting like Rosemary's baby. My nasty mother-in-law was my new best friend.

I'd have given anything for a good astrologer. As far as I could figure, the moon was orbiting Saturn, and poor Pluto was fighting to regain his stature as a planet.

Dodie answered me with, "You don't understand. There's nothing I can say. Or do. Ellen started the meeting by handing me a list of fifteen customers demanding refunds. She said one customer was consulting an attorney about damages! Claims post-traumatic stress brought on by witnessing Yvonne's death."

"Sounds to me like Ellen is stirring the pot," said Bama.

I agreed. Scrapbookers are lovely people. That's why I enjoy what I do. The behavior Dodie described was unheard of.

"Of course she's egging folks on," Dodie nodded. "But as long as this investigation continues, scrapbooking has been given a black eye. I had a call last night from a Chicago television station asking me if this hobby is hazardous. Can you believe it? No wonder everyone wants to distance themselves from us."

The door minder sounded. Bama excused herself to wait on a customer.

I took this golden opportunity. "Dodie, I know this is hard for you, but you can't just lie down and let them run all over you. Is there something else going on? Have you heard any word from the attorney about Horace's job?"

She mumbled, "Not yet, but we have an appointment to talk."

I chewed a fingernail. "How about I take some muffins over for the Gaynor family? Sort of make a sympathy call?" In my navy slacks and dark matching blouse, I could easily pass for a mourner.

Of course, I'd offered my boss a bald-face lie. I wasn't taking that food over to curry favor with the grieving Gaynors. I was planning to nose around and ask their neighbors a few questions. This couldn't go on much longer. Either we helped the cops nail Yvonne's killer, or I'd need a new job.

Today I was supposed to hear back from one of the photographers, and I had a list of retirement communities to contact about giving classes. But none of that would matter, if our doors were shut.

In her current state of mind, Dodie was incapable of resuscitating Time in a Bottle's business. Bama and I were on our own. Since I didn't trust Bama any further than I could track a bumblebee, that left me, myself, and I looking after our employment situation. Oddly enough, less than six months ago, it was Dodie telling *me* to buck up and take responsibility for my life and finances.

Our relationship had taken a real U-turn.

Okay. I could do it. Turnabout was fair play.

And clichés were a dime a dozen. But they were all I had for comfort.

# THIRTEEN

The Gaynors lived across the Mississippi River in Illinois. Folks from St. Louis roll their eyes and say, "Across the river?" as though they are talking about a spot in Siberia, but driving from Illinois to St. Louis can actually be faster than commuting from a western suburb. The drive gave me lots of thinking and planning time. I decided to put together scrapbooking classes for local summer camps. I might be a little late, but it was worth a try.

Checking the address I'd scrawled on a piece of paper, I pulled up to a brick-fronted, three-story home with extensive landscaping and a paved walkway to the front door. Three times I rang the doorbell at the Gaynors' house, but nobody answered. I walked back to my car but couldn't muster up the energy to get in.

Great. I'd driven all the way over here for nothing.

I slammed my hand against my car hood. What a total waste of a morning. I hesitated, my eyes wandering over the similar façades and landscapes of the Gaynors' neighbors. I made a decision. I was not going back without information.

I grabbed the muffins and recited "eenie, meenie, minee, moe" while glancing at the neighbors' houses. "Moe" turned out to be slightly different from the other homes. It stood out with its frontage of white-washed, weathered, and antiqued bricks. Begonias lined the sidewalk in neat geometric lines, alternating white and pink. Vinca surrounded the mailbox. The place was a real showstopper. And bingo! A Neighborhood Watch sign stuck to the inside window of the front door. Unless things were different here in the Land of Lincoln, Neighborhood Watch was a fancy-schmancy way of saying, "Resident busybody."

Fortified with my own perilous logic, and patting myself on the back for my Sherlock Holmes-ian capabilities, I rang the doorbell.

I expected an elderly woman with bad eyesight. A housefrau in curlers and sweat-pants. A matron with French-fried hair. What I got was a dead-ringer for Jackie Kennedy. The woman inspecting me as I inspected her was forty-ish, trim, and wearing a brunette bob that grazed her chin. Diamond earrings dotted her ears, and her A-line shift was of a slubbed silk. If I was a Volkswagen, she was a stretch limousine. Rats. I sure wished I'd dressed better for this encounter.

"I'm sorry," I said with real regret. "I must have the wrong house. I was wanting the Gaynors."

"Jackie" eyed me the way a trail horse inspects a greenhorn rider. In seconds she had my number, zip code, and mailing address. Her fingers tapped the open door. "No one's home," she said in a cultured voice. "I assume you were planning to leave that." And she gestured at the bag of muffins I held.

"Yes, I wanted to drop off these muffins. My friends and I are scrapbookers and we're so sorry about —"

"About that spiteful hussy keeling over? Give me a break. Who would be sorry about that?" Her mouth moved but her forehead stayed perfectly still. Botox, I thought, and lots of it.

I couldn't conjure up an adequate response. On one hand, I wanted to chime in with, "No kidding. Wasn't she a piece of work? I mean, really. Let's talk." On the other, I had a deep fear this woman with her patrician looks and Oxfordian tones was putting me on. Unsure what to do next, I dithered.

"Hmmm." "Jackie" leaned into the door. "I don't suppose you'd like a glass of Chardonnay, would you? Or better yet, seeing it's so freaking hot outside, how about a Campari and orange?" With that she swept me into her foyer and ushered me down a wide hall to her kitchen. I was thankful I was bringing up the rear because my jaw was dragging the floor. This place — and I couldn't bring myself to call it a home — was a miniature Ethan Allen furniture gallery. Each table, chair, mirror, and picture was perfectly placed. Most astonishing, there was nothing, not one dust mote, that told me anything about the people who lived in this showplace. A decorator had chosen every knickknack and accessory. Even the pillows were coordinated, fluffed, and standing at attention. This was like a stage set waiting for the actors to appear.

"I'm Clancy Whitehead," she said, extending a cool and slender hand. "Whitehead like the pimple. Only it really should be Fathead. Because that's what I married. You wouldn't know it to look at me but I lost two hundred and forty pounds of ugly excess weight. I divorced him."

How do you follow a conversational tidbit like that?

She continued with, "I ran into the turkey the other day. Had to back up twice and run over a curb to do it, but I managed."

Unsure how to respond, I offered a handshake and my name. "Gee, this place is really . . . lovely."

She snorted. "Yep. And sterile. Flies have panic attacks when they enter. Come here. Let me show you my cabinets."

Clancy opened a six-foot-long pantry. I've never had another woman show me the inside of her cabinets before, and I felt this sudden sense of shared intimacy. As I waited for the doors to open, I experienced déjà vu taking me back to my best friend in first grade. Her name was Tammy and we snooped our way through every crook and cranny of her house.

Clancy's pantry was stocked with cans, boxes, and plastic containers in alphabetical order. Three risers of varying heights displayed every food item. Patterned paper lined the shelves. A wipe board inside a door listed every food item and where it could be found.

My hostess left me to gaze in wonder. Glassware and ice chinked as she puttered around. The sound of pretzels being poured into a bowl was accompanied by the whisper of napkins pulled from a drawer. I stood and shook my head. Man, was this woman ever organized.

She handed me a vibrant red and orange drink in a tall cool glass. "Cheers."

The taste was unusual. A bitter start, a sweet middle, and a citrus afterglow. I liked it. I probably couldn't afford to drink Campari and orange on a regular basis, but I sure wished I could.

"Pathetic, isn't it?" She clucked at the shelves. "Since I took early retirement from teaching, the kids went off to college, and Mr. Fathead dumped me for a younger model, I have nothing to do but clean house and organize. You know, you say to yourself, 'Someday I'll have the time to get this all squared away.' Then you do. And know what? It's a pathetic excuse for a real life." She paused, took a sip, and examined me thoughtfully. "So tell me, Kiki Lowenstein. What's a nice, sane person like you doing trying to round up the dirt on Yvonne, the Vampire Woman? She really was, you know. She'd suck all the energy out of you in fifteen minutes or less. The world is probably a better place without her. Even though her poor kids will miss her, I have no doubt they'll flourish without that harpy snarling at them." Clancy blinked slowly and took another sip. "By the way, this stuff's potent. I hope you aren't planning to do any driving for another hour or so. Better munch on these pretzels. In fact, let me get you some cheese and crackers."

She put slices of cheddar, crackers, and a pot of chutney on a placemat. We sat side by side in a banquette for a while, enjoying the food while I debated whether to be honest or not. The liquor created a delightful languor in my limbs. A few more swallows, and I'd curl up and nap.

What the heck. I explained everything to Clancy. She was a good listener. Nodding when appropriate and interjecting a quick "go on," she kept me talking. Finally she said, "You need to find Yvonne's killer. The public service aspect of her demise is counterbalanced by the havoc it's creating with your trade."

"Huh?"

"Never mind. Good thing you stopped by my house. No one is home at the Gaynors. If you like, I'll take those muffins over later."

I guess my face betrayed my disappointment.

Clancy saw it and said, "Okay, just so your trip isn't a total waste, here's what I know. Perry is a no good, cheating scumbag who thinks he's a big Texas Hold 'Em gambler. He's been playing online and losing money hand-over-fist. When Yvonne gained back all that weight, he asked her nicely to try to slim down. Said he couldn't get excited by all that blubber. She responded by packing on more pounds. Maybe he was cheating before that. Maybe not. I don't know. All I can say is the two of them seemed bent on destructive behavior. Like it was a race to see who could bottom-out first. His gambling and her eating. And yes, before you ask. I know who he was having his tawdry romance with. Rena's her name."

"Rena Rimmel? But she is — was — one of Yvonne's best friends!"

Clancy smirked. "What is it the politicians say about keeping your friends close and your enemies closer? Yvonne wanted old Rena in her sights at all times."

"But she and another friend, Nettie, said he was messing around with his secretary."

Clancy got up and poured herself another Campari and orange. Seeing me look wistful, she wagged a finger. "Ah-ah-ah! No more booze for you. Otherwise you'll fail the blow test when the trooper pulls you over." She reached into her refrigerator to crack the pop-top on a cold Diet Dr Pepper.

We'd only known each other for fifteen

minutes, and we were already best friends. How'd she know I love Diet Dr Pepper? Huh?

"Our boy Perry was a busy fellow. Yes, he was doing the nasty with his secretary. And with Rena. But he's been having a fling with Rena much longer than with his workmate honey."

I sipped the cola and thought about what she'd said. "You're telling me Rena could be the murderer. She has motive. And opportunity. She was there at the Botanical Garden. There afterward at the crop. She could have brought the scones. Since she hung around with Yvonne, she had access to her purse and the Epi-Pen." I took another fortifying slug of Dr Pepper. It was good, but I hankered for more Campari and orange. "I still have trouble understanding why Rena and Yvonne would stay pals if Rena was having a fling with Perry."

Come to think of it, I couldn't understand why Nettie remained part of this gruesome threesome. It was like that *Sesame Street* jingle about "one of these things is not like the other." The three might have had something in common once upon a time, but not lately.

Clancy washed her glass and mine, dried them, and set them carefully in line with the other glasses in her cabinet. She turned to face me, leaning against her kitchen counter. Her arms were crossed over her chest, and her expression was hard. "Kiki, have you ever realized how tough it is for grown women to make friends? It's tougher than getting dried dog doo off your shoes. I mean, after your kids are out of grammar school? It's dang near impossible. And here? Here in the boonies? Or in a suburb of St. Louis where the watchword is, 'What high school did you go to?' Do you know how much I spend on a shrink because I have no one to talk to?"

She was right. Vaguely I remembered all that. My life changed so much after George died, and I was forced to make my own way that I'd forgotten the loneliness, the lack of purpose. When you have kids, you structure your life around them. Their friends' parents become your friends, if you are lucky. You meet moms at soccer practice. You serve on committees together. But once your child becomes a teen, life does a tilt-a-whirl.

You are as useless as a soggy tissue the day your kid learns to drive.

And finding friends? Shoot, fitting in was incredibly difficult in St. Louis. The only place I could compare it to was Boston — at least that's what I'd heard. There the

Lowells talked only to the Cabots and the Cabots talked only to God. Here, you substituted local names for the same result.

The St. Louis environs has an unusually large population of returning adults. People know where they belong, and where they don't. Each of the ninety-one municipalities has its own personality, own culture, and status. Outsiders could struggle a lifetime and never find a grassy mound to share with fellow revelers for Fourth of July fireworks.

Newcomers circled St. Louis like planes without clearance for landing.

I smiled at Clancy. Yeah, I knew exactly what she was saying. Rena, Nettie, and Yvonne stayed friends because of a combination of inertia and social pressure. It made a weird sort of sense.

But I could also see what Clancy was hinting at, her personal loneliness. I scribbled down my name and phone on the back of a receipt for gas. "I can always use a new friend. This is my cell phone. Call any time. My place isn't fancy, and you have to like dogs, but maybe we can get together."

Clancy's grin was genuine. Her eyes glittered in the fluorescent lights of her kitchen. "I'd like that. I'll bring Campari and orange."

"Sold!"

■ ■ ■ ■

I left Illinois and crossed the Mississippi into Missouri without a state trooper escort. I took Grace for a piddle, nodded to Bama as she took inventory, and thrilled to see the store busy for the first time in weeks. Dodie helped a customer thread a HERMA Dotto dispenser while I matched patterned paper for two women. I was standing at the front of the store ringing up my customer, when a brick sailed past me and hit Dodie in the side of the head.

"Die, Jews!" The invective changed pitch as our attackers raced past in their car.

I raced around the sales counter to reach Dodie's side. Her eyes were closed and a trickle of blood, warm and bright, ran down her temple. Our customers were unhurt. One had the presence of mind to hit "911" on her speed dial.

"Dodie! Are you okay? Talk to me! Dodie!" I yelled to my inert boss. A customer offered a handful of tissues. I dabbed at Dodie's face. The wound looked minor but I had no way of knowing how hard she'd been hit.

"Here," Bama handed me a bottle of ammonia we use to make a solution for cleaning rubber stamps. I waved it under Dodie's nose, and she shook her head violently. I was helping her sip water when EMTs and cops ran through the front door.

As paramedics gathered around Dodie, I called Horace. The police took statements from our customers, which gave me a chance to call Detweiler. I'd just spit out the words, "We need help —" when he said, "I'm on my way."

Dodie pushed me away, insisting, "I'm okay." The paramedic working on her told my boss to lie down while they prepared a stretcher. Dodie raised her voice. "No! No! I'm fine. I will not go to the hospital. No!"

I didn't leave her side. "But look at you! You might have a concussion. Horace is on the way. Maybe he can convince you."

"I'm not going to the hospital and that's final. Leave me alone." When a six-foot-tall plus-sized woman with a butterfly bandage on her temple tells you to back off, you slam it into reverse, pronto.

Uniformed officers started asking questions. Unfortunately, we had nothing to tell them. It all happened so fast and our attention had been elsewhere.

Horace's face appeared between the emergency workers. He muscled his way to

Dodie, cradling her head to his chest and cooing. "I'm here, my love. I'm here."

Wordlessly, Bama picked up chunks of glass and swept ice-like particles into a dustpan. I cleared the sales counter, dumping shards into a trash can and wiping flat surfaces with a damp paper towel.

I paused long enough to see Detweiler talking to the first responders. His face was tight with anger. The emergency workers and local police finished their work and left. I offered our shoppers discount coupons, and they promised to come back another time.

On the way out, I heard one woman mumble to her friend, "These people are jinxed."

Horace and Detweiler moved Dodie from the floor to a chair. She wore a dazed expression, but she answered the detective's questions in a firm voice. No, there hadn't been any more threatening phone calls. No, she knew of no one who wanted to hurt her. At least no one specifically. She asked me to go to her office and grab the list of scrapbookers still wanting refunds after Yvonne's death.

It was Bama who surprised me by saying, "I can't believe it. Who'd do a thing like this? To us?" Her normally flat voice rose to new jagged heights. This was the most emotion I'd ever seen from her. Until that moment, I didn't think Bama cared about any of us or our store.

She and I finished picking up glass and stood by Dodie in a silent show of solidarity. Detweiler asked our boss a few more questions about who might have targeted TinaB and jotted down her answers. Clearly, he had little or nothing to go on.

I thought this was part of a pattern. "What progress is being made on the murder? Nothing like this happened before Yvonne's death."

Detweiler studied his pad silently. "You are right. The timing is too convenient. We need to consider this in conjunction with the murder investigation."

I wondered, what were the police doing? Sitting around on their keisters and eating donuts? While they fiddled around, our business was going down the tubes. Instead of chasing the real culprit, they kept hauling in my best pal. Meantime, the criminals were feeling more and more bold as the flying brick proved too well. I said, "Maybe you and your friends need to quit picking on Mert and start expanding your cast of characters."

He lifted his eyebrows. "We're doing

everything in our power. There's no motive. No one strong suspect. Too many people could have brought the scones —"

I clenched my teeth in frustration. "Have you checked on Perry Gaynor? He was having affairs with two women. Plus, he lost a chunk of change playing poker. Maybe Yvonne had a life insurance policy."

Detweiler's mouth went all tight and flat. "I hope you haven't been poking around. I warned you about this. You better not be interfering with a police investigation." He tapped his pen against his muscular thigh. "The other woman is a rumor at this point, nothing more."

"Let me toss another name into the hopper: Rena Rimmel."

"Rena? But she is — was — Yvonne's best friend." Dodie gave voice to the confusion on Bama's face. They were right: it was a shocker.

"True, but reliable sources suggest she and Perry Gaynor have been involved for a long time. Perry's been playing patty-cake with his secretary, too."

"Reliable sources? SOURCES?" Detweiler said, "Kiki, read my lips. Don't get involved with this investigation. Keep it up and you'll spend another night in jail."

Right. Like he really scared me.

Detweiler continued, "Of course, we're looking at other leads. Mrs. Gaynor seems to have created a wave of ill will wherever she went." A piece of glass dangled from his silk tie. Feeling proprietary, I plucked it off. The grooming allowed me to move closer to him, to feel the warmth of his body.

"When you think about it, Ellen Harmon has the best motive," said Bama. "By killing a scrapper at our event, she's ruined Time in a Bottle's reputation. She keeps agitating the other store owners. She manages to accuse our store of wrongdoing whenever the media interviews her."

"Our" store? Gee, wasn't that cozy?

Bama continued, "None of which is surprising, because Ellen's had a grudge against Dodie for years."

Well, blow me down. My hand flew to my mouth in surprise, and I noticed a dot of blood on my palm. A piece of glass had nicked me. Detweiler pulled a clean cotton handkerchief from his pocket and wrapped it gently around my hand. "You neglected to tell me about that, Mrs. Goldfader," said the detective.

Dodie sighed. "Ellen Harmon started me scrapbooking. She used to be a Memorable Albums consultant."

Seeing how the unfamiliar company name

confused Detweiler, she explained about Memorable Albums and its pyramid marketing structure. A woman recruited Ellen, Ellen recruited Dodie, and so on. A portion of each recruit's sales traveled up the ladder to the person "above" them.

"As long as you worked for Memorable Albums, Mrs. Harmon made money," Detweiler caught on quickly. "But now she owns a store. Surely she doesn't still work for Memorable Albums?"

"No," Dodie answered. "But she feels I owe her for getting me started. She was not happy when I quit. I was her best recruit until I decided to open my own store."

Horace scratched the stubble on his chin. Unemployment destroyed his daily routine. He was no longer the clean-shaven, neatly dressed man I'd originally met. He spoke to his wife. "Remember the time she came by the house? She was hopping mad. *Meshuganeh.* Called you a traitor and everything else. I could hear her screams from the other room. *Oy,* it seems so long ago. I'd forgotten." He sighed. "We'd hoped Ellen had moved on."

I thought about what our suppliers had said. "We heard she was having problems paying her bills. Surely she didn't think our business was hurting hers." I shook my head. "Ellen couldn't possibly be that illogical."

"Scrapbookers shop locally. We're what? Fifteen or twenty miles away from her store? None of her customers would travel here to shop," said Bama.

Horace gave his wife a sideways glance.

Dodie sighed. "You're both wrong. Usually scrapbookers do buy locally, but I've been tracking the zip codes of our customers. We have significantly hurt her business. And we've been getting phone orders from her area, too."

Horace cleared his throat. "Tell them, my love. This has gone too far. You're all in danger."

This was a signal to Dodie. She dropped her gaze. "There's another reason she hates me. Originally, she wanted us to go into business together. But I told her we didn't have the money to invest. That wasn't the real reason. You see, she has no business sense. And . . . I didn't trust her."

Wow. This was a trifecta of hurt. First, Ellen got Dodie started scrapping. Second, Dodie bowed out of the offer to go into business together. And third, Dodie was stealing Ellen's customers.

I thanked Detweiler and handed him his handkerchief. "I need to set up for our crop.

I assume we're still going to have it?"

Dodie nodded.

Horace excused himself to find plywood for covering what was left of our window. Bama moved slowly to help me, trailing one hand along the table and fixtures. Detweiler jingled change in his pocket and watched us. "Okay, Mrs. Harmon has reason to want to hurt Mrs. Goldfader. That I understand. But how does Mrs. Harmon benefit from Mrs. Gaynor's death? She has one less customer."

"People are blaming us for Yvonne's death. We're losing business," I said. "Not to mention our windows are being broken and we're getting threats. These could be hate crimes, but I bet they're because of the murder."

Bama added, "Plus, Ellen's getting tons of publicity and attention. She's appeared on television or radio or in the paper every day since Yvonne died. She's done a great job of positioning herself — and smearing our store in a sneaky way." She paused and said to me, "You know, Ellen is displaying Yvonne's pages and hosting a memorial crop." Then for Detweiler's benefit, Bama continued, "Ellen may have lost one customer, but she's got lots of curious people stopping by to see what Yvonne was doing that was so special. Which, if you ask me, wasn't much."

"Morbid curiosity," Detweiler tucked his notebook away. "Their interest won't last long. Meanwhile, I'll check out other hate crimes in the neighborhood. Even though I hate coincidence, I'm not convinced these things are related. Patrol cars will keep an eye on the store, but you need to be vigilant. All of you." He stopped and pointed a finger at me. "And you better not snoop around. Hear me?"

# FOURTEEN

Our Friday night croppers examined their paper bag bundles curiously. The women were far too polite to ask if I'd lost my mind. At first glance, I'd passed out brown lunch bags stacked with ends alternating open and shut. I let them puzzle over the mess for a moment before holding up my sample paper bag album.

"Holy Moly," said Vanessa Johnson. "I can't believe *that* was once *this*." To underscore her remark, she pointed to my work and waggled her bags in the air.

Mardi Hamilton shook her head. "This is just amazing. I can't wait to show my grandchildren."

"I'm trying this with my scout troop," said Angie Guinness. "They'll love it!"

Nettie Klasser noted, "Wait 'til old Ellen Harmon hears about this. She'll be copying your project faster than you can use a paper trimmer. Probably get a class going before that phoney memorial service. She doesn't care about Yvonne Gaynor — it's all about making the cash register ring. Too bad Ellen wasn't the one who died."

The other women averted their eyes. Nettie was laying it on a bit thick, but she didn't seem to care. She added, "Rena wasn't sure whether to show up tonight or not. She was afraid people'd think her disloyal to Yvonne. Huh! Like Yvonne ever cared about her! Or me!" Nettie punctuated her comment with a loud slurp from a big bottle of Mountain Dew.

Merry Morrison led the others in focusing on the project at hand. She reached for my finished sample. "I'll be jiggered. That's absolutely amazing. I can use up all those bits and pieces of paper I've been saving."

Stacy Czech and her friend Marla Lenzen were excited as well, and Stacy passed the album to Bonnie Gossage.

Bonnie turned the project round and round in her hands. "I love it! I'm teaching a Sunday school class, and this would be perfect. Finally, a project kids can't goof up."

I laughed. This was the part of my job I loved best. "Okay, this is what you can do with ordinary brown bags. Now look at what I made with colored bags, and here we have a project using fancy gift bags."

The corresponding "ooohs" and "aaahs" thrilled me. As I'd hoped, the women were first stunned, then raring to go.

"Can we make one of those fancy ones next time? Oh, please!" Rita Romano nearly jumped out of her chair. The guest she'd brought, a woman named Emma Delacroix Martin, was equally enthusiastic. I'd met Emma before. She had kids who attended CALA, my daughter's school. But this was the first time Emma had come to one of our crops. Together she and Rita plotted all the fun they could have with the elegant gift bag album. The stunned silence that had greeted my initial handing out of materials was now a loud buzz. In fact, the noise level had risen so high, I nearly didn't hear the door minder.

A smiling Clancy Whitehead approached me. "I know I didn't sign up in advance, but can I at least watch? There's nothing on TV —"

"No problem! Girls, say hi to Clancy. Have a seat, kiddo. I always make extras. Here's our project."

The card Vanessa and friends signed supporting Time in a Bottle found a place of honor on our cash register. Dodie gave

Vanessa a big hug and handed discount coupons all around. The raised bruise on her head went a long way toward generating sympathy, as did news of the hate crimes. By the time our crop ended, Dodie, Bama, and I were in a much better mood. The cheerful, supportive, and appreciative voices of our regular customers, plus the new faces, gave us encouragement we badly needed. I noticed Nettie and Clancy chatting quietly. I made a mental note to call Clancy as soon as possible, ostensibly to thank her for coming, but really to find out what new poop she had learned. Clancy would be happy to pass along any gossip.

I picked up paper scraps. "You sure you two can handle the shop while I'm at Spa La Femme tomorrow?" I glanced from Bama to Dodie.

"No way are you getting out of that appointment." Dodie took Horace's hand in hers. After boarding up half our front window, he'd left us, only to show up at closing to drive his wife home. When he walked in, he presented Dodie with a lovely red rose wrapped in cellophane. "I'll put this in water on my desk," she smiled at him and walked away.

Horace turned to me. His eyes were blurry and large bags of purple hung under them.

"Could I pick up Gracie tomorrow? I know you have the day off. Your dog is good company for my wife. I know the police will be watching, but I'd feel a little more confident with the Great Dane here. I'm planning to be in and out. I don't want to worry my darling girl, but I feel like, well, I need to keep an eye on her. In fact, one of my honey-do tasks tomorrow is to buy a big Beware of Dog sign and tack it to the back door. It's not much, but it might help."

"Of course, you can borrow Gracie," I said. "Anytime."

It was nearly dark by the time I made it to Sheila's house. A bat swooped toward her lawn in the dusk. My mother-in-law didn't even notice. Dressed in a pair of tailored rose slacks, an ivory short-sleeved blouse and flats, Sheila was digging holes with a hand trowel and planting something long and round in them. I noticed Anya on the porch with a pack of batteries. Empty boxes were scattered around her. I tied Gracie under a maple tree and moved closer.

"Hi, Mom." My daughter, my eleven-almost-twelve-year-old child, paused while loading batteries into vibrators.

I gawked. I blinked. I had no idea what to say or how to handle this situation, so I tried valiantly to stay calm. But who can stay cool and collected while watching her child activate sex toys? "What are you doing?"

Anya tossed her platinum blonde ponytail, causing the ends of a perky navy ribbon to flutter. She held up a plastic model of a male body part and said, "I'm helping Nana get rid of moles."

I mumbled under my breath. I headed toward her grandmother. "Oh, Sheila? Sheila? Can we talk?"

My mother-in-law wiped her forehead with a delicate linen handkerchief and tucked it into her back pocket. "Make it snappy. I've got work to do." She bent her back to the task at hand, ramming the shovel into the ground, catching it as it bounced back at her, and trying once more until she found a patch of ground that would give way.

"Um . . . please don't tell me my daughter is packing batteries into vibrators."

"Yes, indeed she is. One website swears moles hate vibrators. I let my fingers do the walking until I found an adult toy store up on Lindbergh near the airport that was having a sale. I bought everything they had."

Oh, boy.

"Are you sure this is the kind of vibrator they meant? For the moles, I mean."

Sheila gave me a look I secretly call "the evil eye." "How on earth would I know? And if I don't know, how could a stupid mole tell? The salespeople at the store asked me what I wanted with all these toys, and when I told them, they assured me that a vibrator is a vibrator is a vibrator if you are a mole. They said they had lots of experience with customers and small rodents."

I clamped my jaw shut. No way was I going to share why they might have had this particular experience . . . but I had my ideas.

She continued, "My other choices were lye, Drano, bleach, and moth balls. We've already planted more moth balls. Four entire boxes. That's in addition to the ones you helped me plant. Anya and I planted the new moth balls yesterday after shopping at the Galleria."

Well, that explained the weird smell on Anya's clothes. At least it wasn't dope.

Sheila was on a tear. "Last night I gave pickle juice another chance. I poured eight bottles into these holes, and son of a gun, this morning, two new tunnels popped up. Do you know what they call baby moles? Pups! These moles are having hot and sweaty mole sex and producing more litters as we speak!"

Given her level of irritation — and the

fact that Sheila could go off like a point-and-shoot weapon when angry — I trod softly. "You know, Sheila, I'm not sure it's a good idea for Anya to have contact with adult toys at this impressionable age. I mean, what if she tells a friend she's been playing with vibrators?"

"I told her they're radio transmitters that send out a frequency that scares vermin." A dirty finger jabbed me in the chest. "She has no idea what she's loading unless you blab to her."

I bit my lower lip . . . hard. We'd been swapping off picking up my daughter after science camp for two weeks. Hello? And what were they studying at science camp? Oh, radios and such. I made another stab at convincing my mother-in-law this might not be a fit task for a pre-teen. Sheila turned her back and returned to her digging, so I had to talk fast. I dodged and danced out of her way as she tossed dirt to one side and then to the other with unpredictability. "Right, but that 'radio transmitter' she has in her hand? The one she waved at me when I pulled up? That's an exact duplicate of your late son's finer attributes."

Sheila tossed down the shovel. It bonked and bounced. The woman was a danger to humanity. I managed to step aside before the handle hit me in the shin. My mother-in-law paid no heed as she stomped over to Anya. Plucking the loaded vibrator from the child's hand, she moved the switch from its lowest to highest level.

With an evil grin, my mother-in-law turned to me, waved the vibrator and said, "Really? Just like you know who? That good, huh?"

"Um, yeah."

"Well, poor you. He was not half the man his father was!"

"Okay, sweetie," I said to Anya as she climbed into the car, dragging her ever-present backpack with her. "Let's go home and light the Shabbat candles. I know you lit them with your grandmother, but it has to be sundown somewhere, and I'd like to light them together."

I eagerly anticipated the sense of peace and well-being that came every Friday from thanking God for light, wine, and bread. The short ceremony created a pause, a deep breath of sanity, in a hectic life.

Anya turned big blue eyes on me. "Yeah. I can't wait to tell all my friends I touched real live vibrators today. That is totally cool."

# KIKI'S PAPER BAG ALBUM
## INSTRUCTIONS

Note: These albums are not acid or lignin free, which means they will get brittle over time, and your photos probably won't be safe in them. But they are still fun! Use duplicate photos or photos you have on disk or on negatives.

1. Stack at least three paper bags horizontally, alternating them so that the open end is first on the left, then on the right, and so on.
2. Fold the bags in half vertically and crease.
3. Stitch the bags together in this crease or collate the bags along the spine with staples, stitches, or brads. The flaps at the bottom of the bags can be used for hidden journaling. You can also open up the flaps and treat them as an extension of the "page."
4. Decorate the bags as you like. The front and last pages of your album are the most flimsy and vulnerable to use. Adding cardstock to these will stiffen and reinforce the whole album. Covering the outside pages

with clear plastic adhesive film will also protect your project.

# FIFTEEN

Sheila hired a white Lincoln limousine to pick me up at her house and take me to Spa La Femme. Seeing as how I'd just dropped off my Great Dane at the store and was covered in dog hair, the huge vehicle felt too grand for the likes of grubby old me. On the other hand, my daughter wasted no time adapting to luxury. Leaving her grandmother behind, Anya raced to the open door and peeped in. "It's just like a regular car," she sniffed, a sure sign she sported a bad case of terminally cool. Then she relented with "but the fact you have a driver makes it the bomb, Mom."

Sheila's maid Linnea handed the chauffeur, Howard, a zippered garment bag. Inside were my gown, wrap, and shoes.

Linnea and Anya planned to make chocolate chip cookies while we were at the Opera Theatre dinner. Sheila harbored bizarre worries about Anya getting overweight.

Once privy to my concerns about my child getting too thin, Linnea took charge of the situation, since she'd long since laid claim to Sheila's kitchen as her own personal territory. The maid became my co-conspirator and safety net, making sure my child's diet included more than iceberg lettuce, baked chicken, and apples. "What happens in my kitchen, stays in my kitchen, Miss Kiki," said the stout woman. "I get to decide what to make most of the time. I keep telling Miss Sheila, if she eats too much bunny food, she's going to grow herself a fuzzy cotton tail. I'll make sure Missie Anya gets what she needs to keep shooting up like a weed. You know I will."

The bulging garment bag, the sleek white town car, and the driver standing at attention sent my brain into Queen for a Day overload. I searched the skies for a Disneyesque fairy godmother descending from the heavens to dust me with sparkly stars and shimmering pixie dust. From my childhood memory vault came a sappy theme song. The bouncy refrain of "bibbity-bobbity-boo" gave me pause — and I hesitated, one leg in the car and one on the terra firma of Sheila's massacred and muddied lawn. My mother-in-law showed up at my elbow to give me an encouraging push.

"Is all this really necessary? Our society puts too much emphasis on beauty as it is."

Sheila rolled her eyes. "Get in the car. The staff at Spa La Femme has a lot to do before Howard swings back by to pick me up."

"What if I get done early? How will I get home?"

She rolled her eyes even more and gave a "go on" nod to the liveried driver who was dressed — and was shaped — like a skinny penguin wearing a red tie. The real capper was his hat, a low, flat-topped black affair with a gold braid rimming the bill.

"But without my car . . . I won't be able to get a ride back until, uh, Howard comes for me." I stopped. It dawned on me why Sheila had constructed my trip in this one-sided manner. "You think I'll chicken out."

It was so like her to manipulate me. Somehow, she often got the best end of the deal, which is to say, she got exactly what she wanted. As usual.

She stopped rolling her eyes long enough to stare at me. "The thought had crossed my mind. Why do you think I chose a spa out in the middle of nowhere? Hmm?"

Barbara Walters explained the art of asking questions as the limo rolled over hill after hill, up and down two-lane Highway 94

228

toward Defiance. Howard turned west, following wooded areas bordered with rippling prairie grass, nodding yellow-orange day lilies, and waving white daisies. Along the way, we passed the clapboard-sided two-story home where Daniel Boone dispensed prairie justice to settlers and Indians alike. A mile or so later, Howard pulled into a long gravel drive running uphill through a rolling green lawn. Banners hanging from iron street lamps announced Spa La Femme. I peered around the driver's head at the impressive Victorian farmhouse. The pink pastel siding with lavender, yellow, and green gingerbread trim made me think of birthday cakes. Behind the main house two wings angled, tripling the size of the original building. As we drove under the rose-colored canvas awning, two matrons in white dresses and orthopedic shoes raced down the steps and stood like tin soldiers watching our approach. Their hands were clasped behind their backs à la parade rest.

We rolled to a stop. Howard hopped out and opened my door. Both women rushed forward, one taking me by the hand and the other retrieving my garment bag.

"I'm Suzanne, and I'll be taking care of you today," said the woman holding my elbow. Glancing down at the gold watch pinned to her left breast, my minder noted the time approvingly and said, "Come right this way, we've been expecting you."

For a second, I wondered if Sheila had committed me to a sanitarium. Yeah, we were getting along better, but I still didn't completely trust her. Why should I?

Best to face this head on. "I'm here to have my nails done."

Suzanne and the other woman in white giggled. "Oh, I think we'll be doing a bit more than that!"

Ten minutes later, I stood naked as a jay bird. Other women were also shedding their clothes. We were too embarrassed to strike up conversations, but there was none of the hoity-toity attitude I'd expected at a place as exclusive as this. Nudity is a great equalizer. It's hard to proclaim your status when you're wearing nothing but your birthday suit.

I quickly slipped into a fluffy white bathrobe. My feet shuffled along in soft open-toed slippers. I closed the door on my locker, pinning the key to my robe as Suzanne suggested. I don't know why I bothered. It wasn't like my locker held anything of value. Inside was five bucks, a pack of gum, Chapstick, and a dingy wad of tissues plus the well-worn cut-offs I made out of jeans, a pair of Keds, and a tired Reebok T-shirt that had once been George's.

I joined other stuffed bath towels in the waiting room.

Suzanne tripped in, smiling like a kid the first day of kindergarten. She was very lavender, from her fragrance to the clean look of her. "I think this is a bit extreme for a manicure," I said pointing to my bathrobe. I didn't want the other women to think I was silly. Of course, we'd all seen each other buck naked moments ago. Suzanne consulted her clipboard and chirped, "That's on the list but first we need to exfoliate you."

"Ex-what me?"

"Exfoliate."

"Isn't that what Agent Orange did? In Vietnam? I'm not sure I like the sound of that."

She turned to me, her face clouded with confusion. "We don't have any Agent Orange, but Helga can put citrus aroma in the body scrub."

"Scrub?" I played Little Miss Echo as I scuffed my way along like an octogenarian on her way to bingo in the parlor.

At the threshold of a white-paneled door in an endless row of the same, Suzanne handed me off to Helga, a woman whose musculature and false teeth were ample proof she'd once played hockey for the Boston Bruins. In guttural tones, Helga indicated I was to take off my bathrobe (of which I'd grown rather fond), lie face up on the leather bed, and cover myself with the proffered white sheet. A small pair of panties made from material like kitchen wipes were waiting for me. The smell of bleach and eucalyptus filled the air.

The ceiling was papered with posters of Tom Cruise, Antonio Banderas, and George Clooney. This was instantly and deeply shaming. The last thing I wanted was for these hunks to witness my puny, white, and flabby self in Handi Wipe undies. A quick rap on the door announced Helga's reappearance, and she loomed over me, a mess of gooey orange paste in one paw. "Now, I exfoliate you. We take off dead skin."

When last I checked, all external skin is dead. Helga must have read the same biology text, because she scrubbed me with a vengeance, ridding me of this important outer covering. I gritted my teeth as layers peeled away. Between forceful strokes, she scooped up more nasty mix and slapped it on me. Fortunately, I have a high pain threshold. I could tolerate the sanding down of my upper arms, hands, forearms, and shins, but when she began grinding down my inner thighs, I yelped in pain.

"Could you lighten up, please? You aren't refinishing furniture," I tried to inject levity.

A whisker on Helga's chin drooped as she frowned. "No, is better this way. Better for the mud and seaweed."

"Mud? Seaweed?"

"Makes skin glow. Removes toxins. Drink this."

I grasped a white mug filled with clear liquid and sipped. "What is this stuff?"

"Hot water and lemon. Is natural diuretic. You are bloated."

"I am?" This was news to me. I felt fine. Or rather, I had been feeling fine until I lost that top coat of skin.

Her watery eyes squinted as though I were making a bad joke. "When your last fast? When your last detox?"

"Uh, never. I don't drink much and I don't do drugs. Although either would be welcome right now."

"Chemicals in food and alcoholic beverages build up. Inside. Americans do not eat enough fiber. You need colonic and diuretic to cleanse insides. Alas, we have no time for colonic today."

I had a vague idea of what a colonic was . . . and the thought made me wince.

And I thought people went to spas to relax!

Helga took my cup away with a sniff. "You need detox each spring. Also sauna to sweat out impurities. And you must sauna with no clothes on. No towel, either. Is not sanitary. Finish with plunge in cold water. I know you do not," and she jerked her chin, causing a stray hair to sway, "because I see your skin so murky. Now, you must urinate. After I will apply mud and seaweed."

I pee on command. It's a leftover from being one of three girls. We never left the house without a mandatory piddle-check. Did you go? And you? And you? Once we were in the car, if Dad was driving, it was straight on 'til morning. There was no stopping until we needed gas. Such deeply ingrained habits don't leave you. Even today, you point me at a toilet and I will produce. This time, I have to admit, I wanted to linger in the restroom, figuring if I took long enough Helga would go away. But a discreet knock on the door told me I was making life tough for other clients.

*"Uffda,"* she muttered, slathering on a concoction of brown mud and green seaweed. The plant life had obviously been rotting when added to the mix. I stood in a trance, having given up all my modesty as Helga finger-painted me, touching every-

thing but the little paper panties with a brisk, business-like authority. The mirror showed me an Al Jolson clone. After she judged me "done," Helga wrapped plastic wrap around and around my body, pinning my arms and making me feel like a giant salami. Her bulging muscles came in handy as she lowered me to the bed. The head was slanted higher than the feet, allowing me to view ten dark toes strapped together by the plastic.

"Is hot in here, *ya?*" Without waiting for a response, she opened the window at the foot of my bed about twelve inches. Sheers blurred the outside world, but each zephyr lifted the curtains to provide tantalizing glimpses of freedom.

"Last, I cover your eyes," and as a coup de grâce, Helga lowered a silk bag full of beans onto my worried brow. Now I was immersed in darkness, covered in gunk, and confined like a hog going to slaughter.

"Relax. Sleep. I come back." The door clicked softly behind her.

Relax? Not hardly. I was hogtied, gooey, foul-smelling, and feeling mighty vulnerable. Within minutes, I started itching and twitching. My nose tickled. I heard the putt-putt sputter of a motor rev up outside the window. The angry hum crescendoed and receded as a lawn mower was pushed back and forth in front of my window.

I am allergic to cut grass.

The itch inside my nose demanded relief. My eyes watered. With a whiplash motion, I flipped my head, tossing the silk bag of beans to the floor.

At least now I could see.

The goo on my body had congealed into a semi-hard shell. My arms were wrapped too securely to move, and the drying mixture had glued my armpits shut. Small bits of grass drifted through the window like confetti in a ticker tape parade. Attracted by the static electricity of the plastic wrap, they floated over and stuck to me. I was turning into a chunk of sod, one blade of grass at a time.

My nose ran and dripped with abandon, and no amount of sniffling could restrain the flow. Snot leaked onto my mouth. I ached to wipe it away and rub my tearing eyes. No sound came from beyond the door where Helga had disappeared. Probably taking a steroid break.

The sound of the mower grew more insistent. A man paced back and forth outside my window, only his shoulders and torso visible as he continued his parade.

"Help!" First I directed my call toward

the other treatment room.

Silence. A big echoing silence.

I wiggled violently. The growing desire to scratch made me twitch involuntarily. My body jumped. There was a sound, a noise like ripping a Band-Aid off your skin, and I came unstuck from my bed. My body began a slow inexorable slide toward the open window, starting at a stately half inch at a time but quickly picking up speed. Spatial intelligence kicked in as I calculated height, width, and shape.

Oh boy. I could definitely slide out that window.

I started moving faster. My calves slipped off the end of the bed. Bound tightly by plastic wrap, my legs stuck out like a ledge. I wriggled. Bad idea. I picked up speed. My toes bumped the wooden molding around the window.

I held myself there, gripping with my feet and feeling the pressure of my weight growing, growing . . .

"Help!"

My toes were getting tired. Those ten pinkies were all that stood between me and the great outdoors.

The mowing man concentrated on the area directly outside my window. Muscular sunburned arms marched back and forth.

One of my feet slipped. I wiggled my toes in the fresh air. "Help!" I yelled louder. At this rate, I might even collide with the mower man.

I needed to get his attention! But he couldn't hear me over the noisy engine.

"Help!" I yelled to the door Helga had used.

No use.

I lifted my head and screamed toward the open window: "Heeeelllllllppppp!"

The mower sputtered and cycled down to a stop. "Ahem." A thin sliver of face appeared between my toes. Soft grey eyes peered in. "What the? You all right in there?"

Okay, I told myself. So I look a little like Mystique, the Rebecca Romijn-Stamos X-Man creature. Except I'm brown. And I smell bad. Plus, I'm more ripe than ripped, and more fluff than buff. No need to be embarrassed. Not while modeling poofy Handi-Wipe panties! Wow. Can you say, "Hot! Hot! Hot!"?

"Yes, I require assistance. Please. I . . . uh . . . my nose . . . uh, achoo! I'm allergic to fresh cut grass, and . . ." I sneezed and sniveled, trying to control the snot streaming down my face. Call me Booger Queen. A web of mucous covered my lips, flapping as I spoke, "Please! I need help! Get Helga!"

238

My savior responded with a low chuckle. Using a walkie-talkie, he told the front desk to send someone to the mud wrap room, ASAP. "I think one of our customers is . . . uh . . . finished with her treatment."

"Please tell them to hurry," I whimpered. "My toes are getting tired. They're all that's keeping me from joining you on the lawn."

"Well . . . that might be a bit uncomfortable for you. Seeing how you're dressed and, and covered with . . . with I don't know what." Lawn Boy stared at me. "Can you hang on? I guess you have to, huh?" A pair of thick eyebrows shaded kitten-grey eyes. Crinkles in the corners told me he was smiling. Strike that — grinning like a fool. "If you don't mind me saying so, that baby-baba brown shade . . . it ain't your color, ma'am."

# SIXTEEN

Some people are like toilets: you need to jiggle their handles to get them to work properly. Helga appeared, pronto, uttering a series of guttural noises I translated as abject apologies. Her touch was gentle as she hoisted me, steadied me, unwrapped the plastic, and sponged the goop from my body.

I'll give her this, my skin was baby-butt soft.

Lunch arrived shortly thereafter. Three lonely leaves of lettuce, a half a slice of cantaloupe, a chunk of honeydew melon, braised asparagus, scrambled egg whites, and a bowl of parsley soup sat proudly on a silver tray.

But I'd had all the grass I could eat as an appetizer.

"Ugh." I made a face at Suzanne. "Could we order out for a pizza?"

"Heaven forfend! This meal will help you

shed toxins. These are natural diuretics."

In other words, I was on the "pee your way to weight loss" plan. "Yeah, but I already lost a gallon of fluids with all that sneezing."

Suzanne spoke to me sternly. "You should have listed your allergies on our intake form."

I grumbled to the bunny food on my plate. How was I to know new mown grass was on the docket? Geez. By my calculations I'd lost a half a pound of skin, thanks to Helga's ministrations. One quarter came off as she scoured my body, and the other peeled away with the mud. Evidently what Lawn Boy called "Baby-Baba Brown" both defoliated me and exposed a fresh layer of skin. I'd also given up at least an ounce of oil and gunk to the woman in white who squeezed my blackheads. Who knew that could be a career? Another ounce was torn away by the cheerless gal who'd waxed my eyebrows, my legs, and my girlie bits.

Let me say this: After a bikini waxing, there's nowhere your day can go but up. Nothing else could be that painful or embarrassing. It's right up there with getting a mammogram from a cold-handed sadist with a heavy foot on the compression pedal.

Having hot beeswax spread in places only

my gynecologist had ever seen was a frightening experience. Having the bandage of solid wax and cotton ripped off, hairs intact, was a shock to my system. Afterward, the technician used tweezers to pluck stragglers, thus prolonging my agony.

Here's the worst of it: I had no idea what was coming next. Suzanne followed me around with a clipboard, making check marks at regular intervals. Obviously, when Sheila decided I needed polish, she had an exhaustive regiment in mind. Heck, most of these "treatments," I'd never heard of. Did women really pay to have all this torture inflicted on them regularly? How do you talk shop when you are a hair plucker for people's privates? What did she put as occupation on her credit card app? Bush whacker? And the other lady wielding the metal tool with a nasty ring at the end? What was her job description? Pimple popper?

Ugh.

I knocked back my "hearty" lunch. By my calculations, I downed a whopping 200 calories. Hardly enough to restart hair growth.

Suzanne led me — snarling and snapping for lack of food — to a quiet room where New Age music played. Yet another brawny woman, this one with a name badge that read "TiffanY" prepped me for a soothing foot massage.

I wondered. Did she hit the shift key by mistake or was she really graced with a capital letter at the end of her name? Like all my other minders, TiffanY ministered to me while referring repeatedly to a typed sheet of paper.

"Um, are you a beginner?" I asked cautiously. The foot massage felt good. Really good.

"No," she said. "I'm Bulgarian."

Well, that explained something, but I wasn't sure what.

"Uh, I think I'll be leaving after the pedicure and manicure."

TiffanY cast a worried glance at me over her paperwork, *"Ne! Na kukovo ljato."*

"Uh, you could try that in English?"

"I say 'not in a cuckoo summer.' You need hair highlighted, cut, and styled, and make-up done. Mrs. Lowenstein said this. She is big tipper."

The afternoon hours dragged by. My tummy rumbled in protest. New portions of my body endured manipulations, burnishing, and painting. I stung in parts I couldn't touch in public, and I ached all over.

As a distraction, I puzzled over Yvonne's

murder. Was her gambling spouse involved? Or was the culprit Rena, the good friend who was sneaking around with Perry? And how about his secretary or co-worker? Did Rena and the other-other woman compare details and discover he was cheating on his wife and two-timing them? Could they have worked together to set Perry up? Was Yvonne the real target? Had the tainted scones been intended for someone else? Maybe the brick and graffiti were not generic hate crimes, but specific attempts on her life? Was Yvonne murdered to ruin Time in a Bottle's business? Could the scones have been a food-tampering plot gone wrong? Why were the police hounding my friend, Mert?

I tried to formulate answers, but the lemony cream TiffanY stroked and kneaded into my calves was so soothing. The scent worked on every tense muscle in my body — even ones my masseuse wasn't rubbing.

"What *is* that stuff?" I asked.

"Melissa," she responded.

"Melissa Who?"

Seeing my confusion, she handed me the bottle. "Melissa," it seems, is another name for lemon balm, a member of the mint family.

"Makes good tea, too," said TiffanY. "At

night can help you sleep. Good for upset tummy, gas, and monthly cramps. One cup helps you be calm. Here, I get you some." She returned with a warm drink, which I sipped greedily. It tasted like lemonade.

"More please," I begged. Between ruminating on the murder and gearing up for the night ahead, I was antsy. My nerves were kicking in, big time. I started gulping the tea, and TiffanY brought me a small pot of the brew.

What I really needed was good old-fashioned Valium. There are moments in one's life where having a drug dealer in your Rolodex would be a grand idea. Instead, I would content myself with sipping an herbal brew. By the gallon.

After the pedicure, which felt ridiculously good until TiffanY's puttering around tickled, another woman fixed my nails while a stylist used a rat-tail comb to divide my hair into precision plots. Each area of hair was painted and wrapped in tin foil, leaving me looking like a television antenna's dream date. A makeup artist applied "permanent" false eyelashes, one by one, before lining my eyes, darkening my brows, and "doing" my face. My hair was rinsed, cut, dried, and blown out, only to be curled loosely with a hot iron. Finally, Suzanne led me back to the dressing room and handed me a gift bag tied with ribbons.

"Here are your undergarments and accessories. Howard dropped them off. Your gown is hanging in the locker there. Please hurry," she said as she consulted her watch. "He still needs to pick up Mrs. Lowenstein."

Inside the bag I found a long-line Spanx. Of course, it fit, and better yet, it tamed my wobbly bits into a smooth, taut line. Remember Barbie? And the instructions to dress her the way real models did by stepping into her clothes? It wasn't lost on me. I stepped into my dress.

Suzanne reappeared to help with the zipper. She held my hand as I slipped on my shoes. From the bag came another box. The lid was removed to reveal a small beaded purse in gold. I was smoothing the flowing chiffon of my skirt when I heard excited giggles from the lounge next door. "Please," said Suzanne, "would you show the other staff members how you look? They want so much to see the final effect."

I followed her, more than happy to comply.

"Turn around," said Suzanne, pointing toward a floor-to-ceiling three-way mirror.

I gasped.

The woman in the glass was absolutely beautiful. Her skin glowed, her hair curled artfully to frame her face, her plump lips glowed in a perfect shape. Everything about my reflection was polished to a classy perfection.

Could that person really be me?

"You was like loser from *Survivor*," said Helga in her thick accent. "Now you Swan. Gorgeous! We do this good work." Suzanne, TiffanY, the manicurist, the hair stylist, the makeup artist, and all the other workers gathered to approve the finished product — me!

"Wow, I didn't even look this good on my wedding day."

"We know," sighed Suzanne joining the crowd in nodding sadly. "Mrs. Lowenstein showed us pictures."

It should have offended me, but I knew it was true. Even the limo driver did a double-take as I walked to the Lincoln. Halfway there, I realized I'd forgotten the contents of my locker. Howard opened my door, handed me in, and scurried away to find a spa employee. A moment later, he hustled his way back with word my belongings were being retrieved. I waited in the air-conditioned car, twisting my hands with nervousness.

My door opened. A pale pink shopping bag festooned with ribbons was handed in. The hand holding the bag was attached to a muscular arm. My eyes followed that gorgeous bicep up, up, to a strong chin and a pair of grey eyes. I did a double-take. Lawn Boy, for that's who passed along the bag, was an absolute stud. My breath caught in my throat. Framed by longish auburn hair was the face of a man who'd seen it all, but right at this moment, liked what he saw. Sort of a rougher Billy Ray Cyrus. Resting one arm on the roof and leaning into the interior of the car, he admired me without a shred of pretense. I blushed happily under his inspection.

"My, my, my. That gold you're wearing, that's definitely your color, babe. Definitely."

## LEMON BALM (*Melissa Officinalis*)

This herb was once used by lovers to send messages to each other! Like most members of the mint family, one plant can take over a garden. You may wish to keep the herb in its own pot and sink it in the ground that way so the roots stay confined. The plant produces a lovely, tiny white blossom. The leaves can be dried and stored.

For stomach and digestive complaints, or as a sleep aid, the leaves can be brewed as a tea and taken several times daily. In one study, people who drank a cup or more of lemon balm tea daily found it reduced their general anxiety. The leaves may also be used as an accent in salads or fish dishes.

# Seventeen

"Could you take a photo of me with my camera phone? I'd like to send it to my mom." I offered the Katana George had given me the year before last for Mother's Day to Sheila. With a brief tutorial she was good to go. She snapped my photo. I sent it to my mom and followed up immediately with a phone call.

"Hi, Mom. Can you believe it's me? I spent the whole day getting gussied up for a fancy event with Sheila. See the picture on your screen? Don't I look nice?"

Sheila turned her head to watch the scenery. It was a small gesture designed to give me a bit of privacy. I listened to my mother, before saying goodbye and closing the phone.

"What did she say?" Sheila's eyebrows lifted. "She must have been surprised by how lovely you look."

I swallowed hard and bit my lower lip.

I snatched a tissue from my new gold purse and dabbed my eyes. I lifted my chin and tried to smile. "Uh, she, uh . . . she said you can't make a silk purse out of a sow's ear."

The party tent outside of the Sally S. Levy Opera Theatre was all decked out in tiny white lights, white floral arrangements in silver bowls, and white table cloths. A greeter checked us in and gave us tiny envelopes. Inside was an ivory card on heavy linen stock embossed with our names and table number. I squared my shoulders and stepped into the crowd. Around us swirled women in fairy tale gowns and men in statesmanlike tuxedos. I couldn't help but be impressed by the sight. Sheila and I could barely make it through the crowd for people stopping my mother-in-law to chat. "Photo, please," interrupted a man carrying a large camera with an industrial-strength flash. "Of course I recognize you, Mrs. Lowenstein," said our paparazzi pausing to jot our names in a notebook, "but this is?"

"My daughter-in-law, of course. This is the famous Kiki Lowenstein, scrapbooker extraordinaire. Mother of my adorable granddaughter."

I stood there in shock. From Sheila, this

was positively effusive. But I wasn't taken in. Much of this was about Anya, about making sure I made the right impression so Anya could follow in her grandmother's footsteps socially. Sheila took the notebook from the roving photographer's hands to make sure he spelled my name correctly. (I guess she was concerned he'd spell it KINKY. That's happened before.) "And," she said imperiously, "you will have copies of the photos to my home, right? Please take several more." She posed next to me, whispering, "Chin down, lick your lips, tuck your tummy in and buttocks under, one hip forward, stand straight." The flash went off enough times to temporarily blind me.

As I blinked and tried to get my bearings, Serena Jensen joined us. We chatted in a desultory way until she said, "Speaking of scrapbooking, did you hear about the scrapbooker who was murdered? Wasn't it at a what-do-you-call-it? I hadn't heard about it when I came by your store."

"A crop," I offered, "and unfortunately I was there."

"Really? Oh, Kiki, that must have been awful." She added, "My son works with the husband of the woman who died." She leaned closer to me. "I don't like to gossip, but the word is Mr. Gaynor wanted his

252

freedom. Seems he has his eye on a much younger co-worker."

"Is this common knowledge?" Sheila asked.

"Oh, yes. My Donald — you remember him, right, Sheila? — is a marketing vice president at RXAid. Donald says the human resources director is fit to be tied. Mr. Gaynor hasn't been at all discreet. That sort of behavior is simply unacceptable. People sue so easily, you know."

"You wouldn't happen to know the name of the young woman, would you?" I smiled conspiratorially.

"Let me think. Oh, yes, it's Cindi with an 'i,' Starling. And Perry Gaynor's not the first man Cindi's tried to lasso. The young woman has designs on a wealthy husband. Oh — there's Nancy Parkington. Excuse me. She and I need to chat about an upcoming fundraiser. Nancy, darling!"

Sheila put her lips to my ear, "Do the police know about this? About this . . . relationship?"

It tickled me she was so interested. Methinks my mother-in-law was getting caught up in the excitement of solving a crime! I answered, "I can't be sure. Detweiler's part of the Major Case Squad."

Her mouth tightened. "Your . . . friend?

He's involved in this?"

I nodded. "It's an honor to be assigned to that squad. But he won't tell me everything for obvious reasons. I'd heard a similar rumor but couldn't supply a name." I snatched an hors d'oeuvre off a silver platter proffered by a waiter. It was a puny water chestnut wrapped in bacon. Just my luck to have grabbed something lightweight. My tummy grumbled in protest. When Sheila handed me a flute of champagne, I hesitated. "Maybe I shouldn't. I didn't eat much today."

Sheila waved away my concern. "You'll be fine. This is why I hire a driver for these things. Don't make a fool of yourself, but enjoy it. These events cost enough — and free-flowing liquor is part of the expense. I guess the regime I set up for you was rather Spartan."

I grinned. "I wondered if you were trying to beautify me or kill me. But I sure can't argue with the results. You knew exactly what I needed. I won't ever be able to thank you enough."

A cloud passed over her face, but she held my gaze. I wished at that moment we knew each other better. Perhaps if we did, I could have translated her expression. Was it concern? Fear? An appreciation tinged with remorse for how she'd treated me in the past?

"You are my granddaughter's mother. You must set a good example for the child. As Rabbi Sarah pointed out to me, your best interest is my best interest. At least most of the time."

On that note, we touched flutes and drank. Good champagne tastes a lot different than cheap stuff. The golden liquid dissipates as it touches your palate, leaves no aftertaste and a lovely buzz. The intoxicating shock went immediately to my head, but I wanted more. Everything — my dress, the other partygoers, the décor, the ambience — made this a fantasy-come-true evening, and the champers put the world in a soft romantic focus.

If only, I sighed to myself, if only Detweiler were here.

Sheila craned her neck, searching the crowd. "We must find Police Chief Holmes and tell him what we've learned. But first we should find our table."

Our heads nearly bumped as we walked along conferring. We compared the numbers on our cards to the ones on the tables. The noise level rose as alcohol loosened everyone's tongues and inhibitions. I was the first to spot where we'd be sitting for the evening. The only other people at "our" table were two very, very ancient women, reminiscent of centenarian land tortoises. Their stiff brocade evening jackets formed elaborate carapaces from which their withered necks rotated this way and that slowly. The ladies seemed to be taking turns shouting at each other. One woman's lipstick ran around her lips and up toward her left ear as though she'd slipped mid-application. It gave her a ghoulish grin the Joker would have envied.

"I cannot believe this," said Sheila, "They put the Ryman sisters at my table. I told them they could fill the two vacancies if necessary, but I did expect the organizer to use her head. Next year I'll have to be more specific. No one over eighty-five need apply. I do hope they have a defibrillator on hand. You never know with these old coots when they'll hop the great divide. Even more annoying, you have to scream to converse with them. I can't imagine why they even bother to come. Someone must clean them up, stuff them in their party clothes and send them on their way because neither is sentient enough to know where she is or why!"

Sheila paused to yell to the two old and shriveled-up women. Their gowns must have been built of steel years and years ago.

Actually, I thought the sisters were pretty cute. Lively, too. Sheila introduced me several times over, despite the, "Pardon? What? Sister, did you hear that?"

After a respectful length of time we moved away. Sheila was in rare form. "Annabell left all her teeth at home and Marybell is only wearing a partial. The waiter will have to puree the meal and serve it in a sippee cup!"

I never knew Sheila had such a wicked sense of humor, and I told her so.

"You've also never seen me in my element," she retorted. "Or drunk."

I never even knew she would get drunk. It didn't match my image of my "always-in-control" mother-in-law.

We began another trek through the crowd, with Sheila passing flutes of champagne to me and draining them herself. Man, she could knock this stuff back. I was starting to sway a little on my feet, but I felt darn good.

"Don't worry. The expensive stuff rarely makes one ill the next day," said Sheila, noticing my concern as I eyed my third glass. "That's why rich people make such successful lushes. They can tie one on tonight and make multimillion-dollar decisions tomorrow. Usually based on the financial news they learned from their friends the night before."

We came to a grinding halt when Sheila spotted a familiar face in the crowd. "Ben! Ben Novak! I promised to introduce you to my daughter-in-law, and here she is."

Two rotund men stood between me and Sheila. I steadied myself for being introduced to Tweedle Dee or Tweedle Dum. But Sheila surprised me. She pulled my arm and gently shoved one of the big boys out of the way. I nearly stumbled into the arms of a gorgeous man. Ben Novak was six-feet-two. His dark-blonde hair was shot through with the lighter streaks brought about by natural sunlight. His eyes were a smoky bronze, his chin strong and masculine, and his overall face a chiseled masterpiece of strong planes. Ralph Lauren was missing a model, and I'd found him.

Oh, Lord, a rush of hormones powered by alcohol brought a light sheen to my skin. I couldn't believe I was feasting my eyes on the second highly desirable man of the day. Whatever cosmic alignment caused this surfeit of male pulchritude, I thanked God for it. And I blessed Sheila for getting me in the kind of shape that let me hold my head high as Ben and I stared at each other.

Sheila said softly, "I thought you two

might have a lot in common."

We both colored. Ben seemed to fight a smile.

Yeah, I thought. What we have in common is lust!

Sheila continued, "Kiki likes to be creative with colors and shapes when she scrapbooks, and Ben has always loved to draw as well as write. His father publishes *The Muddy Waters Review*."

Ben suddenly realized he was staring — as was I — and he gave my mother-in-law a small nod and added, "I'm Dad's chief lackey. Not a glamorous title, but an accurate one. Low man on the totem pole, but at least I'm on the right end of the stick if you care to extend the metaphor. Mrs. Lowenstein has told me a lot about you. But her descriptions didn't do you justice."

No, I thought, I imagine not. After all, until today, neither of us knew how good I could turn out with a little polish. I forced myself to smile, which was hard because nervousness made my mouth dry. "You are very kind."

Sheila stepped forward with, "That reminds me, Ben, how is your father? I've been meaning to invite your family over for dinner. Does he still eat brisket? Will your mother let him, is what I should ask. He always loved the way I prepared it." She turned to me and said, "Ben's mother, Leah, is quite the Tartar when it comes to her husband's health. I wish I'd been as smart as she. Harry might still be alive."

Ben nodded and tore his eyes away from me to address her. "Dad would be happy for an evening's respite from his diet. I'm sure we can slip this past Mother. We'd be delighted to come, Mrs. Lowenstein." A small smile curled the corners of his lips as he stared at me. "It would be a pleasure."

The way he drew out that last word caused heat to flood my newly denuded lower half. Wowee. I needed a splash of cold water and fast.

Sheila responded with a courtly nod. "Then consider it done. I'll make arrangements with your parents."

Ben cleared his throat, his eyes never leaving mine. "Mrs. Lowenstein, if memory serves me, you have a granddaughter, right?"

Sheila answered proudly, "Yes. Anya is the daughter of Kiki and my late son, George. Don't get me started about how lovely she is, or I'll show photos and we'll be here all night."

Ben nodded to me, not to her. I caught a whiff of a trés expensive cologne, a spicy scent with masculine undertones. "I see. That's no surprise though, is it? Good looks obviously run on both sides of the family." I started to turn away, but he reached for my hand. "I hope I'm not being forward, but Sheila told us how you refused to accept your husband died of natural causes. You are a remarkable woman."

I blushed. His touch was warm and strong, but kind. He linked a forefinger gently through mine, almost playing with my fingers but not quite. I had a quick vision of how much fun this guy would be, uh, alone. Ben Novak knew exactly how to excite a woman — and his expertise came across loud and clear. I stuttered, "I wanted justice. George deserved that."

Oh, boy.

Ben gave my fingers a light squeeze and dropped my hand. "I hope you'll tell me all about your quest when we get to know each other better."

I watched Ben move away with mixed emotions. He was attractive and interested, but I already had a beau. Detweiler might be moving slowly, but he had kissed me — and we had a history. Plus my daughter worshiped the man. I just wished I knew where we — where I! — stood with him.

Sheila ushered me away. "Well, that was

successful," she summarized while brushing her hands together in a workmanlike manner. "Oh, there's Robbie Holmes."

We came up behind Police Chief Holmes. She tapped the big man on the shoulder. He turned to Sheila, his face breaking into a big goofy smile and his arms opening to embrace her. To my surprise, she stepped right up to him. The police chief gazed down at her with misty eyes. When they stepped apart, my mother-in-law colored. Ah, now I knew. I'd wondered where she had been spending some of her Saturday nights, and what put the spring in her step. She and Police Chief Holmes were more than friends. I watched the woman I'd thought stiff and cold lower her eyes like a shy high-school girl as Robbie put a proprietary arm around her waist.

Robbie Holmes had a face full of character, the visage of a man who'd been through the mill and out the other side. But his eyes softened as he stared at Sheila, and his mouth worked as he struggled with what to say. "Sheila, my, my. Sheila, you always are so lovely, and tonight especially so." A rush of red colored his cheeks. Clearly he was unaccustomed to expressing his feelings.

Sheila told him what we'd learned about Perry Gaynor's girlfriend, emphasizing

Detweiler should be informed as well. As if awakening from a trance, Police Chief Holmes transitioned from smitten school boy to seasoned law-enforcement professional. As Sheila wound down, Police Chief Holmes harrumphed. He stopped. "Speak of the devil."

I turned and found myself face to face with Detweiler. I stepped toward him involuntarily before Sheila grabbed my elbow.

A painfully thin woman moved from behind the handsome detective to slip her arm through his. Her eyes narrowed, and she stared hard at me.

Police Chief Holmes said, "Here they are. Detective Detweiler and his wife, Brenda."

# EIGHTEEN

After that little stunner, I needed a lot more champagne. A magnum might not do it. I aggressively flagged down the nearest waiter, and we all took up glasses. Robbie proposed a toast — but I didn't hear him. I held my flute with a strangled grip, staring into the bubbles and planning to get totally plastered. ASAP. Tootie sweetie. Starting now.

Sheila gave my upper arm a little pinch. "Yes, Robbie, you know Detective Detweiler is working the death of that scrapbooker. I'm sure Kiki's inside knowledge of the industry will be very helpful."

I didn't deserve so much credit, but no way was I about to correct her. In fact, I didn't trust myself to speak at all. What was there to say?

My lips were sealed while I listened to the voice in my head telling me how stupid I was. And how I never seemed to get it right when it came to men.

Police Chief Holmes picked up on my mother-in-law's comment. "Yes, in fact, I'd like to talk with you sometime, Kiki. May I call you that? I was impressed by what Sheila told me about your forensic scrapbooking. Would like to know more about it actually."

I gave him what I hoped was a radiant smile. "I'd be delighted to talk with you. Actually it's amazing what you can learn from photos. Our body language often gives us away, and candid pictures can capture all sorts of emotions — love, anger, trust, and deception to name a few. We can't always trust what people say or do, can we?"

Detweiler winced.

Sheila shot the detective a sideways glance so sharp and dangerous, it hurt to watch. "Well, Detective, doesn't my daughter-in-law look ravishing tonight?"

Meanwhile Brenda Detweiler examined me the way a boy does a fly before he rips the wings off. One edge of her lip curled in a bit of a sneer.

"Uh, yes," said Detweiler. "Kiki, uh, you are . . . Uh, you look wonderful."

I lifted my chin and skewered him with my eyes. "Why, thank you. That's so very kind of you." I chugged my champagne and scanned the room for a waiter, all the while telling myself I had nothing to be embarrassed about. He did. If I hadn't been holding the glass flute, I would have reached over and dope-slapped him. Instead, I turned to his wife, a gangly thing wearing what I assumed was once a prom dress — something very much like I would have worn without Sheila's interference — and said, "It's so nice to meet you, Mrs. Detweiler. Brenda, is it?"

Detweiler ran a finger under his collar.

I hope it feels tight, buddy, I thought. Think of it as a noose, you idiot.

He seemed to be signaling me with a roll of his eyes, a plea to meet later and talk, but I didn't care what he had to say. Or what weirdo motions he could do with those fascinating green eyes. I was not about to seek him out for a chat. As far as I was concerned, if he dropped dead right there and then, I'd step over his body to get more bubbly. Scratch that. I'd have stepped *on* his body to get the bubbly, grinding my stiletto heels into certain vulnerable parts.

Sheila tapped Robbie Holmes on the shoulder. He leaned down so her lips nearly touched his face. She gazed up at him, saying worlds of loverly things with her expression. "And now, dear Robbie, Kiki and I must powder our noses. Please share what we've learned about Perry Gaynor with your *subordinate* here. I'm sure you two have a lot to discuss."

Detweiler caught the inference. The detective jerked his head sharply backward as if he'd been smacked up the side of the face. His eyes blazed in anger.

Good. He deserved it.

As though reading my thoughts, his countenance immediately fell. I steeled myself against his hangdog expression, turning away, trying to clear my head with a little shake. Sheila put a hand on my waist and steered me.

She threw one more jab over her shoulder. "Besides, there are so many lovely single men here that I want my daughter-in-law to meet. We really need to keep moving."

Detweiler blinked fast and hard. "Mrs. Lowenstein, I need to talk with you later about Mrs. Gaynor," he called after us.

Sheila paused, "I don't know who you are talking about." She challenged him with her eyes.

"I meant the other Mrs. Lowenstein," Detweiler said weakly.

I paused, turned slowly and smiled, dropping my chin just a little, tucking my butt under, sucking in my gut, licking my lips, and jutting my hip forward. My mother-in-law and I stood shoulder to shoulder as I said, "Oh, I hardly think I have anything to offer you. Good evening, Detective."

Once inside the ladies' room, I spat out, "How could he have? How could he? I trusted him!"

A couple of women putting on lipstick paused to watch my little drama. No matter. I was mad as a hornet and didn't much care who knew it.

"You cannot and will not make a scene in public." Sheila pulled me into the handicapped stall, slamming the door behind us with a resounding thud. She flicked the door lock, while I paced back and forth, muttering, "He told me he was divorced! He doesn't wear a wedding ring! I thought he lived alone!" I stomped to one end of the small area, spun an about face, and retraced my steps. A roll of toilet paper fell to the floor, and I kicked it down the whole row of stalls. The white line of tissues stared back at me accusingly.

Sheila touched up her blush while leaning over the handicapped sink. "He doesn't live alone. As you can see, he's married."

I stopped storming long enough to lean my head against the cool metal wall. Words, images, thoughts, feelings. Suddenly, the pieces formed a pattern. Click, click, click. I whirled on Sheila, furious and hurt. "You knew! You set me up! That's why you wanted me to come so badly. You did this on purpose!"

Her face betrayed no emotion. She was utterly and totally a blank, a cipher. With her finger pointed accusingly at my heart, she said, "When *my* granddaughter told me about *her* mother's boyfriend, of course I checked him out! What do you take me for? An incompetent old fool? I did what any responsible grandmother would do! I care about my grandchild! She's already had one loss in her young life. I don't want her hurt again! This isn't all about you, missy."

The aquamarine dress contrasted dramatically with Sheila's red and angry face. "What else could I do? My grandchild is mourning her father. Then she tells me how nice this man is. How she doesn't miss her daddy quite so much. It's patently clear she's starting to feel affection for this . . . this man. And you! You let him into her life! You fell for him! Of course I asked Robbie about him. Any intelligent person would have done the same. It's my duty to protect Anya."

I took a giant step back. She was right. I should have asked around. Now my child would suffer for my reckless behavior. I'd let Detweiler become a part of our lives. I grabbed the handrail and eased myself onto the lid of the toilet seat. How could I have been so stupid? So careless? I stared at the tile floor.

Not only was I a sow's ear, I was also a horse's patoot.

"I would never, ever have willingly let my daughter be hurt. You know that."

She huffed. "This was not only about Anya's feelings. How dare he try to pull one over on you? You're a Lowenstein!"

The anger I felt at Detweiler mixed with the hurts I'd endured from her. "A Lowenstein? Gee, that's rich. Let's be honest here, hmm? What's it to you? Since when did my feelings ever matter? Do me a favor and don't insult me by pretending that you care about me. I'm Anya's mother — that's it, that's all. I'm only important as a reflection on you and her." I delivered this salvo to my mother-in-law's upper arm as she smoothed on more lip gloss.

Sheila hadn't wanted her son to marry me. She made that perfectly clear when I'd arrived on her doorstep pregnant. After my marriage, Sheila and George formed a united, impenetrable front with me tagging along somewhere in the rear. But my husband's sudden death upset the delicate balance of our small family dynamics. Now Sheila and I were forced to work together to raise Anya. We'd become equal partners, whether she liked it or not.

Sheila snapped her purse shut. I felt her eyes on me. "Is that so? Has it ever occurred to you that the way people treat you might be your fault? *You* misrepresent yourself. You lead with your insecurities. You lull people into underestimating you. I sure did. If I'd known you then like I know you now, we might have gotten along better from the start."

That knocked the fight out of me.

By golly, she was right. Maybe if I would put forth a little more effort, maybe if I were more honest, maybe if I didn't feel so comfortable playing dumb . . . well, who knew how my life might change?

Sheila said, "Don't you dare cry. You hear me? That *putz* isn't worth it. You will lift your chin and carry on. Never waste your time crying for a man. Ever. Men fall for women who don't need them, not for women who do."

I sputtered, "But you knew! You knew he was married! Why didn't you tell me?"

"You listen and you listen good, young lady. Don't you think I worried over this?

Wondered what to do? What were my choices? Tell you?"

I thought about it. "It would have been better than standing there face to face and —"

"And looking gorgeous? And looking like a million dollars and making him drool? Making him want you? Letting him know you are beyond his reach? Putting him on the spot? Now he can never, ever worm his way out of this. You caught him red-handed! What can he say? 'Oops? Sorry!' His position is untenable and his behavior is inexcusable."

I blinked. Tears gathered, but I blinked hard and — for the second time that day — dabbed them away. I stood and splashed cool water on my wrists. The cloying smell of bathroom spray deodorizer made me a little nauseated. I needed solid food.

I considered what Sheila said. I allowed as how she might be right.

"Think about it," she stood behind me, speaking to my reflection. "Wasn't this best? He couldn't deny her. He couldn't pretend they have an understanding! He had to face you and eat crow. Have you taken a good look at yourself? You're absolutely stunning. Would you rather have learned from a friend at the store? Or bumped into the detective and his wife one day when you were tired and sloppily dressed? Or . . . like this? When you are at your best?"

I watched her image waver. What was wrong with the mirror? Suddenly, I realized she was trembling. Clearly, she was speaking from experience. The words were too hard won. Her face was etched with pain.

Ah, I thought, at least that's something. At least she didn't take joy in this.

"Don't expect me to thank you." I wasn't going to concede her victory so easily. "I don't know what you could have or should have done, but there had to be a better plan. Some other kinder way." I wiped my nose with a tissue. I straightened my posture. I would go on. After all, there was food just around the corner. And champagne. And wine bottles on the tables. And several full service bars with assorted hard liquor. Lots of it.

Sheila said quietly, "Actually I count it a win that you are still speaking to me." She paused, fighting a grin. "Did you catch the look on his face?"

"Uh, yeah," I said and giggled. "He was stunned."

"As well he should be," she said.

We linked arms and walked through the crowded tent, passing Robbie Holmes' table. Out of the corner of my eye, I saw Detweiler half-rising to intercept us. Police Chief Holmes put a hand on the detective's arm, and Detweiler sat down abruptly, obviously chastised.

"And Police Chief Holmes knew?" I whispered to Sheila as we took our seats next to the Ryman siblings.

"Yes. Yes, Robbie knew, and believe me, he was not pleased. He's a good man with strong family values."

"Good," I said, as I slid into the seat a waiter held for me. "I'm really glad to hear that."

I gave one of the Ryman sisters a great big smile and yelled, "How's the salad?"

"Don't go to your house tonight," said Sheila as Howard drove us through the night. The leather seats in the Lincoln were as comfortable as a recliner. I slipped off my shoes and rested my feet on the empty seat across from me. I'd switched to Campari and orange once we began our meal. All that booze suffused my world with a soft, gentle glow. I was happy for the gauzy drape over reality. "Why?"

"Detective Detweiler might stop by to explain himself."

"What's to explain?"

Sheila said, "You really are a babe in the woods. Let's see. There's the 'my wife doesn't understand me' line. And the 'we live separate lives' routine. 'We have an agreement' is also quite popular. Trust me. He'll find one way or another to explain away the small matter of his wife.

"Come home with me. Tomorrow, you'll have your wits about you. If he shows up at the store or your door, you'll have had time to think of an appropriate response."

"Something along the lines of 'drop dead'?"

"Possibly."

She did have a point.

"I have to go take care of Gracie. Dodie and Horace dropped her off after the store closed."

Sheila fiddled with her purse. "Bring her to my house."

If I'd been sober, the invitation would have come as more of a shock. Sheila didn't like animals, and Gracie was a big 'un. As it was, in my mellow state, I rationalized Sheila must really, really be feeling sorry for me. At my current level of inebriation, I'd take all the sympathy I could get. "That's very kind of you. I'll take you up on the offer."

Sheila told Howard the change of plans.

He murmured, "Very well, madame," and I suppressed a laugh. Were the faux British affectations part of his job description? Bully!

If my run-down neighborhood surprised him, he never let on. The Lincoln's head-lights caught my front porch in their triangular periphery. I squinted at something draped over the front stoop banister.

Sheila saw it, too. "Howard, pull into the drive and point your lights at the house. I can't make out what's on the front steps."

Forgetting it was Howard's job, I opened my own car door. I moved along the side-walk slowly, puzzling over the shape, the color, the bulk of the indistinct object dangling before me.

With effort, I could pick out a black and white shape. Howard reversed and reposi-tioned the car. The Lincoln's lights were now trained on the scene in front of me. The blobs of black and white formed a pelt smeared with a red, runny liquid. What was I seeing? My vision adjusted to the inad-equate lighting. I picked out a body, legs, a neck and rope dangling —

"Gracie! Oh, no, it's my dog!" I sprinted forward, my heels puncturing the grass and pitching me to the ground. I scrambled, leaving those blasted shoes behind.

"Wait, miss! Let me!" Howard rushed past.

"No!" I screamed. "No! Not my dog!"

Sheila ran up beside me, panting into her cell phone. "Emergency? We're at 756 Gunterman. Hurry! Send the police!" She grabbed my arm and anchored me, keeping me in one spot. We stood about ten feet from my porch. "Yes, step on it. Hurry or I'll have your head!"

Howard trotted back to us. "Stop. Wait here. There's a flashlight in my glove compartment. I'll get it."

Sheila's arm supported me. My stomach roiled and heaved. She drew me close and patted my back. "There, there. Let Howard get the light. The police are on the way." I tried to stand, but my knees went wobbly. I smelled the damp grass, the floral essence on her skin, and buried my head in her shoulder. A loud sob escaped me. How could this be? Gracie was my best friend, my constant companion. She'd saved my life when my home was invaded. Who would have hurt her? And why?

I turned toward the front step, craning my neck, straining to see. Tears rolled down my face. "No, no, no!" My nose was running and I was crying too hard to speak. Why had I gone to that stupid event? If I'd been home, she'd have been with me!

Did she suffer? Was she frightened? My poor, poor dog!

Porch lights around us snapped on, but no one stuck a head out to see what was the matter. This wasn't the type of neighborhood where people said, "Hello." It was transient, secretive, dark, and brooding. A siren wailed in the distance. Howard ran past, his flashlight beam bobbling along the grass awkwardly. I pushed Sheila away, twisting out of her grasp, following him, my bare feet chilled by the damp grass. She came two steps behind. Howard stopped and focused his light on the harlequin pelt. I shoved him to one side and reached for the long tail. Every ounce of the alcohol I'd drunk conspired to put me in a fog, my own little atmosphere so thick and blurry, that precise motion and thought was nearly impossible. The tail slipped through my fingers, leaving me empty-handed.

"Gracie," I sobbed. "My poor, poor Gracie."

# Nineteen

Howard stepped between me and the mess, blocking my view as he examined the dog. My head began to throb. Sheila pulled me close again and murmured soothing sounds. She thrust a mop of tissues into my hand, and I wiped my face indelicately.

"There, there," she patted my hair. "Shush. Shush."

The driver interrupted with, "Miss? Um, Miss Lowenstein, this can't be your pet."

I didn't even correct him by saying, "It's Mrs. Lowenstein." Instead, I stuttered, "What do you mean, it isn't my pet? You don't know my dog."

He stepped closer to us, his face a study in solemnity. "Begging your pardon, ma'am, but it can't be her. 'Tisn't possible. See, this is fake fur."

"What?" I'd only touched the tail — and that had slipped away so quickly. I reached out again, hesitating, then touching the pelt.

By golly, he was right.

"But who? Why? Wha— ?"

I stood shaking my head, trying to take it all in. If that wasn't Gracie, then . . .

I started for the back door. Of course, it couldn't be Gracie! How could I be so dumb! Horace and Dodie would have put her in the basement. I needed to open the back door to check. My hand shook so badly I couldn't match key and lock.

"Let me," Sheila stepped forward. "Get hold of yourself. The police have just pulled up. Howard will deal with them."

I stumbled across the threshold, tripping on my dress and falling to my knees. Sheila grabbed at me. "You okay?"

"Yes," I stood up, moved forward and tried to open the basement door. It resisted.

I knew why.

A heavy thump, thump, thump told me my dog was right behind the door, her heavy tail wagging. "Gracie? Gracie! Move! Move, baby!" A shuffling noise and the clicking of nails on the stairs followed. I pushed the door again, opening it to darkness. A cold wet nose pressed into my face. Again I went to my knees, but this time to hug her. Belatedly, I thought about my beautiful dress. By now it was probably totally ruined.

Oh, well. Some things are much more

important than clothes. My dog was definitely one of them.

I flipped on the light. While the lazy metronome of her tail beat a rhythm, I examined every inch of the Great Dane's body. I ran my hand around her muzzle, down her sides, across her backbone, down each leg, and under her tummy. She was fine. I crouched eyeball to eyeball with my dear pet. She's not much of a licker, but Gracie nuzzled me and whined.

"Thank heavens," said Sheila, sinking into a kitchen chair. "Anya would have been devastated." Her driver's head appeared around my back door. "Howard? Are the authorities here?"

"Yes, ma'am, they are examining the mess and the note."

"Note?" I turned to Sheila. Very, very softly she said, "It's . . . it's a death threat. The Richmond Heights Police are coming. This is probably the work of that horrible person who killed my son. That monster!"

Howard escorted the officers into my kitchen. My interview went quickly. I explained where we'd been, Sheila told them when we'd arrived, and Howard chimed in with what we'd found. Since it was late, they wrote down Dodie and Horace's number but agreed to call them tomorrow.

I explained about the hate crimes at the store and conjectured this was tied to the death at our crop. Sheila pointed out it could also be the work of her son's escaped killer.

The female officer's eyes narrowed. Her movements exuded an athletic grace. Her questions were thoughtful and thorough. Gracie leaned hard against me, the two of us taking comfort in the pleasant weight of trust, as I talked and the crime investigators processed the scene. Finally, the interview was over, and I led Gracie to the Lincoln Town Car.

Howard opened the door for us, and my pooch stepped in gracefully (as befitted her name), plopping her hindquarters on seat next to Sheila. With her paws on the floor, Gracie sat like a queen, staring out the window, watching the street light playing hide and seek on the pavement. Sheila rapped on the dividing window, which Howard lowered to hear her instructions.

"The exaggerated news of Gracie's demise deserves a celebration. Stop at Ted Drewes." She arched a brow at me. "I hope you don't mind. Harry and I made this a tradition after attending stuffy social functions."

"I'm sorry I didn't have the chance to know him better." My father-in-law died of cancer six months after George and I married.

With a dreamy expression, Sheila said, "You two would have gotten along famously. Harry was an excellent judge of character. His success in business came in part because he could see talent, especially in those whom others might have overlooked." She opened her purse to hand me a moist towelette and her compact. "Touch up your eye makeup where it ran when you cried."

I opened the small mirror and did exactly that, thinking of the unique spot in St. Louis history occupied by Ted Drewes. Since 1929, the Drewes family has been making custard. In 1941, they opened a store on the famous Route 66, and even after traffic was rerouted, the tiny stand remained a popular destination. The frozen custard is to die for. Folks spill off the sidewalks into the street nearly every summer night to buy the concoction in its pure form or in outrageous mixtures.

As a cop waved us carefully into the crowded parking lot, we drove past throngs of customers wearing formal wear. Evidently, the Opera Theatre event didn't so much end, as it adjourned to Ted Drewes Frozen Custard shack. This wasn't surprising. Anya and I had witnessed limos dropping off entire bridal parties and prom groups. Our Missouri state bird is the bluebird. Our flower is the hawthorn. And our dessert is Ted Drewes Frozen Custard. No gathering of St. Louisans is a complete success without a trip to Ted's.

Sheila and I both ordered Terramizzou concretes, a thick concoction of custard plus chocolate, and pistachio nuts. Howard was a purist, a banana-split man, who took his treat back to the car. Gracie daintily lapped at a small paper dish of vanilla which she finished too quickly. Her interest in my treat indicated she'd gladly make a glutton of herself. Sheila suggested I drink several servings of water from the small yellow and bright green paper cups provided for that purpose.

"Part of what we call a hangover is really just dehydration," she said.

I've never been much of a drinker — my initial foray into parties and Purple Passion Punch resulted in pregnancy — so I took her word for this. We stood outside the Lincoln with my harlequin attracting all sorts of attention. Gracie took this as her due, eying other people's custard with a lean and hungry expression. When a giddy young woman dropped her cone cooing over my dog, Gracie doubled as a quicker-picker-upper. Finally I walked the dog back to the limo. "No more treats for you," I said to her sad eyes.

A short time later, the evening that seemed a lifetime long came to an end. Howard escorted all three of us to Sheila's door and made sure we were safely in. I paused in the foyer to thank my mother-in-law.

I put a hand on her arm. "Sheila, you've been very kind and generous. My gown, the accessories, gosh, it's all so lovely. I can't thank you enough for that and for the whole evening, really. Oh, and the day at the spa. I guess I needed sprucing up."

She laughed quietly. "That's one way to put it." Her eyes drooped with fatigue. The excitement of the evening was over. The adrenaline rush caused by finding the fake Fido had worn off; exhaustion hit us both simultaneously.

"I appreciate how you acted about Gracie. Letting her come here. I know you don't like dogs —"

"Pardon?" Sheila tilted her head. "I don't like dogs? What nonsense."

"But you've never warmed to Gracie." I faced my mother-in-law, thinking how she made the best of what God had given her. She was not a naturally beautiful woman. Her nose was too big, her eyes too narrowly set, and her mouth too thin. However, no one who ever met Sheila described her as anything but attractive, a testament to her careful grooming.

She sank down into a chair and shook her head at me. "I happen to love dogs. Before you met George, I had a darling bichon frise we brought over from England. You couldn't get them here at the time. Scooter and I went everywhere together. He slept with me, sat at my feet as I ate, walked right at my heels. Then the vet found a cancerous tumor on his lungs. It broke my heart to hear him cough and gasp for air. Seeing him suffer was too much to bear. I held him in my arms while the vet put him to sleep. I vowed I couldn't go through that again. I cried for months."

"Oh, Sheila, I'm so sorry! How awful for you."

She nodded. "It's odd timing for this conversation. Rabbi Sarah and I talked about Scooter just the other day. She encouraged me to get another dog, a rescue animal. The rabbi says God gave man dominion over animals, but animals have dominion over our hearts. So it all evens out." This last sentence was given extra emphasis by a wave of her slender hand.

I was sitting on her sofa with my head on

286

my hand, thinking. Her revelation surprised me. I didn't know she was a dog lover. I'd known Sheila for nearly thirteen years. Our relationship was an iceberg. Ten percent sat above the water, but the majority was still unknown and unexplored at deeper depths. Just as she didn't know me, I knew very little about her. Tonight I'd seen a tantalizing hint of the woman other people so admired.

Almost on cue, Gracie walked from me to her. Stopping beside the older woman, my dog initiated a low, slow wag of her tail. Sheila and Gracie were face to face. Gracie lowered her big head, pressing her muzzle into the open hand lying in Sheila's lap. At first, my mother-in-law pulled away, but Gracie persisted, lifting her nose and sniffing Sheila's face gently in that probing way dogs have. To my surprise, Sheila raised both hands and began to massage the base of Gracie's velvety ears, eliciting a low moan of pleasure from my dog.

"I've never been around a dog this big. Scooter was portable. He was my baby. Wherever I was, he was happy to be. Losing him, well, it was quite difficult. Of course, it broke my heart to lose Harry and George, but people are different. With people, even those you love, there are irritations. Bothers. Misunderstandings. But Scooter was purebred love. In his doggy mind, I hung the moon and made the sun rise each morning. He woke up each and every day eager to spend every moment of it with me."

Her voice was full of emotion. Gracie leaned in to give Sheila a long, gentle lick on the cheek.

"Good night, Sheila," I said a bit later from the top of her dramatic staircase. With one hand on Gracie's collar, I paused outside a second floor guest room. "Thank you again. For the most part, this was like being a princess in a fairy tale." I gave a small snort. "Except my prince charming was a liar." I had trouble thinking of Detweiler as that, but he was, wasn't he?

She lingered with her hand on her doorknob. Through the opening, I could make out the small sofa in her bedroom suite, and a large enamel vase filled with fresh flowers on the low mahogany table nearby. "It's too bad about that young man. I can certainly see why you found him attractive."

Gracie and I entered the guest room in tandem. Once the lock clicked softly behind me, all the starch went out of my panties. Finally, I had no reason to act strong. I collapsed onto the big bed, burrowed my head into the pillows, and began to cry. All the pent-up emotion of the evening flowed out of me. Egging it on was the raw, angry, pain of disappointment.

Despair swallowed me and sucked me down into darkness.

Gracie's cold nose nudged along my legs where they dangled off the bedspread. She snuffled her way up and down my bare skin, whining softly. I kept my hands over my face and cried and cried. It felt as if my life was spinning in an out-of-control centrifuge, and without the pressure of my fingers to my skin, small parts of me would break off and fly away.

Lord knew, I'd been trying to hold it all together for most of the evening. Now I abandoned myself to well-deserved misery.

"Dang him," I pounded the bedspread. "How could he?" Worried that vestiges of makeup would stain Sheila's bedclothes, I went to the bathroom for tissues. I perched on the closed toilet seat, trying to calm myself down. I'd graduated from crying to sobbing and now hiccupping. My diaphragm spasmed repeatedly, making weird huck-huck-huck noises. Gracie's anxiety about my welfare brought her over to investigate.

That was a mistake. The marble bathroom floor was slick.

Her paws went in four different directions out from under her. Her eyes hula-hooped in panic. I grabbed her collar. She skated around, moving her feet in a cartoonish "woop-woop-woop" of continual motion as she worked to stay upright. I gripped her collar, but her backside slipped down and out. Keeping a hand on her neck, I moved behind her, jacking up her back end. The front end started sinking. I instinctively jerked up on her collar. That had me choking her, so I let go quickly. I put both hands around her neck and lifted. Her head came up but her legs splayed, and her rear end traveled in the opposite direction. Dropping to the floor, I positioned my arms like shelf brackets under her torso. Now she could stand, but she couldn't move. And I couldn't maintain my Atlas-like position. She was far too heavy.

I used one hand to push her into a sit. With my other arm supporting her barrel chest, I crawled along, half-dragging and half-pushing her in that seated position until she made a scrambling leap for the carpet and bounded onto the bed. Her exit pulled the props out from under me. I came down on the tile with a loud, "Ooof."

Something about collapsing on the floor while my dog stared down from a posh four-poster struck me as funny. I looked up at her and giggled. Gracie raised one eyebrow and yawned. Her tail beat the air, and I swear, her floppy lips curled in a self-satisfied grin.

I dragged myself to the side of bed, stripped naked, and tunneled under the covers.

Gracie nuzzled me to say she had to go.

It was half-past six in the morning, and I wanted to sleep longer, but the thought of a Great Dane-sized puddle on Sheila's carpet was a powerful incentive. I grabbed a housecoat from the closet, padded down the back stairs, and headed to the kitchen for Advil and water before leading Gracie into the backyard. Sheila's pool shimmered in the lemon-yellow dawn. Emerald green dragonflies buzzed back and forth, making landings to test the tensile strength of water. Pots of pink flowering begonias, red geraniums, and blue lobelia as well as trellises covered with blooming roses turned the pool into an oasis of calm. I rested on a lounge chair and enjoyed the chip-chip-chip back and forth of two flame-red male cardinals staking out their territory. Gracie finished her business and strolled to my side, parking her carcass with a hearty sigh.

I told myself I could think about Detweiler for twenty minutes and no more. After time was up, I planned to get on with my life.

Detective Chad Detweiler and I met the day of George's murder. He had the unhappy task of telling me my husband died. In the coming months, I convinced him George was the victim of foul play. Another death occurred and Detweiler came to the store to question me. That was the day he met Gracie. I smiled, remembering how his whole demeanor had changed from tough guy cop to the little boy who had long loved Great Danes. Later he brought Anya a big jar of tadpoles from his parents' farm. When the killer carjacked me, chased me through a state park, and shot me, Detweiler was first on the scene, riding along in the ambulance, holding my hand in the emergency room. Since then, he'd become a stable part of my life. Chatting with me about raising Anya. Stopping by the store and our house. Checking whether the killer contacted me.

And finally, he kissed me.

I realized with a jolt I was in love with the man.

I loved his eyes, his body (or what I knew of it), and most of all his devotion to what was right. How could a man with such high morals have misled me? Better yet, why had he? And if he was going to be a cad, well, there'd been plenty of nights I would have gladly taken him into my arms. So why didn't he take full advantage of my ignorance and trust? Why did he stop with flirtation?

Okay, I told myself, enough. I glanced at my watch. This is a waste of time. That's over. Move on. Focus on the future. Figuring out who killed Yvonne Gaynor would go a long way toward improving my life.

So, who did it? And why? The gossip supplied by Clancy Whitehead and Serena Jensen pointed to Perry Gaynor. Who else could it have been? Well, there was Rena. Was she tired of sharing Perry with Yvonne? Maybe she thought he'd marry her and dump his mistress? Or maybe she killed Yvonne and framed Perry for the murder. Maybe there was yet another person involved, someone not part of Perry's love rectangle.

Could Bama have done it? I was still waiting for Bucky to call from Art House. Was Yvonne involved in getting Bama fired? Yvonne seemed to enjoy causing problems for people. Did my coworker bide her time, knowing their paths would cross again? Bama had access to the food. Heck, she'd done the ordering and worked with the caterer. If they knew each other from before, could Bama have had access to the Epi-Pen?

The Epi-Pen. Fewer people had access to it than to the scones. First of all, the food we served was handled by caterers, our staff, and volunteer helpers. But there was the food the scrapbookers brought along. Still . . . the syringe could only have been touched by someone with access to Yvonne's purse. That was a much more specific target. The food could have been tainted to sicken anybody, but the empty Epi-Pen could only affect one person — Yvonne. So whoever touched the pen knew (a) that Yvonne carried it, (b) where she carried it, and (c) how intense her allergic reaction would be.

Something bothered me. Beyond my grasp was an idea. A half-formed thought about Yvonne's allergies . . .

"We have to talk about your house. Your neighborhood isn't safe, Kiki. You've already had two break-ins and now this." Sheila calmly put a thin layer of butter on an English muffin. Gracie and I had joined her in the kitchen.

"I know. You're right. In another area of town, someone pulling a prank like last night would have been spotted, reported, and hauled in by the police. I'd like to move, honest, but my monthly rental is all I can afford. Especially since I want to be close to Anya's school and the store." I balanced scrambled eggs on my fork. My head felt tender, but the water and Advil were keeping a headache at bay. Protein would help. So would the huge glass of tomato juice Linnea placed at my elbow without comment.

Sheila said, "Don't be silly. When I die my money will go to Anya anyway, so it should help her now. I can contribute to suitable housing for both of you."

"But I don't want to be beholden to you. I need to be independent."

"Is your pride more important than your safety? More to the point: Is your pride more important than Anya's safety? Don't be stupid." She took a bite of her eggs and chewed them thoughtfully. "What are you planning to tell Anya about the detective?"

I took a long drink of the hot herbal tea Linnea gave me. Evidently, she had a whole bag of tricks for coping with hangovers. Maybe that had been another reason Sheila invited me to come home with her. I said, "I've thought about that. I guess I should tell her the truth. Otherwise, she'll wonder if his absence has anything to do with her. Knowing my daughter, she'll ask me how the evening went. I'll mention seeing him . . . and his wife."

What else, I wondered, could I do?

Maybe Sheila was hinting she had a better idea. I asked her point blank if she did.

"No. No, I certainly don't." My mother-in-law sighed. It was a sighing kind of topic, the kind of situation that made you feel helpless and sad. "What you're proposing is as good an idea as any. Now," and she seemed to be checking off items from a mental list, "let's discuss her request to wear makeup. I have an idea . . ."

# TWENTY

Traditionally, Anya and I took Gracie to a park on Sundays. We left Sheila's with every intention of doing just that, but the inside of my car was so stuffy, Anya turned to me and said, "Mom, could we pass? It's too humid to be outdoors."

She was right. The heat index was hovering near 105, and the air quality was orange. With her asthma, a walk outside was not a good idea. A part of me loathed letting our tradition slide for even one time, not because I didn't think she was right, but because my child was growing up before my eyes. Soon, her excuse for not wanting to take that walk would be "I want to be with my friends." I was trying to postpone that moment by entrenching our routines.

"Okay-dokey, Anya-Banana. What would you like to do instead?"

She turned cornflower blue eyes on me and said, "Call Detective Detweiler and see if he'd like to go roller skating. He told me he's really good at it. The kids say that rink over on Manchester is lots of fun."

Crud. I wasn't quite ready to discuss this yet. I needed a little more time to process last evening, to practice what I'd say, to consider any alternate approaches. But . . . here it was. I said, "I don't think that will work, honey. You see, he's married. I met his wife last night."

Anya stopped twirling her hair and turned to me in horror. "Shut up! You have to be kidding me."

Thank goodness I knew "shut up" was teen-speak for "no way!"

I sighed, "No, honey, I'm not kidding."

"Wow."

"The good news is I wasn't dating the man. Right? I mean he was only a friend. And I suppose he can still be our friend. It's just . . . it's just that maybe I misunderstood the kind of friend he wants to be." I didn't like lying to her, but I wasn't about to share that he'd kissed me. It was too humiliating. I had to focus on what was best for Anya.

She stared at me with huge eyes. "Mom, that's total bull. And you know it."

The inside of my old BMW suddenly felt too small, too cramped. The leather seat stuck to the back of my legs. I couldn't get a good deep breath of air. I directed an air conditioning vent toward my face and swallowed hard.

My perceptive daughter wasn't finished. "Well, this is baloney. I don't care what you say. Maybe it wasn't the kind of dating with him picking you up and taking you out, but he sure acted like he was interested. I'm not stupid, Mom. I might be a kid, but I saw the way he'd look at you. Even Daddy didn't look at you like that."

"Like what?" My voice cracked.

"Like you were the most important person in the world. Like he thought you were just perfect. Like he wanted to hug you and kiss you and all that yucky stuff. He looked like that. Like they show in the movies. And he didn't even try to hide it."

I was surprised by how observant she'd been. Surprised and saddened. "Maybe. Or maybe that's the way you wanted to see it. I can accept responsibility for not being more . . . uh, proactive and asking him what his intentions were. I guess I misinterpreted his behavior."

A snort came from the other side of the car. Anya said, "You need your head examined."

"Anya, you will not speak to me that way.

That's disrespectful." I knew exactly who she was channeling; she'd been spending a lot of time with her grandmother, and that expression was one of Sheila's favorites.

"Okay, all right. But Mom, you need a serious rethink about this. Honest, you're always telling me to trust my gut. Does your gut think he only wanted to be your friend?"

I didn't answer her.

She made a disgusted sound. "Right. Does Mert know about this yet?"

"I plan to tell her tonight at the cookout."

"This ought to be good. She'll track him down and slap him up the side of his head seven ways to Sunday. You know what Roger told me? Once there was this bully at school, a senior? And Roger was, like, a middle schooler. And the bully kept slamming Roger into lockers in the hall when teachers weren't watching. Mert goes to the principal, but he said they'd never seen it happen, and like, they couldn't do anything? Besides the kid's family was real important and all. One day, Roger came home, and his eye was black because the kid pushed him into an open locker. The edge of the metal door ripped the skin around Roger's eye. The next day Roger stayed home 'cause, like, his eye was swollen shut. But, see, after school, Mert drove to the school parking lot and waited. When that boy came out, Mert called him over to her truck, and like, he was walking around and strutting and showing off for his friends. Roger was slumped down in the car watching. He said he was really, really scared — for his mom. Next thing he knows — wham! Mert grabbed that boy by the hair on the back of his head and slammed his face into the hood of her truck. That boy's nose was broken and everything. So like, Mert says to him, 'And whatcha gonna do about it? Tell everyone a woman half your size wearing a skirt broke your nose? You better not, 'cause next time, I'll break your arm and both your legs, too'."

Anya concluded this recitation of Mad Mert and the Thunderdome with a satisfied nod. "Yep, she did that. I can hardly wait to see what she'll do to old Detweiler. She is *not* going to be happy about this."

Out of the mouths of babes. What was it Mert said when she returned from being questioned by the cops? Something about Detweiler being a sleezeball and not to trust him?

"Well, I'll be," I mumbled to myself. I bet Mert already knew he was married.

But I was being totally ridiculous. If Mert had known about Detweiler, she'd have told me right away. And the idea that she'd knock him silly, well, that was almost laughable.

Or was it?

I knew her to have a temper. She was fiercely protective. And not afraid of anything or anyone. Once over a bottle of wine, she told me about a fight she'd gotten into at a bar. The other woman was taken to the hospital. And what was it she suggested when her neighbor turned up with a black eye? Mert said, "Iffen my husband ever dared lay one hand on me, I'd wait 'til he done fell asleep and take a cast iron frying pan to the side of his head. That'd stop that nonsense for sure."

I'd thought it a funny story.

She'd never hurt anyone. Never.

Or would she?

All traces of the fake Gracie were gone from our front porch. An officer at the Richmond Heights P.D. called to say they learned nothing from interviewing my neighbors. He promised patrolmen would make extra passes by the house.

Huh. Like that would do a lot of good.

"Mrs. Lowenstein, our records show a few months ago your house was burglarized. Twice. And now this. Ma'am, maybe an officer should do a security canvas. Tell you how to make your place less appealing to the criminal element. You know, when word gets around that a house is vulnerable . . ."

I didn't listen to the lecture that followed. I couldn't. I knew exactly what he would say. My house had become a target for every miscreant in the greater St. Louis area. Even my Great Dane couldn't offer enough of a deterrent to keep me and my child safe.

There was only one option: I had to move to a better neighborhood. Which would mean paying higher rent. Which would mean accepting help from Sheila. Which would mean giving Sheila more input and control over my life.

I groaned.

Any money she contributed would undoubtedly come with strings attached. Maybe even with steel cables.

But what other options did I have?

I covered my face with my hands and fell back on my bed. Peering between my fingers I noticed a wet spot around the light fixture. Great. My roof was starting to leak. What else could go wrong? Crud. I did *not* want to be in debt to Sheila. Double crud. I could *not* continue to expose my child and my dog to danger. Triple crud. I had to do something.

I spoke to the weird stain on my ceiling. It

was vaguely shaped like Bill Clinton in profile. "I know! I'll marry a rich man who can take me away from all this."

Huh. Did that. Got the T-shirt, the kid, and the photo album.

Okay, I'd marry anybody with a job. Or a steady salary. What was it Dodie once counseled? Find a spouse with great benefits. Like a school teacher. Or a postal clerk. Or a cop.

Not.

Bad plan.

I hated this. My inability to take care of myself, my child and our dog made me sick, but the queasy feeling quickly changed into a lump in the pit of my stomach. Last night, my tormenters left a calling card. Lucky for me, it was only a prank. But it could have been the real deal. Then what?

Was I willing to put Gracie and Anya at risk?

I had to face facts. I could no longer go it alone. I didn't have the resources. And I couldn't put my loved ones in jeopardy. I needed to swallow my pride and do what had to be done. It wasn't fun or pretty, but I'd be gracious and grateful and work like the dickens to make enough money to pay my mother-in-law back. I dialed Sheila's number.

"Uh, Sheila. I've been thinking about your offer to help me find another place to live . . ."

The finished outfit seemed a mite skimpy. Dress code for Mert's party was decidedly different from Opera Theatre. I pulled on cutoffs, a white tank top, and a pair of flip flops.

Then came a flash of inspiration. I rummaged through the few clothes of George's that I hadn't given away and found a navy blue vest. Thrown over the tank top, I had myself an outfit. Not wanting to seem too dressed down, I added a pair of big gold hoops and a couple of bracelets. This felt way more comfortable than last night's apparel, and yet, I had to admit, there'd been a sea change in me. Typically I wouldn't have taken the time to consider how my clothes looked. Today, I did.

My Spa La Femme transformation taught me the power of polish. Taking those extra minutes to add the vest and jewelry definitely gave me confidence. The extra grooming I'd endured — my shaped and dyed eyebrows, fake lashes, exfoliated and buffed skin — all contributed to a more attractive me.

Sheila had thoughtfully planned the timing of my meeting Detweiler's wife. Not only did I meet Brenda Detweiler on a night when I was at my best, I was able to face this new day, the morning after, knowing I looked terrific. I was primed to meet Mert's brother Johnny. And if he and I didn't hit it off, maybe there'd be another man at the party who struck my fancy.

Right, I thought. Girl, you lie. First, you better get over that detective.

Okay, I'd work on that. I'd take it one step at a time.

I'd mixed up a big bowl of my Hoosier Daddy Kidney Bean Salad the day before — it needs time for the flavors to blend — so Anya and I were good to go when the phone rang.

"Got a minute?" Clancy's voice sounded needy. I checked my watch. Arriving on time wasn't really important. For a casual event like this, we could be a half an hour late and not be rude. Anya was absorbed in a TV program. She'd probably appreciate a little delay.

"Sure. How are you? What's up?"

"I ran over to Ellen Harmon's store this morning. That woman is making a killing off Yvonne's demise. Gives the term 'good grief' a whole new meaning."

"That's fascinating. Tell me more." The

Barbara Walters tape suggested this conversational encouragement. I tried these exact sentences on the Ryman sisters, but after shouting it three times I gave up.

"She's plastered the whole store with scrapbook pages dedicated to Yvonne, by Yvonne, and about Yvonne. I mean, you can't find an inch of blank wall. And displays? She lit a tall white candle and put it next to this big photo of Yvonne along with a bouquet of red roses. And, there's a collection box for contributions to the Gaynor kids' education fund. Plus, a big book where mourners can sign their names and leave remembrances. On the marquee outside it says, 'We mourn the passing of our friend, Yvonne Gaynor.' She's hung an American flag at half-mast from a flagpole stuck in concrete blocks. I swear, Kiki, it was positively ghoulish — and effective. Man, that place was wall-to-wall people.

"I've never seen such a well-orchestrated sob fest. I wouldn't be at all surprised if Ellen Harmon was behind Yvonne's death. Heck, she might have even done the deed herself. At the very least, she could have planned it. It's enough to make a maggot puke. I thought I'd toss my cookies before I could get out the front door."

"Wow." I pulled up a kitchen chair. Gracie

ambled over and set her big head on my lap.

"I ran into Nettie in the parking lot. The display in the store really upset her, too. Nettie called Ellen everything but human. And I agree. That woman is one sick puppy. You have to see this place to believe it. Nettie and I got to talking while she had a cigarette, and I mentioned you'd dropped by to get the scoop on Perry. I googled you, girlfriend. Why didn't you tell me you're the same gal who outran a murderer last spring? Wow! You are my kind of hero! I told Nettie if anyone could crack this caper, it'd be you."

I laughed. "Clancy, you are giving me too much credit. I'm no Nancy Drew." We chattered a little longer, making a date for coffee. Since her schedule was more flexible, she offered to drop by the store.

I closed the phone and rubbed Gracie's ears thoughtfully. Like I said, I am not a girl detective. But after my husband died, I found myself thrown into the role of amateur sleuth. And it was kind of fun. While I'd never admit it out loud, I found solving crimes exciting. Working on Yvonne's murder would definitely take my mind off Detweiler.

And if I found the killer before he did, it

sure would show him a thing or two.

Mert lived in a small house not far from mine, but in a more stable neighborhood. Up and down her street were working-class families struggling to survive. Their shared values kept the block secure from mischief makers. A couple neighbors owned Doberman pinschers, and one house kept a pit bull behind a tall fence. I knew for a fact several of the men kept shotguns in closets.

A home invader didn't stand a chance. He'd be wearing buckshot and pulling canine incisors out of his jugular a hot half-second after breaking and entering. And that would have been the warm-up act.

St. Louis is a city of neighborhoods. This particular neighborhood was so tight that when one family fired up the grill, everyone dropped by to throw their steaks on the barbecue and crack a brewski.

As Anya and I climbed out of the car, strains of country western music drifted back to us. My kid smiled. Under ordinary circumstances, she'd have taken a beating before listening to "hillbilly" music. But the lure of Mert's darling son, Roger, made both country and western tolerable to her.

Gracie led the way, eager to visit Elsa and Red, the mother and son yellow labs Mert rescued years ago. Anya raced off to find Roger. I closed the cyclone fence gate behind me, put Gracie in the dog run with her friends, and searched the crush of people for my best pal. I didn't spot her right away, so I let myself into her kitchen to add my bowl of bean salad to the other food. I was removing the plastic wrap when I felt a tug from behind. Mert pulled me into a quick hug. "I been telling Johnny all about you. Did you get any pictures so's I can see how you looked at that fancy dinner last night?"

A deep voice startled me. "Don't need to see the photos. I was there to get a look at the real thing."

I turned and behind me was Lawn Boy. The man who rescued me at the spa, who found me naked, covered in mud and grass, was Mert's brother Johnny.

I could have crawled under the kitchen table and never come back out. My face went hot with embarrassment.

"Nice to meet you, formally," he extended a hand roughened by work but gentle with consideration.

"Johnny's been working for Butler's Landscaping and Lawn Service, and I figgered he might run into you out at Spa La Femme. He's always loved plants and animals. That there's the perfect job for him. And get a load of that farmer's tan," Mert turned loving eyes on the heart throb I'd met the day before, pointing to the brown skin that stopped at the edge of his polo-shirt collar and sleeves. The soft blue of his shirt warmed the gray of his eyes. A quick up-and-down scan proved him to be trim, on the side of muscular, with long legs in classic jeans. With a white tee and cigarettes rolled up in a sleeve, Johnny could have been a James Dean clone.

"Right," was all I could croak as I followed my friend's fingertips as she traced her brother's bulging bicep.

Johnny rewarded us with a slow, lazy grin. "Like I told you, babe, brown is not your color. But dark blue does amazing stuff to your eyes. If you'll excuse me, Mert's got me fixing the burgers and dogs."

She laughed. "He's the Grill God," and she winked. "He's really somethin', ain't he? Got all the looks and brains in the family."

Grill God? She had that right. Her brother belonged up on Mount Olympia with Zeus and company. I got a great gander at his backside. Woowee. Suddenly I felt hot all over.

Mert chuckled. "That's my baby brother. Now, what was it like? I never been to a fancy party like that. Tell me everythin' about it."

We set out food, arranged serving utensils, and chatted. I told her about Detweiler and she froze with a big spoon stopped in mid-air.

"You knew he was married, didn't you?" I asked softly. I was busy arranging paper napkins in a wicker basket. I couldn't bring myself to face her.

She cleared her throat. "His wife came into the station when they was questioning me. I was hoping to find out more — like if they were really together or if they was separated, you know? But I didn't have the chance."

Mert stepped in front of me. "Honest, girl. I woulda tole you if I'd'a been sure. I wouldn't have left you to find out with old Sheila." Searching my eyes, her mood changed abruptly. "That no-good skunk, next time I see him, I'm a gonna —"

"Do nothing," I said quietly. "Don't you dare. He's an officer of the law. You don't need that kind of hassle, especially with Johnny trying to get his life in order. And after the interest the cops are taking in you for Yvonne Gaynor's murder, messing with him would be counterproductive."

She glowered at me. Her lip liner followed

her lips in a turndown. Those thick lashes with their generous helping of mascara narrowed into a furry line of black. "Well, just so you know, he ain't off my sic 'em list. He better beware." Then she paused and added softly, "But I gotta say, that man loved you, baby girl. I saw him look at you, and it was the kind of expression a person gets when he sees his whole life in front of him and cain't hardly stand for it to get started. This don't make no sense. There's gotta be more to this here story, Kiki."

I let my shoulder rise and fall quickly, carelessly. "Maybe so, but I can't be bothered to find out. He's married. End of discussion."

"Oh, sure. And you was married. Folks can still be hitched and not be joined in spirit. Maybe there's extenuating circumstances. You never know."

"I can't go there. Correction: I refuse to go there. Now let me tell you what happened last night with Gracie." I related the events surrounding the scare with my dog. I finished with my decision: I needed a new home. Mert nodded. She is the most eminently practical person I'd ever met. Her favorite saying is, "It is what it is," but with her southern Missouri accent, it sounded more like, "Hit is what hit is." Mert lives by

313

the philosophy that lying to yourself won't change anything, but it will make your life more dangerous and less satisfying. She'd long since convinced me she is right.

"Yeah, no two ways about it. You gotta move. I hate to give Sheila credit, but even a blind pig finds an acorn once't in awhile. You're lucky she's willing to help. I got news, too. They took in one of the catering staff for more questioning. I heard all about it from one of my friends who does clean up. See, there's this woman at the caterers who used to cook special events for the Gaynors. Like dinner parties and all? Yvonne fired her butt. Stuck her with a big bill for a whole lotta food and such. I guess the cops done took this gal to the station for intense questioning." Mert picked up a carrot stick and chewed on it. "Oh, and one more thing . . . you'll never guess. That Bama? Her sister works for the caterers. Turns out she got a bonus for bringing in the Time in a Bottle business."

"You are kidding me!"

"No, ma'am." Mert took a hefty slurp of her beer and burped discreetly. "I kid you not. You see what that means? Bama had a way to mess with the food."

We decided to ask around about Bama and her sibling on Monday. I picked up a deviled egg, admired the paprika before popping it into my mouth whole. Yum, a touch of mustard and bacon bits were mixed with the yolk. I swallowed and said, "That's certainly another line of inquiry that bears scrutiny. Not that I plan to let Detweiler in on it."

Mert turned thoughtful. "Did you tell the squirt about him? Anya's awful fond of the man. She'll need to know why you gotta put distance between yourself and him."

I repeated my conversation with my child.

Mert laughed at Anya's rendition of her slamming Roger's bully into the truck. "It's a mite exaggerated, but she's got it in one. I don't take to people messing with the folks I love. Won't stand for it. Never would. There ain't that many I really care about, and you and her are part of that special group. You gonna be okay without this guy in your life? You was awful lonely after George died."

I told her about Ben Novak. "I have high hopes," I added.

"I also noticed my baby brother cain't keep his eyes off'a you, neither. Baby girl, I'm thinkin' your lonely days is long gone."

There was way too much to eat at Mert's. Anya shadowed Roger, who was cheerfully good-natured about her overeager attention. I thought I'd burst eating the grilled burger Johnny put on my plate, the potato salad mixed with cucumbers, the gazpacho, the seven-layer Mexican dip, the innumerable desserts including a huge Texas sheet cake and fudge. The country western music set my toes tapping. I mingled with Mert's neighbors, listening in on their conversations. Even though the Barbara Walters book had enhanced my courage socially, I was still reticent.

Johnny hovered by my shoulder. He'd been trying to induce me to dance, but I'm no good at line dancing. I can't remember the steps long enough to stay in sync with a crowd! Then Roger slipped one of his CDs into the music mix. The first strains of Gnarls Barkley's "Crazy" made me sway to the rhythm.

I make it a rule not to dance in public.

There's a reason.

A very, very good reason.

This time I blame the beer, my sadness over Detweiler, and Johnny's urging.

It won't ever happen again.

Growing up, I was kicked out of ballet, tap, and jazz classes for my style of dancing. As a young woman, I caused fights to break out at school sock hops. And in college, I woke up the next morning pregnant.

It's too dangerous for me to dance in public. I told Johnny I shouldn't. I told him I couldn't. I tried to hide, to stop the involuntary tap of my toes. But Johnny would not take no for an answer.

"What? You feeling shy? I think we know each other better'n that. Come on, pretty lady."

One minute I was moving with restraint on the edge of the crowd, the next I was in the middle of a large group dancing with my eyes closed. The beat took over. I lost all inhibitions. I threw my arms around. I twirled and whirled. I opened my eyes briefly and shut them again. Totally unaware of my surroundings, I cut loose. I was hopping and skipping and again, I closed my eyes and tossed my head to the music.

I fell backward over a flowerpot.

All was silent. I blinked and faced a couple dozen shocked faces. I sat up and tried to brush dirt off my shorts. Johnny offered me a hand. His mouth was contorted with an effort not to laugh.

Anya's voice broke the quiet with, "Ah, Mom. I can't believe you did that." I was still picking leaves and plant parts off my body.

Mert asked, "What did you used to be?

An understudy for Big Bird? You jest cut loose and ran wild there, girlfriend."

The expression on Johnny's face told the whole story. He was biting his bottom lip for all he was worth. The corners of his eyes crinkled with amusement. "Uh, I can see why it might be best for you to dance in private. Babe, that performance will long be remembered."

With that, he volunteered to drive Anya and me home in my car. Roger was to follow in Mert's truck. "I better check your house," he said as he turned the key in the ignition. "After what happened to your dog and," here he paused and ran a hand through his long hair, releasing a scent of male, "because half my sister's neighbors think you're a menace to society. I'm just not sure the control tower at Lambert Field's got you cleared for flying."

"Lambert Field?" I mumbled. Then I remembered. That was the original name of Lambert-St. Louis International Airport. I let my head rest on my seat and closed my eyes. I was soooo tired.

After walking through the house, Johnny waved an all clear. Anya scooted inside with the dog. She and Gracie were also exhausted. I walked Johnny to my front door where he stepped closer and closer, pinning my back against the wall. It felt dangerous, but I knew I was in good hands. Those gentle gray eyes turned hard as flint before it strikes a spark. As he pressed gently against me, I nearly melted. All of me turned to butter. "You," he said with his lips against my ear, "are one darling little girl. Next time you want to cut loose, why don't you call me? Hm? Dancing by yourself might be hazardous to your health, babe."

Then he kissed me.

# TWENTY-ONE

The next morning as I pulled out of the parking lot at the Science Center after dropping off Anya (and reminding her that Sheila would pick her up), a car with tinted windows followed on my bumper. A couple of blocks later, it remained glued to my rear end.

St. Louis drivers might be the worst in the country. In fact, cops in other towns joke about "St. Louis stops," where drivers give the stop signs a cursory slow-down rather than coming to a complete halt. Being tailgated was nothing new. Dropping into defensive driver mode, I signaled far in advance and added a few extra lane changes on our way down 40. The dark SUV stayed with me. At the exit, it nearly tapped my bumper.

Now I was beginning to feel scared. Really scared. We turned off on Brentwood, and waited for the stoplight. The driver revved his motor behind me; the big car lunging and lurching as the engine roared full throttle.

Hairs on my neck stood at attention. My gut weighed in. This went beyond reckless driving: it was a threat.

I opened my cell phone.

But whom would I call?

Not Detweiler.

Traffic congested near the Galleria but eased the next three blocks. Using the timing of stoplights as an aid, I put three cars between myself and the SUV. Feeling safer, I zipped into the parking lot of Time in a Bottle.

The SUV passed me and drove off. I tried to get the license number, but the back of the vehicle was so mud-splattered, I couldn't even read the state name. I backed up and realigned my hood with the white lines of a parking space. Glancing over my right shoulder, I saw the SUV zoom past, this time facing toward me. They must have made a U-turn. The car slowed as it came closer. Only the sidewalk formed an imaginary barrier between us.

I dropped sideways into the passenger seat, managing to reach my right arm behind me to shove Gracie's head down. Fortunately, she didn't resist. I punched 911 into my phone.

Pop! I heard a sound like a firecracker. A million pieces of glass sprinkled over my arms. A glance up told me my windshield was shattered. I yelled to the operator, "Gunshot! Emergency! I'm at 1415 Kirlin, three blocks south of 40!"

"Are you alone in the car? Do you need an ambulance?"

My shaking hands lost purchase on the phone. Another pop rang out. More glass sprinkled around me. I undid my seat belt and twisted toward my dog. The moment my grip on her loosened, she pulled away. A small rivulet of blood ran down my wrist.

"Gracie!"

I rolled all the way onto my belly, my feet under the steering wheel, and peered around the passenger seat. I could only see a patch of fur. She didn't move. Heedless to danger, I threw open my door and yanked back my seat. My dog was on the floor, whimpering. "Gracie? Gracie?" I reached down and my fingers came up sticky with blood. Hers or mine?

That's when I dialed Detweiler.

He must have been two blocks away. Detweiler roared into the lot, sirens and lights splitting traffic. He checked me over. Tiny cuts marred my arms and hands, but I didn't have the patience for him to examine them more closely. "It's Gracie," I said, "I think she's hurt."

Detweiler coaxed Gracie out of the car. By then an ambulance had joined us. The dispatcher had heard me cry "Gracie" and assumed another person was in my car. After asking me a few questions and rinsing off my superficial wounds, the EMTs bent over my dog. Detweiler pulled me close. My face was buried in his chest. I couldn't look, I just couldn't. I was crying hysterically, soaking the front of his shirt. He smelled of soap and starch and stark masculinity. The harder I shook, the harder he held me, murmuring in my ear, "Shhhh. You're safe. She's going to be okay."

A voice chastised me for allowing him to provide comfort, but panic and fear overruled it.

The sirens and lights had brought Dodie racing out of the store. She spoke to the cop and the paramedics right as a Richmond Heights P.D. car pulled into our lot.

At last the male paramedic rose and walked over.

"Mrs. Lowenstein? Your dog must have a guardian angel."

Gracie wobbled to her feet. A tall, thin

paramedic walked her in a circle, observing my harlequin carefully. My dog's ear was bandaged, but she was alive. The EMT continued, "Splinters of glass cut her. We picked 'em out of her ears, washed the surface good, and put butterfly bandages on one area. Rinse those with hydrogen peroxide. You might want to check with your vet."

I knew EMTs didn't ordinarily fix pets, so I was extra-profusive with my thanks.

"No problem, ma'am, we're both animal lovers," said the one medic as he gave a nod toward his partner.

I pushed away from Detweiler and knelt by my girl. Gracie licked me and whined. Her heavy tail moved back and forth slowly. Her bandaged ear cocked with a jaunty air. Detweiler moved closer, and she shoved her muzzle into his hand. I heard Dodie discuss with him and Richmond Heights officers how best to handle the increasing violence. I offered a description of the SUV. When I mentioned mud-splattered plates, Detweiler's expression darkened. "Must be someone with experience evading law enforcement officials."

Detweiler suggested Dodie hire off-duty policemen for the store. "They can watch from unmarked cars on the street. Get a security camera hooked up."

Dodie said, "But I don't want anyone in a uniform scaring people off. Besides, inside the store isn't what I'm worried about."

"They don't have to wear a uniform. At least let someone escort all of you in and out of your cars."

Dodie's face was a worn-thin gray. "Get the dog inside. God only knows what might happen next."

Detweiler caught me by the arm, pulling me closer. His lips brushed my ear. "We need to talk."

"I appreciate all you've done, but I don't think so." Now embarrassment ran rough-shod over all other feelings. I couldn't face him. I couldn't hold my head up. Even with what I knew, he'd been the one I'd turned to for comfort. He offered his protection with no preamble, no caveats. He'd run to my side and taken me into his arms without comment.

And now I pushed him away. My weakness, my dependency made me angry with myself. I grabbed Gracie's collar and started toward the store.

"Kiki!" Detweiler reached for me.

Dodie stepped between us, "Go on in to work, Kiki. Detective, I appreciate your help and guidance. However, the party's over between you and my employee. Leave her alone. Don't even think about stopping by her house."

"What?" he barked. His face colored.

I watched Dodie put both hands on her hips. How did she know what I'd only learned on Saturday? I didn't want her fighting my battles. On the other hand, her response signaled the return of the old Dodie. Her protective instinct trumped her depression. Now, she had a cause. Maybe that was what she had needed after Yvonne's death and Horace's employment problems. A focus. A reason to step up to the plate. A way to shake off her blues.

And I had a good reason to go inside and cry, but not until after I called a car repair service.

Detweiler blazed back, a sharp edge to his voice. "Sorry, ma'am. That's not your decision to make. I will talk to Mrs. Lowenstein when and wherever I choose. You have no choice in the matter." He added, "Mrs. Goldfader, there's a murderer out there. This might or might not be connected. And I have a job to do."

Ah. There it was. His mantra. "I have a job to do." It wasn't about his feelings for me. It never had been. A muscle pulsed along his jaw. "Incidents aimed at you, your employees, and your store have escalated. You've received death threats. Don't forget the graffiti, and a brick through your window. You both need police protection. This might all be related to Yvonne Gaynor's death, or it might not. But right now, all I can say for sure is you are in danger."

I'd stopped and stared at both of them. Gracie's tail thumped my leg.

Dodie shrugged. "Of course we will cooperate with you as a law enforcement official. But I'm warning you. Do not bother my employee."

His face turned stony. "Don't tell me how to do my job."

We were getting nowhere. He had a point. We needed to get to the bottom of this. Only after this was over could I really and truly say goodbye and good riddance. I came closer and said to him, "Okay, maybe we do have to talk, but Dodie's right. I prefer you talk with me here when there are other people in the store." I thought a second. I added, "No dropping by the house. Anya knows about your wife."

"What? How could you have done that? Why did you tell Anya?" His green eyes spit sparks. Oh, boy. He was ma-ad.

"Why not? It's true. She needs to understand why you aren't coming by anymore."

He let loose with a string of curses. Each word was bitten off and spat out. He stomped away.

Dodie and I heard his car door slam all the way across the parking lot.

"Harrumph," she said. "That went about as well as could be expected without loss of life or limb."

We walked Gracie into the store and closed the stockroom door behind us.

Two Diet Dr Peppers later, I got my groove back. A mobile windshield repairman assessed the damage to my car and explained he could fix it on the spot. I eyed my dwindling total in my checkbook and gave him a reluctant go-ahead. That plus my need to repay Sheila for my upcoming move — provided I found a suitable place — fueled my desire to get cracking with new business ideas.

Two photographers had asked me to make customized but standardized albums. The best way to be efficient was to design the pages and then break down what was needed into parts I could mass produce.

I had appointments for the next week with three nursing home administrators.

Meanwhile, I needed to keep coming up with unique projects that would keep our regulars happy — and get a positive buzz about our store restarted in the scrapbooking community.

Boutique pages offered a way to add sparkle and jazz to ordinary scrapbooking. They were also tricky to pull off. Adding glitter, flowers, buttons, ribbon, and trinkets could overwhelm the photos and make a page look trashy. The best approach was organizing the space. Hand-drawn frames — like picture frames but two-dimensional and of paper — could do exactly that.

I was deep into doodling designs on the frames when a mellow voice interrupted.

"Hey, babe."

Johnny draped an arm over a nearby fixture. There was a languorous, graceful line to his body. I wondered if he had any idea how powerfully attractive he was.

I bet he did. Not even Helen Keller could have missed his sensuality.

"A little bird named Mert told me you got a long evening ahead of you. With the crop and all. I put a picnic in my truck. How about we run over to Tilles Park and sit outside with Gracie? Figured you might need a break."

I was happy to go with him. There was an element of the unknown and unknowable about him that set me tingling. This sort of distraction would make it easier to wean myself from Detweiler.

On the way to the park, I told him about the shots that were taken at my car.

"I wondered what that bandage was on your dog's ear," he said. "You need to be careful. Look, anytime you need help, just give me a call." He was silent for a while. Then he said, "You know about me being at Potosi."

"Yes, Mert told me." His introduction to a topic I'd rather avoid was spare, laid out without preamble. I said, "I have a daughter. Anya."

"I know. I met her, remember?"

Okay, it was a non sequitur to him, but to me it followed. I was trying to say I was worried about the impact of bringing a felon into our lives. Even if this wasn't a segue to dating, it was the opening of a door. Johnny didn't need to spell out his thought process. Or maybe he did. Maybe jail defined him. Maybe this was the "getting to know you" discussion that preceded ongoing interaction on any level.

Johnny shifted, restive in the driver's seat. "She's a wonderful girl. My sis talks real highly of her. Roger thinks she's cute as a new pup."

And I am her mother. Responsible for her.

What would happen if the Venn Diagram of our lives included Johnny as an overlapping circle? How might we then color in the shared space? Would we be endangered by his past? Could I possibly be in more danger than I was now? Would Anya be shunned by other kids if word got around her mother was dating a former inmate? Would Johnny's presence bring into our lives an undesirable group of friends? And, I couldn't suppress a thought I skittishly avoided, what would Sheila say?

Suddenly I felt totally tongue-tied and inadequate. That's how conflicted, how confusing were my thoughts. They rendered me dumbstruck.

He searched my face. Then he laughed, a sound as rich as roasted coffee beans. "I'm not a child molester, Kiki. Is that what worries you?"

"No! Not at all, it's just . . . it's just . . . I worry about your friends, and if you are safe, and there's my mother-in-law. Her reaction. How Anya fits in, and what her schoolmates might say." Now the words came out in a torrent.

"I don't remember proposing marriage."

"Right. I know. I mean, I realize I must seem . . . overwrought. I'm protective."

"You should be. It's not easy to be a single

mom. Mert told me about your husband. I'm sorry for your loss." This politeness felt deeply, thoughtfully genuine. He added, "I need to get everything out in the open. No games. I'm starting over, so to speak, and want a cleanness, an honesty to my life. You deserve that, and I respect your situation.

"See, I'm not good enough for you. There's my past. I don't have a good education or prospects. But —" and his withdrawal seemed shamed and painful, "but here I am. I take care of my own, and at the very least, I'd like to build on my sister's friendship with you."

My thoughts jumbled and rolled over each other. I didn't say, "It's just that I've never dated a convict before." I wondered if this was a new low? Or was I simply being true to my belief we all deserve more than one chance? Was this the right time to invite someone like Johnny into our lives? While my husband's killer was loose and threatening me? Was I begging for more trouble? Or might Johnny have the inside track (whatever that was) on criminal behavior?

On the other hand . . . he was so luscious. Maybe he could help me forget the monster-sized hole in my heart left by Detweiler. (And I could only imagine what Detweiler would think about me cozying up to Johnny.

That alone would be worth the price of admission.)

Johnny parked the truck and dipped his head level with mine. His index finger raised my chin. "Say the word and I'll disappear." When I hesitated, he moved closer, closer, and kissed me very, very lightly on the lips. "Or stick around. Up to you. We can see how it goes. Now, what do you say we eat? Mert had all sorts of leftovers and I hate for them to go to waste."

I've always been a sucker for bad boys. Who isn't? The thrill of danger mixed with the hormonal rush of desire is heady stuff.

But my inexperience always caused me to hang back. In my youth, my innocence was at risk. I lost that to a good man, or so I thought, who had done me wrong. What could a bad boy do? Besides use a heightened sense of awareness, of fear, of the unknown, to awaken my Sleeping Beauty of a romantic life?

All we did was eat. But . . . my legs were wobbling and my knees were knocking, as I entered the store. And I hardly ate a thing. I wasn't that kind of hungry. I went straight into the bathroom and splashed my forearms with cold water. That didn't help much, so I tossed cold water all up and down my neck. All we had was cold water, because Dodie wouldn't turn on the miniature water heater again until the fall. But cold water was all I needed.

Liar.

I needed something more. I was, after all, human. And lonely. And in the prime of my life. My motor was racing and my engine was pointed toward the Indy 500 Speedway of Desire.

Johnny could do all this with one kiss and a lot of innuendo?

Oh, boy.

"Have you seen Yvonne's pages on the magazine website? Gosh, I didn't know she was that talented. Last time she and I went to a crop, she could barely manage one of those packages of coordinated paper and embellishments," said Bonnie Gossage as she copied my boho page. "I hate to speak ill of the dead, but I thought I was a better judge of talent than that. I mean, after all these crops, I thought I had a pretty good handle on other people's ability." Baby Felix dangled on her knee as she scrapped with one hand. Every once in awhile, another scrapbooker would snag Felix and love him up. He was our resident pass-around baby. The duckling down of his hair was as kissable as his fat little arms and legs. Women cooed over him and wistful expressions blanketed their faces.

If a baby boom started among our group, Felix bore the responsibility of being the trigger and catalyst.

Emma Delacroix Martin was attending her second crop, her old St. Louis pedigree indicated by her French middle name. Like dog breeders, the hoi polloi of our town industriously kept their breeding lines straight. Surnames regularly appeared as first names and conjoined last names drew straight lines of genealogical descent. Someday soon I'd run across an Elizabeth out of Gerald or some nonsensical nomenclature. Intermarriage kept money and power within the family. It also spawned imbeciles, but those problems were kept behind closed ranks.

However, Emma exemplified the best of good bloodlines. Her queenly carriage, her good manners, her patrician intelligence made her someone I wanted to know better. She was everything I aspired to be. She smiled and said, "My teenage son helped me find the website featuring Yvonne's pages. They certainly are impressive. Of all the winners, I think she has — had — the most talent. But, Bonnie? You didn't see her like that? In real life, I mean?"

Nettie blew her nose loudly and hocked up a loogie. "Sorry. The mold count is unbelievable. The air quality is yellow. The color of pollen. Geez, my allergist wants me to keep puffing on my inhaler, taking Claritin, and he's after me again to quit smoking." Nettie copied my page and finished a greeting card. I also noticed she brought along an album. That was a first. She never brought her original work to a group session. At the next break, I wanted to ask her discreetly if I could see what she had. Looking over our customers' work was a great way to get to know people better and learn what appealed to our consumer base. After all, scrapbookers usually scrapbook what matters most to them. So each album is a glimpse into their psyches, their value systems, and their world.

Nettie reached into her purse and rattled a pill container. "Could I have some water, please?"

I retrieved a bottle of water from the back. As she fiddled with the lid of the bottle, I noticed Dr. Andersoll's name on the label. Anya's allergist.

Emma signaled for my help. "I don't know how to do a design transfer."

"No problem. I'll show you how to do one on light or dark paper."

Markie Dorring added glitter glue to her frame. She was working to create an album for her nieces and nephews, and the frame I'd created would be perfect for spotlighting their photos. She talked as she worked. "Has anyone gone to Memories First to see Yvonne's pages? The ones for the Scrapbook Star contest?"

"You know I've been meaning to do that, but I don't want to run into Ellen Harmon," I admitted. "Until all this is settled, it seems like a good idea to steer clear."

Markie said, "That store is packed all the time. Ellen is on top of everyone, asking questions about Yvonne's death. I keep expecting her to waltz out of the back room wearing a deerstalker cap and smoking a pipe. Perry's employer is offering a $10,000 reward for information leading to Yvonne's killer."

Nettie wiped her nose. "Are you saying you think Ellen will try to pin this on someone? So she can collect the reward?"

Markie shrugged. She wore her hair in a short cut that hugged her head the way a receptacle cradles a flower blossom. "Why not? I heard her bragging. She's as greedy as they come. I suppose she's got as good an idea who did it as anybody. She was there when it happened. She knew Yvonne. She has access to all those people trooping into her store and a reason to ask them about Yvonne without seeming inappropriate. Seems to me that she's got the ideal set up for tracking down who dunnit."

Before anyone could respond, Dodie commandeered the head of the table and cleared her throat. "Since you are among our favorite customers, I wanted you to be the first to know our news. We're launching a Design Team. Bama and I are working out details."

News? I'll say. It was a surprise to me. Usually we discussed ideas and refined them together. Why had she left me out? A sudden anger at Bama rose within me. Once Dodie and I were a dynamic duo. Now I was just another employee.

The table buzzed with chatter. A Design Team offers page designers a forum for their work and a steep discount for supplies. It helps a store stay up-to-date with trends. Designers display new products, add excitement, and sometimes teach classes. Before our fiasco with the CAMP outing, Dodie and I had discussed the possible merits of a Design Team. But she hadn't said anything since then. Her announcement took me by surprise.

Get over it, I told myself. It is, after all,

her store.

Dodie explained she wanted a variety of talents and experience levels on the team: newbie scrappers, card makers, artist trading card makers, altered items specialists, and seasoned scrappers. To be considered, she asked each woman to submit six of her best pieces of work by e-mail or in person.

"Who'll be the judge?" asked Nettie. "You and your staff?"

Dodie's bushy dark hair swayed around her olive-complected face as she shook her head. "Not just us. Fellow store owners around the country will help choose. That will be more fair, and we can't be accused of favoritism."

The women at the table found her methodology pleasing. We all knew of contests biased by personalities or pocketbook, as in, you buy enough stuff from me and I'll treat you like a star.

"What if we don't have a scanner?" asked Nettie.

"Bring in your work, and we'll scan it. But please know, if you are selected, we will want to display your work in the store."

Nettie nodded. "That makes sense. It's just I don't like to leave my work where everyone has access to it unless there's a reason. Otherwise people can copy my ideas."

Markie agreed. "Yep, I'm with you, Nettie. A lot of people try to pass off other people's work as their own. Anyone catch the chat on that one list-server where a scrapbooker copied another woman's journaling and then entered it in a challenge?"

A challenge is a sort of mini-contest. Scrapbookers are "challenged" to use a certain technique or theme in their work. Sometimes the winner gets a prize; sometimes it's just recognition. Usually all the responses to the challenge are posted for others to see and appreciate.

The group responded with a chorus of "No way!" The women chimed in with their opinions and swapped viewpoints on scrap-lifting — authorized or unauthorized use of other's ideas and designs — until time to leave. Dodie called our rent-a-cop to escort our customers out the back door. That's when I realized that Dodie's announcement had distracted me from seeing Nettie's work. "Nettie, are you giving thought to being considered for the Design Team?"

Through our broken and mostly boarded-up front window, and under the glare of new security lights, we watched the other women climb into their cars under the watchful gaze of our new rent-a-cop. In addition to the lost revenue from our

CAMP disaster and from the bad publicity, these security measures were costing Dodie a bunch of money.

Nettie paused. "Maybe."

"I hope so. I haven't seen your pages, but I'd like to."

She wavered. "How about I come in tomorrow? I'll bring my favorite layouts."

The off-duty officer lingered by the front door while Dodie and I cleaned up. I could tell Dodie was feeling more like her regular self. It seemed as good a time as any to ask her again. "What's been going on? It can't just be Yvonne's death and Horace's job. You've been through tough times before. Maybe it sounds like I'm prying, and you've been evasive, but I care, Dodie. I know you're my boss, but I consider you a friend." Perhaps I sounded a tad manipulative, but what I said was true.

She pushed a pile of small odds and ends of paper into her palm and stared at the random pattern. "I found a lump in my breast."

For a moment, my heart contracted in my chest. A chill spread over my body. The big "C." Oh, no! I forced my voice to sound conversational. "And you are going to the doctor, right? Tell me you have an appointment."

She rearranged the pieces of paper. "No. I can't."

"What? You have to!"

"Not until we get this thing with Horace's job squared away. If we can get his old employer to pick up our insurance, great. If not, and if I go to someone now, the new insurance company will call it a pre-existing condition and refuse to cover me."

A slow, painful understanding crystallized. "You mean to tell me Horace doesn't know? Dodie, we're talking your health. You can't worry about insurance. You need to get to a doctor as quickly as possible. My Lord, Dodie. Don't you realize the longer you wait —"

"Stop!" Her face was agitated, fierce. Her hairy brows formed storm clouds. "Don't start. I know exactly what the complications are. My mother and sister died of breast cancer. I am not sending my husband and my daughter to the poor house over this. Especially if it isn't curable."

I sputtered. My voice rose to such a pitch that our security guard turned to stare at me. "Are you nuts? Breast cancer isn't a death sentence anymore. We aren't living in the dark ages. And as for going to the poor house, Horace would . . . would . . . well, he'd just curl up and die without you. And your kid can put herself through college. Your priorities stink, Dodie. Money isn't everything —"

"The heck it isn't! You of all people should know that. I can't get proper treatment without do-re-mi. Loads of it. And I won't do that to Horace!"

"Then I'll tell him!"

"You better not!"

"I will do exactly that."

"And I'll fire your scrawny butt."

"That's fine because I'd rather be unemployed than sit here and watch you die. Your health means more to me than my job. I can live without this place, but I can't live with myself if you get cancer — if you've got cancer — and . . . and . . ." I couldn't go on. The fright with Gracie, the news about Detweiler, the strain with my daughter, being second to Bama, all snowballed inside me. I'd had enough. I started to cry. "Please, Dodie, please. Don't do this. Don't make me stand by and watch."

"That's exactly why I didn't tell you. But you wouldn't leave it alone, would you?" Her voice was ragged.

We glared at each other, speechless, both shocked by the violence of our disagreement, and by the passion in our voices. I was the first to turn away, which meant, I'd lost. Something in that willingness to blink gave Dodie permission to calm down.

She put a heavy arm on my shoulders. "Don't cry. *Oy,*" and she rattled off a Yiddish saying.

When I said, "Huh?" she translated, "They bury better-looking ones. Hey, scout, I didn't think you'd take it this way."

"How did you expect me to take it? You aren't making sense. You must have thought I'd be upset or you would have told me sooner."

She stepped back to an arm's length. "I didn't know. I guess . . . I guess I thought, well, I'm your boss, and that's it. I figured you'd try to fix it. That's what you do."

I had no idea what she meant by that, and my face must have shown my confusion.

Dodie gave me a gruff hug. "It's one of the things I like about you, Kiki Lowenstein. You really believe you can fix things . . . even when it's clear they are hopelessly, irrevocably broken. You just keep trying, don't you? You're the *tikkun olem* queen, sunshine."

*Tikkun olem.* Repair of the world. I didn't know whether to laugh or to cry. Yeah, she was right. I set for myself impossible tasks. I was a real idiot, through and through.

She sighed. "Here's the plan. We'll find

out Friday what the attorney thinks about a settlement. Horace has been job hunting and has an interview in Chicago next Wednesday. Give me until next Thursday. That's not long. Promise me you won't say anything to my husband, okay?"

I nodded, reluctantly, and we went back to picking up. We were nearly through when she said, "I have a confession to make. Sheila called me about Detweiler. I didn't tell you, but I knew what she was planning."

I stared hard at her, unsure of what to say and not trusting myself. So she was in on it too. The perfidy of my inner circle amazed me. What was that old joke about it isn't paranoia if they're really after you? Life is a series of solo experiences made bearable by the comfort of friends. Now I saw my support net differently. I was surrounded by arrogant do-gooders manipulating me. I responded with a disgusted sound and shoved chairs up to the worktable hard. I wanted out of here, to pick over my sore feelings in the company of my dog. At the very least, I needed to change our bandages — my psychic ones and Gracie's on her ear.

Dodie sighed in response. "Detweiler's a good man. I have no idea why he led you on. Sheila and I talked it over."

Without me, I supplied mentally and

angrily. It was my turn to share a pithy little saying: "Better a good enemy than a bad friend."

"Maybe we were wrong, but we thought if you felt like a million bucks, at least you could walk away with your head held high." Her face sagged. "Sorry, but you had to know. You deserved to know. I hope we did the right thing."

I grew hot under the collar. "It doesn't matter. After all, you two made your decision without consulting me. Why care now about how I feel? What if I told you I knew all along he was married? You two could stuff that in your little red wagons, huh?"

I was well and truly peeved. I'd had my limit. Their internecine plotting was as painful as Detweiler's deceit. After all, he was a man. What was Dodie and Mert's excuse?

Treelike and immobile, Dodie planted herself next to me, her bulky polyester shape blocking my path. Her voice was soft. "You care about me. You think you know what's best for me and Horace." She ran a shaky, thick hand through her porcupine hair. "And I care about you. And Anya. We both have good intentions. Maybe we're equally right . . . and wrong."

Put that way, I couldn't maintain my irritation. "I guess you two did the right thing. I don't know. Maybe I'll never know. But it sure is hard." I paused to bite my lower lip. "I really, really liked him."

Her voice faded out. "I know. So did I. Life sure can stink."

# Kiki's Tips for Boho (Bohemian) Style Pages

Boho is a state of mind where anything goes. Mainly, it's about mixing rich textures and funky found objects with abandon. Here are some tips for making your own Boho page:

1. Start with one large photo. Because the pages have a lot going on, it's easy for your images to get lost unless they are prominent. A 5" × 7" is a good size that won't get lost.

2. Use richly patterned paper for your background. In fact, it's best if you can find two or three patterns that work well together. Concentrate on mood, more than color or pattern. If you need to darken a paper, try a thin wash of acrylic paint dabbed over it.

3. Assemble the items below. Play with arrangements until you find something pleasing to your eye.

    • Ribbons and fabric. Dig through your sewing supplies. Any pieces of fabric, ribbon, or buttons will work on a boho page. If you have a wide piece of fabric, use the selvage like a ribbon or tear a strip to use like a ribbon.

- Flowers. Silk will work, but you'll need at least three, or any odd number. You'll want various sizes. You can make a flower out of fabric by sewing a running stitch along the strip of fabric, pulling it to gather it into a circle. Overlap the open edges. You can also crochet a flower or make one out of felt.
- Add odd found items such as postal stamps and bottle caps. These are part of the charm of a boho page.
- Finish by adding sequins, "jewels," old costume jewelry, tiny mirrors, and chains.

# TWENTY-TWO

Horace came to get Dodie, and they followed me home. He walked through my house to make sure I was safe. I wanted to tell him Dodie's secret, but I held back even as I waved while they pulled out of my driveway.

I'd made her a promise.

Sheila called bright and early the next morning. She and Anya had driven past a few rentals after science camp the day before. I agreed to go house hunting with my mother-in-law over a long lunch hour. We decided Anya's involvement should be minimal at the outset. She was so emotional these days, and we didn't want to add more uncertainty to her life.

At half past noon, Sheila pulled up in front of Time in a Bottle. I climbed into the back seat of her silver Mercedes. In the passenger seat was Abigail Thorgood, a real estate agent who belonged to the same country club as my mother-in-law. I'd dressed up for the look-see, wearing neatly ironed navy slacks and a lacy white blouse. Through my belt loops ran a pretty scarf in colors of blue, purple, and white. This was part of my new gussy-up policy. The enchanted evening at Opera Theatre taught me nice clothes and makeup constituted a modern suit of armor. I needed all the external fortification I could get. My whole ensemble came from Target — or Tar-Gzay — but as long as Sheila didn't shop there she would never know. From the driver's seat, my mother-in-law handed me a sack with an Einstein Brothers salad inside.

"You eat. I drive," she said, sending back a tall iced tea. "Abigail navigates and narrates."

Sheila pre-empted the need to think or fully participate. My job was to obey. I was glad she didn't know about Gracie getting shot in the TinaB parking lot, or we'd have been job hunting as well. I had no idea what sort of employment she could find for me, but given her resourcefulness, I was sure she'd find some poor soul who owed her a favor and call it in. I munched the lettuce quietly, imagining how bored I'd be spending eight hours in a cubicle.

Since Sheila doesn't allow Anya to eat in her car, my meal was a big concession. My housing problem obviously mattered greatly to her. I wondered how far apart her idea of suitable places and mine might be.

Her short list was three houses, one located a few blocks from her home. On a small spit of land sat an older home that should have been — and one day would be — demolished for resurrection as a Mc-Mansion. Anya could walk to Sheila's from this place, which was a plus. We mentioned this to each other as though we'd actually let my child wander the open streets. Ha! Oh, the deception we shared. We both knew her walking anywhere alone was impossible. But still . . .

The teardown's price was outrageous. The lot alone was worth a million bucks, so the house was just lagniappe. Welcome to Ladue, where everything — including egos — is inflated. The second house was farther away, on a quiet street in Rock Hill. My excitement about the big yard and a more reasonable price tag disappeared with one sniff of the damp, dark, mildewed interior.

Mrs. Thorgood noted my disappointment and said quickly, "Not to worry, dear. Don't scowl. I saved the best for last."

House Number Three was a barn-shaped,

converted garage in Webster Groves. Exuding charm, this house sat on the grounds of a larger home owned by a local author. I'd heard his name but never read his books because people call them "gritty." I think that means the story features blood, guts, and truths about life I'd rather not face. Mrs. Thorgood and Sheila wandered around with me, as we inspected the large, fenced-in yard. From the outside we could see that the high windows would allow a lot of light. Inside, a serviceable neutral carpet complemented plain walls. I loved the place because I saw a blank canvas. Best of all, Anya and I could stroll with Gracie to the small old-fashioned downtown in Webster Groves. Another plus, the house's overgrown garden hid tangles of herbs, wild blackberries and strawberries, plus climbing roses. I was eager to get my hands on those plants, and I knew someone who could help tame them. However, the price was the highest of the three we'd visited.

"By the way, Sheila," I said when we'd returned to the car. "I found a person to help you with your moles," and I handed over Johnny Chambers' phone number.

Sheila told Mrs. Thorgood we'd "think about it" and dropped me off at the store. Our plan was to confer later that evening.

"It never pays to be too eager," my mother-in-law reminded me earlier in the day.

I was decorating House Number Three in my mind when Nettie suddenly appeared at my elbow. I didn't see her approach. All in all, she was a drab house sparrow of a woman, a person you could easily forget. Her graying hair was twisted with a rubber band into a ponytail. Her eyes were small, and since she wore no makeup, they sort of disappeared into her bland face. Her manner of dress didn't help. She wore polyester slack sets with matching over-blouses in washed-out colors. Nothing fitted. Everything hung big and loose in muddy tones. To be truthful, I didn't expect much from her pages.

"You surprised me. I was deep in thought." I took the album from her hands. We moved to an empty crop table so I could review the memory book with its creator.

What I saw blew me away. I was stunned.

"Nettie, I had no idea you were so talented!" Then I remembered a study I'd read linking bipolar disorder with creativity.

Not for the first time did I marvel at how the good Lord evened things out in life. Whatever the mental disorder had taken from her, perhaps she'd been somewhat compensated by her extraordinary creative genius. She had a sure hand with color, a magpie eye for adding unexpected articles, and a careful and meticulous way of pulling everything together. Her style was sophisticated, daring, and eclectic. Here I'd worried about Bama taking my job, and I should have been concerned about the woman at my elbow. "How have you managed to keep this a secret? I mean, you are fantastic! I would have thought you'd be bragging like crazy."

She gave me a weak smile. "I haven't been making layouts much lately. Um, health issues. But that's really nice coming from you. I like your work too."

"Why all the secrecy?" I was mesmerized by her pages and had a hard time conversing because I didn't want to look away. I wanted to feast my eyes on her albums. My creative juices were flowing. I was itching to try some of her ideas on my own pages.

For a long time, she didn't respond. I thought she hadn't heard me. Finally she started talking, but her eyes never left the floor, "I hate having other people scraplift my pages. Beginners do it to learn. That's fine, I suppose. And it's okay when you are stuck. Especially if you just take one element, give it a twist, and make it your own. That's being creative. But, it's wrong when you steal other people's ideas wholesale. Especially if you do that and pass the work off as your own." She peeked up at me to see my reaction.

"Yeah, I know."

"Has that happened to you?"

I laughed. "More often than I care to think about. Almost on an hourly basis." I thought about the phone call I'd taken only a few minutes ago. Ellen Harmon now offered a paper bag album class. One of our customers received an e-mail notice from Memories Forever, and she was checking to see if we had a similar offering. All I could do was shake my head. Ellen had taken all of, what? A few days to copy us?

"Doesn't it make you mad? It's theft. Couldn't you just — just strangle the copycats?"

"I guess I'm used to it. I have younger sisters. They always wanted whatever I had. My mom told us imitation is the purest form of flattery. Besides, there's always another idea. I'll wake up tomorrow and think up something new. And the people who copy —" and I paused, thinking of Ellen Harmon, "— they're always a step behind."

She nodded and reached for her album just as Ben Novak walked in. In a button-down shirt and a tight pair of jeans topped with a well-made navy gabardine blazer, he was everything a man should be and more. There was a lankiness to him that could turn to skinny if he lost weight. As it was, he had the strong, lean musculature of a cyclist, which I later learned he was. Ben had a confidence about him that was very, very appealing.

Nettie scooped up her albums. "See you later, Kiki. I've got to go."

"Make sure you apply to be one of the Design Team," I called after her. She gave a quick nod and practically ran out of the building.

"How are you? You're looking marvelous, Kiki. How was the rest of your weekend?" Okay, it was banter, but his eyes locked into mine and he seemed to really care. I told him briefly about the party at Mert's, in part because I was curious. Was Ben too sophisticated for that sort of fun?

"That must have been terrific. I love St. Louis' multiple-personalities. It's amazing, really, how diverse our neighborhoods are. Think of how artistic and hip U-City is. Compare that with the scrubby Dutch of the south side. And I love the Hill at Christmas. Have you ever viewed the *presepi,* those terracotta Nativity scenes? I first saw them on the roadsides near the Amalfi coast in Italy. An entire scene would be tucked along a hillside. Imagine how shocked I was to learn I could drive across town to enjoy them here! You know how it is, we all tend to stay in our comfort zones."

His effusive manner was infectious. I longed to live a more worldly existence, one this man obviously knew and took pleasure in sharing.

"Hey, listen to me. I'm going on and on. Point being, this is a great place to live. I regard St. Louis as one of the best-kept secrets in the world."

"I agree," I said. "Come talk with me while I work." I needed to get cracking on my sample albums for the photographers. We had a great response, but the businesses would each need an album to show customers — and without those samples, I couldn't finalize any plans.

His frank, guileless smile touched me. I liked Ben, really liked him. Then I remembered Detweiler and came up short. Hadn't I learned anything? After the sting of the detective's lies, I needed clarity. "What brings you to my neck of the woods?" If he wasn't interested in me as a person, I needed to know pronto. No way was I letting down my guard again.

"Whoa," he laughed. "It's not like I paddled a pirogue with Lewis and Clark to get here. Considering my office is in Laclede's Landing, that might have been feasible once upon a time. You'll have to visit — our area is absolutely outstanding. And the cobblestones on our street are completely fabulous." He stepped closer, bringing along his expensive cologne. Really, the man was a preppy poster child in all the best of ways. He didn't take himself too seriously, and I sensed a frat boy's exuberant joie de vivre. A youthfulness clung to Ben, and a pang of poignancy for the years I'd given over to life as a young mother swept through me.

"Here's the thing," he grinned. "We have a long-time employee who's retiring, and I convinced Dad an album covering his tenure might be nice. Is that the sort of project you'd take on? If I coaxed you?" His eyes were golden in the light, and his lashes were thicker than mine would ever be.

"You've come to the right place," I said crisply. This was about business. Well, we needed business, so I was on it. "Let's start by seeing what you have."

"Okay, work before pleasure," he repeated the cliché. "Your mother-in-law warned me you wouldn't fall for my charms. After I called her this morning to get the store's address, I purposely only brought a few photos and articles. That gives me a reason to come back and see you again. For lunch maybe?"

To paraphrase Mae West, I like a man what plans ahead. This guy had all the angles covered. "Yes," I said, "you'll need to come back with the rest of your photos. Plan for lunch and at least another hour."

We consulted our calendars. Talk about how different we were — mine was a photo-copied stack of papers stapled together while his was a BlackBerry. Ben said good-bye, taking my hand in his cool, slim fingers for a handshake that was more than a handshake. "Okay, play hard to get," he growled. "Make me work to get to know you. I've never been one to back away from a challenge," and he stopped short. "By the way, what in the world happened to your window? Sorry, but the reporter in me is curious."

I explained about the brick, the graffiti, the fake dead dog, and my busted-up car window. Ben switched gears faster than a sports car into overdrive. "When? Tell me again exactly what happened."

I did.

"That's odd, we had a window broken at

the newspaper, too. By a brick. And we've had graffiti on the side of our building. It doesn't make sense that we'd have such similar problems at two locations miles apart. This must have nothing to do with our respective neighborhoods. You know, I'd heard rumor of an anti-Semitic cell. My sources tell me they're financed by well-organized groups in other states. Introduce me to your boss, please. If I'm right about this, we need to call Police Chief Holmes. With all these separate municipalities and police forces, things can slip through the cracks."

While he chatted with Dodie in her office, my cell rang. Bucky from Art House said, "Hey, you owe me for this one —"

"No problemo. The next time we need art supplies, I'll come to you. If you want, we can even distribute Art House brochures with your business card."

"Yeah, that's the ticket. Great idea. I'll mail you a handful. Here's the scoop. Yvonne Gaynor ratted out Bama to our boss. Said she was taking drugs — and Yvonne offered to prove it."

"Oh-ho-ho," I mumbled to myself. I thanked Bucky as Ben and Dodie walked together out of the back room. Dodie gave me a happy smile. I hadn't seen her so joyful in weeks. "Ben knew my son, Nathan. They were in youth group together." She and Ben took turns explaining Police Chief Holmes thought our hate crimes might be traced to *Strahlend Weiss,* a local white purity group. The name translated into "spotless white." Thanks to Ben spotting a linkage, Holmes was on top of the situation. Ben bade us both farewell, leaving Dodie to watch him leave longingly. "He knew Nathan," she repeated over and over. The friendship seemed a sign, a talisman she rubbed her hopes against. "My boy. I miss him so. But someone else remembers him. Isn't that wonderful?"

After she went back to her office, I called Detweiler. Yeah, I hated it. It seemed like even when I tried to break contact with him, I couldn't. I got his answering service and left a message with what I'd learned from Bucky. I'd no sooner finished when the door minder announced Johnny.

"I hope you don't mind me visiting you here."

"Not as long as you don't mind me leaving when a customer walks in. Let's chat while I cut out letters."

"I wanted to say thanks for giving my name to your mother-in-law." From behind his back, he pulled a single, perfect pink rose. I filled a bud vase and gave the flower a place of honor on my worktable. Johnny explained he'd already been by to see Sheila's lawn. She'd certainly made a mess of it, but he was confident he could whip it into shape and rid her of the moles.

"Trapping them is an art. You have to determine which tunnels are active and place the traps exactly right. Believe it or not, I'm apprenticing with the best mole killer in the area. If a trap springs and doesn't catch a critter, he makes me study where I set it so I don't make the same mistake twice. It's worth the trouble 'cause this dude alone nabbed more than eight hundred of the little buggers last season. His company charges $69 a mole."

"You are kidding me, right?" I made a mental calculation. Clearly, I was in the wrong line of work!

"Nope. You saw what Mrs. Lowenstein did to try to get rid of them. People who care about their lawns get frantic when they have mole infestations. Those critters can turn a beautiful green lawn into a map of raised brown furrows. And of course, since the moles keep multiplying the problem only gets worse. Which of course, is what God intended them to do." He winked at me. "Actually God intends all his creatures to go forth and multiply — that's why he makes it so much fun. Burrow, eat, and make babies. That's the circle of life."

Johnny leaned on the worktable to watch me. "The moles aren't the problem. Not really. We are. We're encroaching on their land. Destroying their habitats and natural enemies. This whole area once was home to coyotes, foxes, and wolves. Not to mention owls, hawks, and eagles. And it's not only moles affected, it's all wildlife. Out in the western suburbs there are more than eight-nine deer per square mile? Herds are starving to death, but they have nowhere to go. And they keep multiplying. Hunters and cars are their only method of population control." Johnny's face grew more and more animated, more passionate with concern.

How odd, I thought. This didn't sound like a man who could easily hurt anybody — any living creature — much less take part in a crime. That doesn't make sense. I'd read about criminals who began by torturing pets. Johnny clearly was not like that — not at all!

He paused, and I asked, "What would you suggest we do?"

But before he could answer, the door minder buzzed yet again, and in strode Detweiler. Speaking of animals, the detective walked like a cougar on the prowl, eyes focused, jaw set, and every step filled with aggression. I started to introduce the men, but the cop waved me away, training his sights on Johnny and saying, "We've met." For a long moment, the two stared at each other. Neither spoke. Detweiler took in the single rose. His green eyes turned nasty cold. Testosterone thickened the air. Any minute now, this could get ugly.

Johnny backed down first, but after all, Detweiler carried a badge and a gun. Mert's brother turned to me and said, "Actually I came by to ask if you'd like to go with me to a concert at Riverport Friday night. Why don't I call you and we'll work out the details?"

Steam came out of Detweiler's ears. His emotional radiator was busted. I thought he'd throw a rod right then and there.

And what could he do? He was a married man. I'd seen the proof.

I gave Johnny my best smile. "Great. I'd like that. A lot. We had such a super time on our last date."

If Johnny was surprised by me calling a quick lunch "a date," he didn't show it.

But Detweiler did. He positively glared at both of us. That muscle in his jaw twitched fast and hard. He harrumphed, crossing his arms over his chest, tapping his foot impatiently on the floor, scalding me with evil looks. He was not a happy camper.

After writing down the website address so I could check out the concert, Johnny leaned over and gave me a peck on the cheek. "Take care, babe. I'm still dreaming about your dancing. Maybe we can even have ourselves another picnic, and I'll bring the music, huh?"

My mouth twitched. Dreaming about my dancing? What a hoot.

Johnny might as well have reached out and twisted Detweiler's, uh, nose. The detective's angry stare followed the other man out the front door.

Detweiler wasted no time, launching into a rant as soon as the door slammed shut. "Have you lost your mind? You've got to be kidding. You can't date that man! He's a felon! He's on parole! Good grief, use your head, Kiki. Think about Anya."

"I have thought about Anya," I said. "This is none of your business. Now are you interested in information I have about the murder? Or should I phone it in to Robbie Holmes?" He flinched and sputtered and tried to interrupt, but I raised my palm to him. He carried on, cursing quietly under his breath. I told him what I learned about

366

Bama being fired after Yvonne Gaynor told the boss at Artist Supply that she was on drugs.

As I spoke, Dodie ambled out from the back room. She was on her way to give the cop a piece of her mind, when a flock of customers showed up. It happens that way. For hours you've got nobody, and then boom, the place is packed. Detweiler was taking down specifics of my conversations with Bucky when I noticed Nettie carefully examining metal embellishments in the next aisle. Here, I'd thought she'd left.

Detweiler tapped his notepad with a pen. He leaned close and said, "How about we go together and take a look at Yvonne Gaynor's scrapbooking pages? We can do it tonight. I can pick you up and —"

"No. Huh-uh. I don't think so, Detective." I wasn't falling for that. He wanted the chance to get me alone. He wanted to explain away his dishonest behavior and lecture me about seeing Johnny. Luckily, there was a way around making a site visit with him. "I don't need to go to her house. A few of her pages are online at the magazine's website, and others are on display at Memories First. I'd rather start there. Believe it or not, I'm not eager to be in your company."

He reached over and took hold of my forearm. "How badly were you cut?"

I gave him a cold "Hands off, pal."

He shook his head, his eyes full of pain and his face stricken. Whatever was happening beneath the surface went beyond feeling competitive with Johnny. Detweiler felt pain, real pain. "Kiki, we have to talk. It's not what it looks like. You need to let me explain." Those amazing green eyes took on a hurt puppy expression.

Worst of all, I wanted him to explain. I teetered on an emotional edge. Oh, how I wanted to fall into his arms. I wanted to be with him. I wanted to tell him how much I cared —

But I saw Brenda in my mind. I swallowed and said, "It is what it is. I have nothing more to say." I spun and walked away before I lost my nerve. He could be replaced with two new men. A two for one special. I was so done with him and his lies.

His hand grabbed my retreating shoulder. He said softly to my back. "Tell the kid I . . . I asked about her, and for goodness sake, at least tell me how Gracie is."

I froze. I didn't turn around to face him. "Fine. My dog is fine. I am too. We're all doing very well, thank you." I didn't trust myself to say more. I pulled away. I took my supplies for cutting letters to another table, went back to work, and didn't raise my head as I heard him walk away.

I blotted my eyes hurriedly.

"Ahem." Nettie stood at the foot of the table trying to get my attention. "I came back because . . . see, I was planning to go over to Memories First on Friday. Ellen is kicking off a weekend dedicated to Yvonne. Would you like to drive together?"

I answered, "Yes," and we started to make the arrangements when my phone rang. Sheila was breathless with excitement. "He caught one! The trap went off. Anya and I saw the dastardly thing wiggle. Those were its death throes. Johnny got a mole! They'll all be dead soon! One by one, he'll kill them, ha ha!" The call ended with a maniacal laugh.

She'd lost her mind.

# TWENTY-THREE

Anya spent the night with her grandmother. The two of them set a timer and ran out into the front yard at intervals to check for dead moles. Pretty sick if you ask me.

Horace walked through my house to make sure I was safe before saying good night. This was getting old. My boss agreed that one of us — and I was the most likely prospect — had to go over to Memories First and see what Ellen was doing — mainly whether she was casting aspersions on our business.

Okay, and I wanted to solve the mystery. I was sick and tired of dealing with fallout from Yvonne's murder. Once the killer was found I would never have to talk to Detweiler again. If we were really lucky, within the next day or two Police Chief Holmes would nab the hate-mongers who were vandalizing our store and terrorizing me and my dog. Suddenly the weight of what I was dealing with hit me hard. Gee, no wonder I felt like I'd been wrung through my grandmother's old wringer washer. I stopped by a convenience store and bought a big bottle of cheap wine on sale.

At home, I took a long, hot shower. I sat down at my old computer and worked on handouts for the retirement home classes. I planned to present the handouts with a project sample to several administrators. I'd put in a couple of hours when Johnny called and we made our plans for the day of the concert. Sort of. I committed to going, and we decided to firm up details later. He couldn't talk long, and I was too tired to be sociable. I got off the phone, poured a glass of the wine, sipped it slowly, and went to bed with Gracie and one of my mysteries borrowed from the library.

The next morning, I added a spoonful of raspberry preserves to peanut butter on a whole wheat English muffin, sliced up a banana, and settled in to plan my day. First, I needed to call Ellen's store to check out their weekend schedule and report back to Nettie. Second, I would view Yvonne's pages on the magazine website. Third, I would take my daughter for her return trip to the allergist. At 3 p.m. I was scheduled to work the store. There I needed to check in a big shipment that had arrived late yesterday, tag it, and set it out. Our current inventory would need rearranging.

I finished my muffin and washed my plate. That house in Webster Groves was very, very appealing. By my calculations, I was $1200 short of the first and last month deposit, and a couple hundred short of the rent each month. I tried to imagine being indebted to Sheila and felt uncomfortable. I could easily foresee the two of us disagreeing — and she'd hold the money over my head.

Was my neighborhood really so unsafe? Would the house in Webster Groves be safer? I scrubbed my tub and thought.

The prominent author was in residence most of the time in the main house. The setting was small town. Webster Groves maintained a real, live downtown, and as a result the surrounding neighborhoods had a 1950s "we know each other and help out" type of feel. Meanwhile this neighborhood grew steadily more transient.

I mopped with Mr. Clean and thought about Detweiler. My tears plonked into the rinse water. I tried really hard not to get upset, but memories flooded back. I remembered him laughing with Anya about an incident at science camp. I thought about how he loved to wrestle with Gracie. She heard me sniffle and poked her muzzle under my chin. That's when I broke down and cried in earnest, big gulping sobs. "It's going to be all right, isn't it, girl? Think of the two new men I've met. Pretty soon, I won't even think twice about that old cop, will I? And you won't either, right? We're tough, eh? You and me?" But Gracie only lifted sad brown eyes to mine.

She didn't agree; I could tell.

I threw myself into cleaning. After a while I was cried out and my housework was done. This place was small enough I could clean it top to bottom in a couple of hours. I let Gracie out, rinsed the cut on her ear with hydrogen peroxide, and booted up the computer.

The website for *Saving Memories* magazine was full of articles to read, sample pages, books to buy, links to products, and the winners of the Scrapbook Stars contest. Yvonne's bio noted she'd scrapbooked for six years. (I found that very hard to credit.) Her favorite technique was acrylic paint on pages. (That surprised me. I'd showed the ladies how to use big foam letter stamps with acrylic paint, and she'd made a real mess of everything. I remembered mopping up after her.)

Yvonne's layouts were the biggest shock.

They were extremely sophisticated, eclectic, and bold. Her use of color was skillful. Her incorporation of found elements was imaginative. How could I have misjudged this woman's talent? I closed down the computer and stared at the blank screen. Here I'd thought she was a little below average in her skills. But the work she'd turned in was terrific . . . and I had this weird sense of déjà vu.

Still . . . I see a lot of pages, and everything runs together in my mind. I was putting on lip gloss when it hit me. Yvonne's pages bore a startling resemblance to Nettie Klasser's work. Well, no surprise. Scrapbookers who crop together regularly teach each other skills. They consult on choices. They share tools and attend classes together.

I tackled my #2 item on the "to do" list. I phoned Memories First. Minnie Hertzog answered the phone. I knew her from an altered books class we attended at Artist Supply last year. Minnie chattered happily, "We've got lots happening. Yvonne's pages will go on display Friday. As you know, the magazine website only shows four of them — we've got the rest. There'll be a big memorial candle-lighting ceremony starting at dusk. Ellen has asked Nettie Klasser to say a few words."

That threw me. Nettie hadn't mentioned she would be eulogizing her pal.

Minnie added, "We're offering drop-in classes featuring the techniques Yvonne used on her pages."

"Gee, that'll be a little hard without her, won't it? I mean, sure you can figure out how she did the stuff, but it's a lot more complicated without the artist."

Minnie lowered her voice. "Promise never to tell anyone I told you this . . . but I bet Ellen or somebody here at the store helped her. I really don't know who. It wouldn't be the first time a winner had assistance, would it?"

I thought of the chat I'd seen online about one woman stealing another's journaling — and about how much scrapbookers helped each other in general. "Yeah, seems to me I've read about women working together on contest entries. Sort of a support group, I think."

"That's right," said Minnie. "In fact, we've had crops where people worked on challenges together. Frankly, I don't know where the line is between authorized and unauthorized help, do you?"

"No," I said honestly.

After that call, I drove to my mother-in-law's, thinking and thinking the entire time.

It was the kind of aimless thinking like when a dog circles a spot before deciding where to lie down. I just couldn't find my spot.

Whatever.

Something bothered me, but I couldn't grasp it. The subconscious mind knows no master. I'd simply have to wait.

Sheila sat in a rocking chair watching what resembled croquet wickets all over her yard. A foot high stake topped with an orange flag marked each metal hoop. She gave me a tour of what was left of her lawn.

"A trap shaped like a pair of scissors extends under the ground. The mole pushes the trigger as he moves along. The blades are sprung and cut him in half. It's wonderful!"

"Ugh. That's awful."

"No! It's effective and works fast. A mole can extend a tunnel by 100 feet a day! A good mole trapper knows exactly where to set the trap. Johnny figured out which was the main runway."

"Runway? Like an airplane?"

Sheila peered at me carefully. "You aren't laughing about this are you? Think of all the damage these pests have done to my yard."

Frankly, Sheila had inflicted the majority of the damage. Those hills were nothing compared to the holes she'd dug. I bit the inside of my lip and responded vigorously. "No, ma'am. I'm just trying to make sure I've got this all down."

"He figured out which was the main tunnel by flattening all the rest and watching. Those horrible animals returned to the main tunnel. When it popped back up, he knew where to set the traps."

I scanned the area. She was right. Not all the tunnels had traps along them. "Why not put traps on those tunnels too? Or are they like extra rooms the moles don't use?"

"Those might be feeding tunnels for finding grubs or worms. Where my lot edges the woods out back, Johnny found another set of tunnels, probably where the mole nest was." Sheila's eyes sparkled. Oh yeah, the hunt was on. "Got two of them so far. Cut those nasty suckers right in half!"

# Twenty-Four

Anya raced to the car. "Mom, we have to go home. Now. Before the allergist. It's an emergency."

I started to argue and then thought better of it. Instead, I told Sheila goodbye and backed out carefully.

"What's up, Anya Banana?"

"You told me I could wear makeup when my periods started. Guess what? They started!"

My baby. My little girl. I forced myself to concentrate on the traffic. Months ago, I'd collected the paraphernalia a woman needs when she has her monthly cycles. I'd boxed and gift-wrapped it. Today was a red letter day. George, I said silently to my dead husband, can you believe it? Our child is now a woman.

We stopped at home and ran inside. With trembling hands, I pulled the package from its hiding place and gave it to Anya. "Pass your underwear to me, honey. I'll get the stains out."

"La la la," she sang from the other side of the bathroom door. Good. I had wanted this to be a great experience rather than a negative or frightening one.

"After the allergist can we go buy makeup? You said I could when I started. There's this party one of the girls at camp is giving next weekend, and boys will be there. I don't want to look like a baby."

"It depends on how much time we have, honey."

She handed her panties out the door. I stared at them. "Hey, by the way," I asked casually. "How was your day with your grandma? Did Linnea buy that Faygo Red Pop you wanted to try?"

"Yeah, it was good. I drank it with a straw 'cause otherwise you get a funny smile. Nana knows lots of tricks like that. Why?" Anya opened the door. I said nothing. Her eyes darted to the ceiling, the floor, and back to me. She couldn't face me.

"Nice try, kiddo. Did you think I wouldn't recognize Faygo Red Pop on your undies? No makeup. No way. And there will be a consequence for being dishonest."

She stomped past me. "Aw, Mom!"

I kept my back to her, trying hard not to

giggle. Boy, how strong it was, this urge to grow up quickly. I clamped my mouth into a straight line and led the way to the car. She pouted the whole way to the allergist. Under her breath, she grumbled and snarled.

I didn't pay much attention to her, but I did do a lot of glancing around at other cars. I watched my rearview mirror. The events of the last few days had made me nervous about being followed. I kept my cell phone open and accessible, but I didn't want to worry Anya.

What was I going to do? I wasn't safe at home and I wasn't safe at work. I didn't have the money to move, and I needed my job. The gunshot through my car window was the final straw. That and the fake, bloody dog. Danger had found its way to my doorstep. Really, this was grinding me down. Could I live with the possibility of one of us — and I included Gracie — being hurt? And now that Detweiler wouldn't be dropping by, were we more at risk?

Oh, George, I cast a thought again to my dead husband. Why didn't you plan better for our future? I trusted you, and you blew it.

Yeah, well, so much for my good taste in men.

■ ■ ■ ■

Seeing how irked Anya was, I let her go alone with the nurse into Dr. Andersoll's office. When my daughter got like this, it was best to give her a clear berth for a while. Besides, I had sleuthing to do.

"Who introduced Yvonne Gaynor to your office? This is sort of far from where she lived." The receptionist raised an eyebrow. I needed a reason I was being nosey. "I'm one of the scrapbookers putting together a book for her children. We're trying to contact all her friends. You can imagine how difficult that is. We don't want to leave anyone out. Since Yvonne was a patient, whoever recommended her must be another friend who might want to share a memorial sentiment. For the album. For her children. And family."

The receptionist smiled. "I see. I heard a group of women were working on that project." She glanced around. "I can find the name. I really shouldn't do this though . . ."

She disappeared for five minutes and returned with a slip of paper.

Whoever recommended Yvonne would have known about her allergies, and maybe about the Epi-Pen. But the name I was holding was not one of the people at our crop. In fact, it wasn't anyone I'd ever heard of. There goes that idea, I mumbled to myself.

Anya begged to go over to Nicci Moore's house. I called Jennifer, Nicci's mom, and she formally invited my daughter. Interestingly, my daughter's language had changed. She no longer wanted to "play" at a friend's house. The new operative phrase being the more nebulous "go over to." I dropped her off and made a mental note I needed to get a life.

The store was quiet. Dodie was back to her down-in-the-dumps self. Maybe she was back to thinking about her lump. I sure was. I tried to busy myself to get my mind off both our troubles. I would keep my promise about not telling Horace for a while. I said a little prayer they'd have good news on one front or another.

I found cool imprintable paper for my retirement home class handout. I made up a folder with all the materials I'd need to "sell" my idea to an administrator. I un-boxed more paper for my customized albums for photographers. I worked sorting the papers, and making die cuts so I could create more wedding pages in an efficient manner.

Dodie was at her desk, and I'd just come out of the bathroom when Bama marched into the back room. Her face twisted into a mask of rage. Running one hand along the wall she invaded my personal space, stopping inches from my face and shaking a finger at mc. "You sicced the police on me! I didn't do it! I have vertigo! I am not on drugs. I am not drunk. I have a medical condition. Dodie!"

Dodie rose slowly and lumbered over. She surveyed both of us. "Get a hold of yourself, Bama."

But Bama was livid. "A hold of myself! I have never been so insulted in my life. How dare she?" Spittle flew from her lips. "This is outrageous!" And she repeated herself with, "Absolutely insulting!"

Dodie edged herself between the two of us. Thank heavens she is a big woman.

Bama screamed, "How dare you? What colossal gall!" and she jammed her finger toward me, white saliva dripping from her lips, her eyes bulging out of her head. "You, Miss Smarty Pants, you go stirring things up with my old co-workers. Thanks a heap. I finally get to put all that behind me —"

"Put what behind you?" asked Dodie.

"The old news about how Yvonne Gaynor told my boss at Artist Supply that I was on drugs."

"Oh, that," said Dodie.

Uh-oh.

Bama continued, "And when Miss Hotshot told her married cop boyfriend about the gossip, I was hauled in for questioning! Never mind my old boss apologized and gave me a raise. You didn't know that, did you, Smartie Pants? No, you set out to embarrass me!"

"If he offered you a raise, why did you leave? Huh? Answer that!" I countered, yelling over the barricade of Dodie's body. I felt a false sense of safety with her between Bama and me, like a kid hiding behind her mother's skirt.

"Because I don't want to work with people who don't trust me. That's why I told Dodie what happened before she hired me."

Our boss turned to me. "That's right, Kiki. I knew all about Bama. You are way out of line here."

I sputtered. "But what about her sister? Huh? Explain that. Dodie, her sister works for the caterer!"

Gnashing her teeth, Bama stood on her tiptoes to yell at me. "My sister? She has three kids to support. Three, Kiki! Not just one like you do. Think it's hard making ends meet with one? Try three! I called her about catering for CAMP, but Dodie knew all about it. Dodie didn't pay one cent more. Katie got a bonus. Big deal! A whole twenty bucks! And when the cops questioned the catering staff, that stupid twenty didn't compensate for the half day of work she lost. They grilled her like a quarter-pound hamburger!" Bama was running out of steam. Her voice wasn't as shrill and her motions a lot less threatening. Flecks of spit were drying on her lips.

Dodie said quietly, "Bama told me about the commission. I was glad to help." The level way she talked made my gut go liquid. Dodie was mad. More than mad. She was seriously ticked at me.

And I deserved it.

"You should fire Kiki's butt." Bama's mouth sank into an angry red slash. "For all the trouble she caused me. I never did anything to you, Kiki Lowenstein. Ever. All I want to do is design work. That's what I went to school for. And you've been hateful to me from day one."

She was right. I pretty much had been. I never saw it that way, but she was right. I stared at the floor. I'd screwed up. I'd hurt her, disrespected Dodie's authority, and jeopardized our store.

"I apologize." I swallowed. "I was out of line. My intentions were good —"

"Good intentions? Hah! You wanted to send me to jail!"

I continued, "I worried about the business. The police weren't getting anywhere, so I played amateur sleuth. But I was wrong. I should have brought my suspicions to you, Dodie. I've been jealous of you, Bama, so I found fault. And when I did, I didn't do the right thing."

Dodie spoke wearily, slowly. A meaty hand rubbed her temple, and she squinted. "I really did not need this right now."

That did it. I could handle Bama's anger and my guilt, but knowing I'd made life more difficult for Dodie was too much to bear. I was two steps from the bathroom. I hustled my sorry self inside and locked the door. I turned on the tap, running water from both spigots and under the cover of the noise, I cried. I sobbed about my stupidity, Dodie's cold fury, Detweiler's lies, Gracie's ear, moving, Anya's rejection of me, Dodie's health, and my mom's "sow's ear" remark. My bushel basket of misery was full to the brim. Of course, crying couldn't fix any of that.

But I couldn't either.

I was at the end of my rope.

I was a royal screw-up. A bad, incompetent person. My kid didn't want to spend time with me. I couldn't afford safe housing. I stuck my nose where it didn't belong. I hurt innocent people. I hurt those who had trusted me.

As usual, my sobs devolved into hiccups. I washed as much smeared mascara off my face as I could. I straightened my spine and stepped out, fully expecting Dodie to fire me.

What a pitiful two-fer. I'd lost both my job and a friend.

# TWENTY-FIVE

Dodie called me into her office and gestured toward an empty chair. "Dumb move, scout."

"I understand you have to fire me."

Her pallor accented the dark smudges under her eyes. "Fire you? It just cost me a bundle of goodwill to educate you. You have learned a valuable lesson. You didn't trust me to do my due diligence. Hey, I checked Bama out before I hired her. And if I hadn't been so distracted, I would have done a better job of managing you two and noticed your animosity. This is a team effort, but every team needs a coach. My head was up my butt instead of on the playing field."

I felt cautious optimism. "That mean you want to keep me?"

"I need help running the store. You are trained. Horace and I have that appointment with the attorney. And I need the floor covered." She wagged her shaggy head.

"Plus, I still want you to go to the Memories First memorial service for Yvonne Gaynor. Given Mert, Bama, and my history with the woman, you're the only one of us who won't cause a problem just by showing up. That is, if you can behave yourself."

"I'm on it. I've learned my lesson." These responsibilities might allow me to get back into Dodie's good graces.

For the moment, I was still gainfully employed. The phone on her desk rang and I rose to leave, thinking it was Horace. But it wasn't. Dodie greeted Ben Novak. Her side of the conversation was peppered with "uh-huh" and "really?" Finally she hung up and said, "Go get Bama." I did as I was told, wondering if my co-worker would ever forgive me. But Bama acted like nothing had ever happened. Maybe her style of anger was like a summer storm — fast, furious, and quickly over. On the other hand, maybe she was planning her revenge.

Dodie handed out cold colas. "Good news, girls. The police found our hate crime pal. Lives down the block. He's a twenty-three-year-old man who lost his job to an Arab. But this dope thought the Arab was a Jew because the man was from Palestine. He confessed to all the damage at our store and at the *Muddy Waters Review,* plus a few more Jewish-owned businesses around the area."

"But what about faking Gracie's death?" I asked. "And Yvonne's death?"

Dodie dropped her voice, "Sorry, sunshine. Seems this nut-case bragged about what he'd done — and neither Yvonne's death nor your fake pooch made his hit parade."

I drank my Diet Dr Pepper slowly. Our store was now safe from one miscreant. But if neither our graffiti artist nor Bama killed Yvonne Gaynor, who did? Even if Dodie let me keep my job, could she keep the doors open? My husband's killer was still out there and cast a dark shadow over my world. And now Yvonne's killer threatened more of the same.

Either or both obviously knew where I lived and how to get to me and those I loved. The bloody pelt had been a warning shot over my bow.

That did it. Time to grow a spine where my wishbone had been.

First, I dialed Sheila. We agreed to talk over the weekend about the house in Webster Groves. Oh, and Johnny had killed three more moles. She hired an artist to paint a tally for an inside garage wall.

Then I tackled that other procrastination-worthy item on my "to do" list — Yvonne Gaynor's memorial event. It would be easier to go if I didn't have to show up alone. I called Nettie.

Nettie apologized. "I'm afraid we can't ride over together. I need to get there early. I have things to do. And I have to leave before the candle-lighting ceremony begins."

She still didn't mention giving a eulogy. Maybe it was to be a surprise. She added almost as an afterthought, "You get a look at Yvonne's pages on the magazine website? Notice anything odd about them?"

"Her style is a lot like yours."

"No kidding! Yvonne was a thief. She swiped ideas. My ideas and my designs. Those were my pages she turned in. Mine! She just swapped out the photos. Ellen was her accomplice. Now we're all supposed to show up and feel bad that that two-timing, backstabber is dead."

I shook my head. I didn't have the energy to pursue this.

"If I were you," she said, "I'd stay home. Trust me. You don't want to be there."

I explained I had no choice.

"That's a shame, because I like you," she said sadly. "You've always treated me fairly."

At least one person didn't think I was a

complete idiot.

I called Mert and begged for girlfriend time after work. With Johnny back in town, we hadn't seen each other much. As per usual, she was there for me. With a bottle of Shiraz. And a plate of stove-top cookies, which are really nothing more than peanut-butter and chocolate fudge with a little oat-meal.

There are many roads to Nirvana. If chocolate, sugar, and alcohol don't lead there, I can't make the trip.

"I'm done sleuthing. All I've gotten is a broken heart, a bullet wound, and a mad co-worker. Not to mention, possibly a pink slip," I sipped my third glass of wine, grate-ful I didn't have to drive anywhere. Mert sprawled out on an overstuffed chair from my previous life. She got up to pour more wine and patted my shoulder.

"Yeah, you behaved like an ignoranus," she said.

"That's ignoramus," I corrected.

"Not how I mean it."

Thanks, I thought. I needed that.

Mert's hot-pink halter top with sequins around the neckline contrasted nicely with her crisp white short-shorts. On her feet were raspberry sandals with three-inch high heels. I wore an old T-shirt of George's and a pair of drawstring cotton pajama pants. I was half-propped up on my sofa with a pillow under my armpit so I could keep on drinking. My plan was to go from slightly buzzed to unconscious without a scintilla of sobriety in between.

"I'm coming to grips with being indebted to Sheila. That's the only way I can swing a move. I can't go on living here, Mert. It's not safe. And it's not fair to Anya. Or Gracie." I sucked on a cookie, letting the sugary confection melt in my mouth. "Gosh, this is good."

"I'll leave you to wallow in your misery. I got houses to clean tomorrow." She gazed down at me benevolently. "I can tell you like them cookies. That's your sixth one in two minutes. Don't worry none. I'm leaving you a plastic container to get you through the weekend."

Huh. That little care package wasn't even going to last me through the night.

# Twenty-Six

Without needing to get my daughter up and to camp, my morning was leisurely. Which was great because my headache was powerful. I sipped a cup of tea with my Advil.

I was busy all morning with summer activities pages to be displayed throughout the store. Dodie buzzed in around noon. "Could you watch the store the rest of the day? Horace and I need to chat about his Chicago trip."

Time passed quickly. I had completed four sample albums for the photographers, and I was working on a presentation outline and a sample page for the retirement homes. I also dreamed up a "Summer Magic Class" and managed to use the new Disney shaker box embellishment we had tons of, as well as the metal adhesive word "soccer." Our customers were always more likely to try a new product after seeing it on a page. Dodie would be pleased with my progress. The mail brought responses for custom albums from yet another couple of professional photographers.

I tried not to think about my troubles. It would all be much easier if I had someone to talk to, someone like . . . Detweiler. I missed his friendship, his dropping by, and his good counsel. There was a quality about him, a reasonableness tempered with empathy that made tough times easier. Unlike most men, he didn't try to solve my problems. Instead, he would listen carefully. "I can tell you are worried," he'd say. "I have confidence you'll make the right decision. Is there anyway I can help?"

A splotch on a piece of cardstock I'd been working with told me I'd been crying.

It was nearly closing time when Johnny stopped by. The band he'd proposed we see on Friday was a country and western group. I didn't care. Being on a date was the highlight for me. I was flexible when it came to music. And since I couldn't dance to country or western, we were safe.

While we chatted, Dodie called.

"Please open tomorrow and work until you leave for Ellen Harmon's. Bama has a doctor's appointment the same time as Horace and I are meeting with the attorney."

She didn't ask. She told me. This was a

new low. But I was in no position to complain. After I hung up I realized it would be tough to get from Ellen's store and back to my house in time for Johnny to pick me up.

He drawled, "No problem. They owe me a couple of hours at work because I came in last weekend. How about I drive you to the other store, and we go from there to Riverport? That'll give us more time together."

Anya spent the night at her grandmother's, giving me my second morning in a row to putter around uninterrupted. I started laundry, pausing after my cup of tea to fold whites. With my hands busy, my mind wandered. As far as I knew, the police hadn't made any headway with Yvonne's killer. And I'd sure learned my lesson about playing detective. The CAMP stores posted notice of the $10,000 reward. But the flurry of tips must not have yielded anything solid.

Well, it really wasn't my problem.

I decided I'd better make myself indispensable at work. The first order of business was making an "I'm Sorry!" card for Bama. Then, I tackled next month's class calendar. Every so often, I checked my image in the bathroom mirror. I was wearing a tight pair of embroidered jeans and a sleeveless surplice top in blue. The jeans might be a bit warm, but it was better than being exposed to mosquitoes. I'd taken special care with my makeup. This was my first real date in nearly thirteen years, and I was nervous.

I also wondered if I was doing the right thing. I loved Mert, and I trusted her. But Johnny was her brother. What if I wanted to quit seeing him or if we quarreled? What would Mert do? Did I really feel comfortable dating a man with a prison record? No. I'd rather be on the other side of the law with a cop. But I remembered Detweiler's dishonesty. The fact the detective warned me away from Johnny encouraged me to take perverse joy in dating the man. All things considered, Ben Novak would be a more suitable choice. But he hadn't asked me out. His visit had been strictly business.

My track record with men stunk. First George, then Detweiler, and now a felon. Suddenly the excitement of having a date evaporated like so many fizzy bubbles.

Oh, well. I'd made a commitment for one evening, and one evening only. One night at Riverport would not a romance make.

Clancy phoned. "Have you heard about the memorial ceremony? What a pile of poop! I swear, Ellen Harmon is a dirty-fisted grave robber. She's lower than a maggot in a dumpster. There's a page on her website about 'those in the scrapbook community who can't possibly understand the grief we feel.' Can you believe it? Behold, the new Queen of Tacky!"

"You planning to attend?"

"If I don't go, I won't have anything to gossip about, will I?"

"No, you won't. I'll see you there."

"I wouldn't miss it. Hey, guess who snuck into the Gaynor's house last night under the cover of dark? Rena. How's that for a motive? Out with the old and in with the new, eh? She and Perry didn't even wait until old Yvonne was cold in her grave."

"No kidding," I said. "Well, my sleuthing days are over, but that sure is interesting."

At a quarter of one, Bama came in to relieve me. I handed her the card I made and apologized once again.

"Whatever. Forget it."

I hoped not. I wanted to remember how out of hand my snooping had gotten. Jealousy, not the desire to right a wrong, had been at the root of my investigation. Even as we talked about the calendar for the next month, I realized how hard it was for me to give up control. I liked being the person in charge of the classes and crops.

It didn't help that Bama wasn't a warm and fuzzy type of person. Our personalities were oil and vinegar. Still, that was a lousy reason to suspect someone. And I hoped I'd learned my lesson.

Johnny showed up at two on the dot. Bama eyed him with unconcealed interest.

"I have my cell phone on, if you need anything this evening," I told my co-worker as we paused by the front door.

Johnny laughed, "Babe, I doubt you'll be able to hear the ring over the band. Take a night off. This woman seems perfectly capable."

She was. And that was the problem. Correction, that was *my* problem.

St. Louis suffered through another muggy summer day. Humidity drove the heat index to an uncomfortable three-digit temperature. Johnny stopped at a drive-up window and bought us large colas for the ride.

Memories First was a long drive from our store. By the time Johnny and I arrived, and after drinking all that liquid, I needed the facilities. I started toward the back of the store and noticed Nettie studying a wall display of Yvonne's work. Considering how negative she'd been, I wondered why she agreed to say a few words. As shy as she was, it seemed totally out of character. I wanted to ask her why she'd bothered, but I needed to use the bathroom first.

A huge sign over the sink read: "Careful! Hot water!" A bit of acrylic paint under my nails had lodged there after working on a page title. I scrubbed carefully, being vigilant about the water temp. It stayed cold. That was odd. What was the deal with the big warning sign? I sniffed the air. What was that smell? Bathrooms could get funky, but this one smelled funny. I didn't see a drain. The little room held a hot water heater and a small tin storage cabinet for sanitary supplies and cleansers.

Knock it off, Kiki, I told myself. No more snooping!

I rejoined Johnny, and we stood in line to view a collection of Yvonne's winning pages. When my turn came, I stepped up, stared at the layouts and realized I had seen every one of these designs before . . . in Nettie's album. Oh, boy. I backed into Johnny, pulling him away. "We need to step outside."

On my way to the door, Minnie Hertzog intercepted us. She nattered on about how nice it was to see everyone. By her calculations, almost a hundred people were jammed into the small building.

"Is Nettie giving a eulogy?" I asked.

Minnie shook her head. "No, she begged off. Said she has to go before we get to the candle-lighting. That's weird because she asked to be a part of the ceremony. She was after me nearly every day for a schedule of events."

Crud. I had a sick feeling I knew exactly why. All the pieces were starting to make sense. "Minnie, is the water in your bathroom really hot?"

"I burned myself just this morning. It rushes out scalding first thing because the sink is right next to the water heater. I keep telling Ellen it's silly to waste money on gas in the summer, but she never listens."

I pulled my phone from my pocket and excused myself ostensibly to return a call from my daughter. Johnny raised one eyebrow but blessedly didn't ask questions. I hustled us out the front door and off to one side where we could speak privately. More and more people streamed past us into the store. The parking lot was full. Visitors were finding spaces farther down the street.

If I was right, this was bad. Really bad. The more people who arrived, the worse the situation became. My face must have reflected my alarm.

"Babe, what's the deal? You okay?" Johnny slipped a loose arm around my waist. I leaned on him for a second, trying not to panic.

"I'll tell you in a minute." I dialed the allergist's office. "Hi, this is Kiki Lowenstein. Remember that album I'm working on? Right. The memorial album for Yvonne Gaynor. That's it. Yes. I was wondering . . . I know Nettie Klasser is one of your patients. Who introduced her to your practice?" I waited for the answer, my heart in my throat.

"Why, Yvonne Gaynor, of course," said the receptionist before I rang off.

I sketched out my idea to Johnny. His face turned serious, but he volunteered to walk back into the store and check out my concern.

"You were right." He swore under his breath. "The water heater pilot light isn't lit. What you smelled is natural gas. I turned it off, but no telling how long it's been leaking."

"We have to get those people out of there! Any minute now, they're going to light candles!"

"And they need to leave in a calm, orderly fashion. Shoot, Kiki, there's little kids in there. If there's a stampede, someone's going to get hurt." He ran a hand through his long hair, his fingers tangling at the ends, and swore. "The cops won't listen to me. Sorry, babe."

I dialed 911. I gave the dispatcher our address and the business name. "The building is about to blow up. There's a gas leak. About 100 people are inside."

"You sure?"

Okay, I wasn't sure, but what were my options? Better to apologize than to be wrong. "I'm positive, send help — it could go any time!"

The dispatcher confirmed she'd have someone on the way immediately.

"You must get everyone out of the building," were her last words before hanging up.

"That's a problem," I told Johnny. "Ellen Harmon will think this is some ploy Dodie and I cooked up. She'll never believe me. She's like that."

"Well, we've got to think of a plan — fast!" His eyes were dark with concern.

I had an idea.

"Could work," he said. "It's our best shot."

I slipped into the store, and Johnny went to his truck. Fortunately, Ellen had started to talk, microphone in hand. Thrilled to be the center of everyone's attention, she was not about to relinquish the limelight quickly. To prolong her fifteen seconds of fame, she called various people to the microphone to talk about what Yvonne — and her store — meant to them. The crowd listened intently,

403

becoming a bit restless as she nattered on. Perry Gaynor and two children, a boy and a girl, bookended Ellen. I rose on tiptoes and scanned the crowd. Nettie hunkered down in the rear of the building, right next to the back door.

Normally I would have been thrilled to see Clancy. She waved and worked her way through the crowd to my side. I put a finger to my lips to signal "be quiet" while I pocketed a package of letter stickers. No one else saw me; everyone was watching Ellen.

I motioned Clancy to come outside. Johnny had changed into his work shirt. After briefly introducing them, and telling Clancy what I suspected, I peeled off one sticker letter at a time to spell out "Gas Company" and stuck the words under the embroidered Spa La Femme logo. It was pretty schlocky, but because Johnny's neatly pressed dark jeans looked like regular pants, my plan just might work. He held a clipboard full of papers in one hand and said, "Give me a kiss, babe. I'm going in."

"I can help," said Clancy. "Uh, not with the kiss. But to manage the crowd. We need to get everyone out of there fast."

We decided our best bet was to keep people away from the back where the water heater had been leaking gas. I'd read about cell phones sending up sparks. I didn't know if that was true, and I didn't want to find out.

Right before I walked in with Johnny, I dialed Detweiler. He picked up first ring. "There's a gas leak at Memories First. We're here. I've called 911. We're trying to clear the store. And Yvonne Gaynor's killer is inside."

"I'm on it," he said. "Don't try to be a hero. Kiki, get the heck out of there."

# TWENTY-SEVEN

I went to Minnie and told her what I suspected. She gasped and turned pale. "I . . . I smelled something . . . I didn't stop to think . . . oh, no!" I whispered our plan. She and I and Clancy watched as Johnny worked his way to Ellen Harmon's side. He interrupted her midsentence, taking the microphone and covering it with his hand. He whispered in her ear and pointed to the letters on his shirt.

Ellen was so surprised she temporarily shut up.

Johnny turned to the audience and spoke into the mic. His voice rang with authority. "We need you to leave the building. All of you. We have plenty of time. Just stay calm and walk outside in an orderly fashion. Go through the front doors or the side. Thank you."

Minnie had gone to the front double doors and locked them in the open position.

Clancy worked the side door like a traffic cop. "Keep moving. Stay calm," she said in a no-nonsense voice. "That's right, please keep moving. Come along." The teacher in her kept order with, "No dilly-dallying. Move along."

Ellen Harmon tried to talk, but the noises of people moving were too loud. She opened her mouth to shout, but Johnny slipped a palm over her face. She struggled mightily, fighting him. Finally, she peeled away his hand. She made a grab for the mic, but he reached over and pulled the plug. Her face was red and her voice shrill. "What is the meaning of this? Get back in here everyone! Now!"

The sound of sirens arriving outside drowned her out.

Johnny shook his head and tried to drag her toward the side exit. I continued to wave people toward the front with, "That's right. Stay calm."

I could see the rotating red lights in the street. Walkie-talkies crackled, and more sirens wailed in the distance, becoming louder and louder.

Ellen called Johnny names. She kicked and screamed at him. He kept moving her toward the door. Over the thinning crowd I heard him saying, "So if I'm wrong, you can be mad, okay? And your party will start late. So what?"

Almost everyone was outside. I climbed up on a stool behind the cash counter so I could search for Nettie. She had flattened herself near the far back wall, behind a fixture. Her agitated eyes moved around the room. She spotted me — and it dawned on her what I knew. She pushed open the back door. I hopped off the stool and hit the ground running. I darted around an elderly couple moving slowly out of the building.

Memories of my last encounter with a killer served me well. I knew I needed a weapon. Something, anything. The more unexpected the better. On my way past a set of shelves, I grabbed a spray can.

I was so *not* letting her get away.

Two months ago, a killer had escaped me. Every day since, I lived with fear. One idiot with a grudge against me was enough. I would not spend the rest of my days worrying when and how Nettie might strike back. Nor would I put my child and dog in further danger. This was going to end right here, right now. My conviction made me fast and furious. I ran out the back door, holding the can in one hand. There was no time to call for help.

The sirens had stopped, and I assumed the police were taking care of people in the front of the building. I wasn't sure what they needed to do to make sure we were safe. There was no time to ask for their help. Besides, pointing out shapeless, forgettable Nettie would take too long. She would melt into the crowd or disappear into the surrounding neighborhood.

So I sprinted around the back. Detweiler's plea rang in my ears. He did care about me. I hadn't been fooling myself. As I ran, a warm feeling of hope took seed in my heart. He cared! An overwhelming sadness joined that seed of hope. Why is it always too late? And what did he matter? He was still married.

But I loved him. I knew I did. My thoughts were of him and Anya and Gracie. And that gave me strength.

My feet skidded on gravel. I slid to a halt. Facing me was a dumpster and nothing else. A low retaining wall of concrete blocks rose to cordon off enough space for three cars and the trash bin before making a right turn into the main parking lot. A rickety sign on the wall said, "Employee parking only." I crept my way around the vehicles, listening carefully. Watching the ground for crushed grass or footprints. I moved slowly behind each car. There was no room in front of them. Not much room in between either. Nettie wasn't there.

I crept to the dumpster and squatted on the sparse grass. I leaned down, head brushing the ground to peer underneath the metal box. I could hear heavy breathing. Was it mine? Or hers? I held my breath. Definitely someone was panting.

I rose from my crouch, touching the cold metal for balance. Easing one foot quietly in front of the other, I shifted my weight, rolled my foot, and repeated. I snuck alongside the big green bin. At the next corner, I rested my face against the metal and gripped the edge with one hand. Slowly I craned my neck around the other side, leaning onto my left foot. My body was flat against the dumpster.

"Got you!" Nettie threw her purse strap around my throat. My free hand yanked at it. The leather tightened. I pulled and pulled at it, trying to get enough room to breath, but I did not let go of the spray can.

"You can't stop me, Kiki. They have to die! All of them! They deserve it! They think she was so great! She tricked them! She tricked me! I hate her! And now they're all crying for her. Idiots! They're all idiots!" Nettie maneuvered herself behind me, her knee in my back. My lungs burned for air. Gasping sounds came from my throat. Black edges framed my vision. Stars — and fire in my lungs — and pain. I started to sag, pulling the purse strap tighter as my body weight choked me.

"Tell me . . . about it . . ." I managed. What had saved me before was a killer's need to brag.

Nettie yelled in my ear, her hot breath moist on my skin. I could smell the alcohol and tobacco on her. "She stole my pages and put her name on them! She turned my designs in. My work won the contest! All those hours! All that work! Yvonne Gaynor was a creep! She deserved to die! You want to avenge her? That worthless slut! You're just like the rest of them!" Her spittle landed on my cheek.

"No, not avenge," I managed.

Lack of oxygen made my vision fuzzy. My lungs were screaming, begging for air. I opened my mouth to call out but could only gurgle. In front of the store a policeman with a bullhorn urged people to move across the street while the gas company examined the building. His voice grew faint as he ushered the crowd away from the danger. No one could see us back here. No one would know I was struggling with a killer.

More sirens wailed in the distance. I heard arguing and commotion — and Nettie breathing heavily from fighting me. My free hand clawed at Nettie's fingers. I scratched her good and she loosened up. I got a lungful of air, then two.

I had one chance, just one. It was all dependent on my right hand, and the can I held. I sagged again — this time on purpose — to throw Nettie off balance. But her anger made her strong. I did manage one more gulp of oxygen.

You can do this, I told myself. Stay strong! I squeezed the can lid with my right hand. My eyes felt like they were popping out of my head. I let my weight go to my knees, sagging again, and this time she tumbled with me, rolling over my head. We somersaulted over each other, once, twice. But Nettie didn't turn loose of the purse strap.

We landed with me on the bottom. I wedged my knee between our bodies, bumping her in the groin. For a moment, she eased up. I gulped another small taste of blessed oxygen. Come on, I told myself, you're nearly there!

She yanked the strap, and we flipped over in tandem. Now she gouged me in the gut. She crawled over my body, digging her knees in as she climbed, and got a better purchase on the leather. She pulled back and twisted the strap — hard. It dug into my skin, into the muscles and my neck. I heard myself coughing, gagging. I couldn't give up. Not yet. With my right hand I was working and working the can lid, trying to give my thumb leverage. I squeezed; I pushed. My hand was slick with sweat. I squeezed again. Finally the lid popped off.

But . . . the can slipped from my hand and rolled out of my reach. My lungs hurt. My ribs ached. A sharp pain shot through my side. Suddenly I was tired. I wanted to give up. I wanted to give in. I couldn't fight much longer. I wanted to sleep. To let it all go.

Anya's face came to me. Detweiler's kiss. Gracie's soft muzzle.

I mustered one last surge of strength and bucked my body, pushing up with my feet and arching my back. Once, twice. Nettie fell off me. Bits of gravel and broken glass gouged me. Again, she eased up on the purse strap as she struggled to regain her balance so she could finish me off. Her body stunk of a sour sweat. I twisted and turned, trying to get away. She yanked the strap and began to twist again, turning the purse into a garrote. This was it. I couldn't do any more. I couldn't.

I had to.

Wildly, my arm swept the ground beside me. My fingers stretched and stretched — searching. My arm wiped snow angels in the dirt, back and forth on the gravel, and I tried to roll to the right. All I did was claw up gravel. I felt the grit under my nails.

I couldn't reach the can. I stretched and stretched.

The stars swam in front of my eyes. The dark was closing in. It was all going black.

Anya. Anya! Anya, I love you!

I pushed at Nettie's face with my left hand and again, she loosened her grip for an instant, barely long enough for me to gulp air. This time I smelled the rot of garbage and the thick gross scent of old grease.

I arched my back, planting my feet, and rising again. My searching fingers touched the can. I grabbed it. Nettie was inches from my face. I squeezed my eyes shut. I raised my hand, aimed the nozzle and pressed the button. I heard the hiss of the spray and her voice screaming, "My eyes! My eyes! I can't see!"

A blast of Carolyn's Scrapbook Protectant Spray with the clearly written warning to "avoid contact with eyes and skin" had done its job.

I passed out.

# TWENTY-EIGHT

The rest is pretty fuzzy and maybe I dreamed this, but Detweiler was in the ambulance with me. He wiped the back of his hand across his face. I thought I heard him blow his nose. The EMT stepped aside, and given that opening, he knelt beside the gurney, stroking my hair. He took my hand and kissed my palm and curled my fingers closed to hold the kiss. "You're going to make it," he said in that no-nonsense voice of his. "You have to. We're not done yet, sweetheart. Not by a long shot."

But like I said, maybe it was just a dream.

I woke up to Mert and Sheila arguing. Anya was sitting in a chair in a corner watching them with an anxious expression on her face. The place smelled like burned popcorn and rubbing alcohol. The sheets were so stiff, they hurt like sandpaper. An institutional TV hung from the wall. At my side stood a stainless steel tray and a pole holding a bag of fluid. I figured I was in a hospital, and I was right.

"She's coming home with me, and that's final," said my mother-in-law. Her lipstick was faded and her hair was all askew. Mert didn't look much better, and she was six inches from Sheila's pursed mouth, spoiling for a fight. "No way. I'm taking care of her. I'm not letting her out of my sight."

Anya saw my eyes open. She jumped to my side. "Mom! You're awake!" Very cautiously, she leaned against the bed to kiss me on the cheek. "You're okay. The doc said it would be a good sign if you woke up fast. I was worried about you."

Mert and Sheila stopped arguing long enough to see that I was, indeed, back to the world of the living.

"Great Jehoshaphats. Gosh darn it, girl, you had us scared," Mert's face was creased with worry lines. She was wearing her work uniform. Her mascara was smeared, and she looked tired.

Sheila motioned to Anya. "Call a nurse. Tell them your mom has come around." She paused, "Thank goodness you are all right. Robbie Holmes told me to call him the minute you woke up." She touched my shoulder gently, leaned as if to kiss me, stopped herself, then stepped away and out the door.

"Johnny was beside himself," Mert said in a low voice, patting my hair. "He blamed himself for not watching you closer. He's been miserable as a dog with a double case of pinworms. I'm going to tell him you're right as rain, and I saw it with my own two eyes."

I tried to smile. Talking was difficult. I rasped, "So . . . everyone . . . got . . . out? And . . . Nettie?"

She took my hand and put a cool palm to my forehead. Her skin was rough from work, but her expression tender and caring. "Hold off, Sweet Pea. The doc says your throat's in perty rough shape. That woman nearly strang—" she stopped herself and shivered. She took a quick glance to see if Anya had returned. "Iffen it weren't for you and my baby brother, a whole passel of folks'd be jest little bitty pieces by now." She offered me a sip of water from a glass with a straw. "That stupid Ellen Harmon was a fussing and carrying on to high heavens about you was purposely ruining her get together. But the police done set her straight how you saved her bacon. Believe you me, they was right short with her and her nonsense."

Under her eyes were bags of worry, and her nose was red and chafed. In her expression was a mixture of tension and relief, as though she scarcely dared believe I was all right.

Robbie Holmes came barreling in with Sheila two steps behind. The crisp creases of his uniform matched the sharp intensity of his gaze. "I know you can't talk," he pushed Mert to one side brusquely, "but if you can write, your answers will help us gather evidence to build our case against Mrs. Klasser." A nurse appeared at his elbow.

"Sir, she needs rest. She's had a shock." She scolded him.

"Let . . . me . . . take . . . care . . . of . . . this," I managed. "Then . . . rest."

His cap was tucked under his arm when he handed me a clipboard and a pen. At first, my hand didn't cooperate and the writing instrument rolled onto the faded cotton blanket. Sheila retrieved it and carefully folded my fingers around it. Her hand trembled as she did, and she gave my fingers a small, encouraging squeeze.

"How did you know it was her?" Chief Holmes' face turned quizzical. "Johnny Chambers and Clancy Whitehead told me about the gas leak. What gave it away that

Mrs. Klasser was the murderer?"
This is what I wrote:

Nettie would have known that Yvonne loved orange scones. It would have been easy to mix a little orange baby aspirin into the orange-flavored frosting and reapply it to the pastry — you'd never notice! She could have put the tainted scones out on the table of food while everything was being set up — other scrappers also contributed goodies. Nettie must have snuck her tainted treats past Yvonne and Rena by hiding them inside her Cropper Hopper. There was so much commotion that she just added her offering when no one was watching. She wore gloves at the crop to swap out the Epi-Pen. She and Yvonne had the same allergist — but she lied to me about knowing Yvonne had allergies. Nettie didn't worry about anyone else getting "sick" from her scones because she knew it was a pretty rare allergy — and that Yvonne would make such a pig of herself that no one else would get to eat one! The catalyst: When Yvonne won the contest and her pages appeared on the magazine web site. Nettie realized her "friend" had stolen her work. That was all she had in life — and with the brain lesions she suffered, Nettie didn't have long to live.

He stroked his chin thoughtfully. "You're telling me — and you expect me to believe — that a scrapbook contest was that important? With all due respect, that's the most ridiculous thing I've ever heard."

Anya stepped to the foot of my bed. She lifted her chin and spoke with patient authority. "No, it's not, Chief Holmes. You haven't met these women. Most of them have very busy lives taking care of kids, their husbands, and their homes. Thankless jobs, mostly. You don't know how important a little recognition is. Or how much effort these ladies put into making beautiful pages. And that particular contest has launched a lot of careers. Hasn't it, Mom? So, of course the contest was important."

That was my girl. A bona fide daughter of a scrapbooker. She knew her stuff, and I was proud of her. I nodded. "Ow." That hurt.

Mert put an arm around Anya and added, "That's the long and short of it, Chief Holmes. Jest because something don't seem important to you or your cop buddies don't mean it don't mean the world to someone else. Besides, it weren't just that there contest setting old Nettie off. Mainly, it were all about being betrayed by a friend."

Chief Holmes shook his head. "If you say so. I'd have never guessed this . . . this motive. I've got to hand it to you, Kiki. You are really something."

Sheila's house was a good place to recover. Linnea loved fussing over me, making me soups and purees, plumping my pillows — a service I'd always read about but never experienced. Gracie and I had our normal "guest" room, but I suspected Sheila now considered it ours because she purchased a dog bed and water bowl that matched the room's décor. While I was healing, the whole world trooped through my bedroom doors.

Dodie stopped by to tell me how much she appreciated me solving the mystery and redeeming the good name of the store. Ellen's lawyer advised her to apologize to us and she did, publicly. Scrapbookers were showing up at Time in a Bottle in droves, praising me for saving lives and wanting "the straight scoop." The newspaper was full of how Minnie, Johnny, Clancy, and I managed to evacuate Memories First without incident. Dodie also shared her own news — Horace accepted a job in Chicago and would be commuting. I asked about the lump in her breast, but she evaded my question with all the finesse of a bull in the streets of Pamplona. Frankly, I didn't have the energy to press the issue. My body was covered with bruises, one of my ribs was cracked, and my throat muscles hurt whenever I talked.

She grinned. "Well, sunshine. I'm planning on your new celebrity status counteracting all that bad P.R. that Ellen heaped on us."

Bama came by with a basket full of how-to books. She also brought me a calligraphy kit and coached me in making the letters. The secret is letting the pen turn in your hand. Who'd have guessed? Clancy came by several times. She brought me a book on tape she thought I'd like. It was about an amateur sleuth, and she handed it over with a warning, "Don't get any bright ideas. That sure was a close call."

Ben Novak sent a dozen pink roses. He brought me a book on the history of St. Louis and joined me in a dinner Linnea made for us — and Sheila orchestrated. We ate off trays by candlelight although he joked that he'd checked all the water heaters first. He had steak, and I had soup and other slimy food designed to put minimal stress on my throat. I was embarrassed to think how bad I must have looked. Sheila refused me a hand mirror, and she covered the mirror in my bathroom, so I knew it couldn't be good. I could feel how puffy my face was and I imagined a lurid purple and green necklace of bruises around my neck. Ben's expression was not one of disgust, but of admiration. "I can't believe you. This is the second time you've managed to outwit a killer. I mean, I understand about adrenaline, but that — that woman — outweighs you by sixty pounds at least. She had the advantage."

"No . . . I have Anya."

He shook his head. "You are amazing."

I tried to shrug but it hurt too much. Muscles I'd never met were issuing formal complaints. I said, "A child changes everything." And I thought someday I might tell him exactly how my child changed my life's journey.

"Sheila told me about the rental house in Webster Groves. The owner is Leighton Haversham, an author and a friend of my father's. Turns out, Leigh has a pug and another pet that occasionally need babysitting while their master is on book tours. If you are interested, the monthly rent can be reduced in return for being on call to watch

Petunia and Monroe." Ben named a negoti-
ated rental fee.

"Petunia?" I whispered. "Monroe?"

Ben laughed. "Can you believe it? And
Petunia is a he who's scared spitless of his
own shadow. That's one reason Leigh
doesn't like to leave poor Petunia at the ken-
nel. He comes back sick . . . as a dog.
Monroe is a donkey. I guess it's hard to find
someone to come over and feed Monroe. Is
it a deal?"

As if on cue, Gracie ambled over to stare
at my guest. Tentatively, he patted at her,
and she leaned against him, before putting
her head on the side of my bed. Ben smiled
an uneasy smile. Lord knows, the man was
trying hard. And Gracie is a good judge of
character. She liked him even if he was
unsure about her.

I was thrilled about the author's offer. It
put the converted garage within my budget.
All I needed now was deposit money, which
I could repay Sheila over time. Ben enter-
tained me with snippets about a program
he heard on NPR and an article he read in
the *New York Times*. I liked hearing how his
mind worked, and how big his world was.

As he was leaving, Ben kissed my forehead, and then leaned closer, his lips brushing mine. It wasn't a kiss so much as a

promise. "I'll be back. I don't want to tire you out, and we have all the time in the world."

Or not, given my ability to attract murderers.

I should have been delirious with joy. But I wasn't. I felt mildly depressed.

Johnny stopped in with a bouquet of white daisies mixed with orange, red, pink, and yellow zinnias. He'd taken Clancy to Riverport once they'd gotten word I was all right. I didn't mind at all. It was silly for him to waste the tickets — and given his limited resources, that was a lot of money. He talked a mile a minute about the evacuation, Ellen's wild accusations, the crowd's initial angry rumblings, and finally their appreciation.

"I can't ever forgive myself for not keeping an eye on you. I was so focused on helping everyone else. Mert liked to kill me. And I feel like a real dope that you got hurt. If I'd caught up with that hag before the police did, well . . ." And he stopped.

I was left wondering exactly what he might have done. My best friend and her brother both displayed alarming propensities for retribution, a trait I needed to consider more carefully at a future date.

On the other hand, Johnny's killer instincts

for tracking down moles pleased Sheila to no end. She kept a tally of dead furry bodies with permanent marker on the new scoreboard in her garage. Mr. Sanchez decided to stay on in Mexico indefinitely, clearing the way for Johnny to care for Sheila's yard in addition to his regular job. "I need to repay Sis for her help with my legal fees from before. The money's real helpful, and there's a lot to be done here to get it prettified. A whole lot, if you catch my drift."

No doubt. Sheila had pretty much torn up every inch of her grass with her mole removal antics.

"Listen to this. I found two adult toys planted out there in the lawn! I asked Mrs. Lowenstein about them, and she told me the craziest story." He rubbed his eyes. "It's awful hard to credit."

He too kissed me when he left.

I know I should have been thrilled. Not one, but two available men were vying for my attention. I was going to move into a nice house in a better neighborhood. TinaB was back to ringing up sales. Bama seemed to have forgiven me.

But mainly I was sad.

I stayed at Sheila's house for a week. I appreciated the visitors, I really did, but I missed more keenly the visitor who didn't come. The last time I'd suffered trauma like this, Detweiler had been there, sitting beside me for hours. I knew this was for the best, but still . . . the ache in my heart hurt more than my neck, shoulder, and ribs put together.

And broken hearts can take forever to mend.

# Epilogue

I was leading Gracie into the store when a woman hopped out of a Subaru and ran toward me. The hairs rose on the back of my neck and my stomach fluttered. Gracie froze, her ears pricked in alert. The killer I'd tracked down was still free, and who knew but that Nettie Klasser had relatives vowing to avenge her? Around my dog's neck, a ruff of angry fur stood *en garde.* A low growl rumbled deep in her chest.

But a second look told me I had nothing to fear.

It was Brenda Detweiler. She was as rangy as I recalled, and she wore a baseball cap, a golf shirt and jeans, and a clunky pair of Reeboks. Her gait, her awkward walk, was more like that of an adolescent boy than a grown woman.

"We need to talk," she said, crossing her arms over her flat chest.

I hesitated.

The back door of the store swung open. Dodie appeared there, with a trash bag in hand. She saw us and stopped.

I sighed and tried to step around Detweiler's wife. "Not today."

"You don't know the whole story," she stepped closer, using her body to intimidate me. I noticed her hands were balled into tight fists. Her T-shirt bore a softball league logo, and her jeans were worn and faded. She spoke more loudly. "I said we need to talk."

"Please . . . not now." I wasn't up to a quarrel.

Dodie took one look at my expression, Gracie's wary demeanor, and yelled to me, "Kiki? You need help?"

Brenda passed me, letting her shoulder bump me hard as she moved on. A referee would have called foul, personal contact. "There's more to this than you know. I'm telling you —" she hissed, "he misses you."

I walked away.

I missed him, too.

# AUTHOR'S NOTE

On Sunday, March 8, 2009, a man opened fire in a church in Maryland, Illinois. He had been fighting mental illness caused by the bite of a tick infected with Lyme disease. According to the news media, the shooter had taken a variety of medications for the problem, and had developed brain lesions.

# ACKNOWLEDGMENTS

The idea for the Scrapbook Stars is based loosely on many scrapbook contests, but the one closest to my heart is "The Best of British Scrapbooking Contest." I founded it in 2004, and it is now administered by Rosie Waddicor and the terrific folks at *ScrapBook inspirations Magazine.* Visit them at http://www.scrapbookinspirationsmagazine.co.uk.

Kiki and I invite you to bring your family to St. Louis, the gateway to great times and memorable moments. We have so much to offer! Check it out at http://www.explorestlouis.com. The Missouri Botanical Garden is more magnificent than I described in this book. Learn more at http://www.mobot.org. The Science Center is a terrific free attraction that will amaze you and your kids — and in the summer they do hold camps. Visit them at http://www.slsc.org. Opera Theatre of St. Louis continues to create "magic on the Missis-

sippi." Their website is http://www
.operastl.org. And no trip to St. Louis would
be complete without stopping at Ted Drewes
Frozen Custard (www.teddrewes.com).

The whole Archivers' ScrapFest 2008
Team gets big hugs for their help and
enthusiasm in launching *Paper, Scissors,
Death,* the first book in the Kiki Lowenstein
Scrap-N-Craft Mystery Series. If you
haven't been to ScrapFest, you're missing a
massive party (go to archiversonline.com).
Tina Hui of Snapfish, Lara Starr of Mrs.
Grossman's Stickers, Katey Franceschini of
ANW Crestwood, and Doug Dvorak of the
St. Louis Convention and Visitors Commission have been incredibly generous with
their support of this series. Mary Anne
Walters and Fi Whittington at UK Scrappers (ukscrappers.co.uk) put together a
super all-mystery virtual crop weekend to
tell my UK friends about Kiki Lowenstein.

Jenn Malzone helps me with contests and
email lists. Her dad Gerry Malzone is my
graphics go-to guy. Karen DiGasbarro
kindly proofed galleys. Pat Sonnett is my
queen. Hugs to my best pal, the incompa-
rable Shirley Damsgaard, author of the
Ophelia and Abby series, for being on
speed-dial. "Casey Daniels" (author of the
Pepper Martin series) contributed stories

about her dog Oscar, who became Guy in this book.

Scott Creech from Critter Control has been killing moles in our yard for years. He was very generous with his information, and he's the guy who caught eight hundred moles in one year! And yes, there really is a donkey in St. Louis named Monroe.

Kari Murphy was kind enough to loan me her beautiful harlequin Great Dane, Orion, as my stand in for Gracie. Robert George of Robert George Studio and his colleague Martin Schweig were very patient with Orion and me. Okay, Orion was a super-model and I was . . . a problem.

Congratulations to Merry Morrison, Raquel V. Reyes, and Mardi Hamilton who won character naming contests. Stacy Czech won the Scrapbooker's Dream Weekend in St. Louis and brought her pal Marla Lenzen.

Special thanks to my sisters Jane Campbell and Margaret Campbell-Hutts for looking after me when I needed help last summer.

As always, I am grateful for the support of my wonderful husband, David Slan, a guy whose logical mind is the perfect complement to my more "out there" thinking.

Want more Kiki? I know you do! To see samples of her projects, visit my website:

www.joannaslan.com. Sign up there to receive the free quarterly online magazine I share with Kiki. In the magazine we offer contests, freebies, and lots of terrific craft ideas. You'll find recipes such as Hoosier Daddy Kidney Bean Salad and Snicker-doodles on my website, as well as book club and trivia questions.

I love hearing from you, so email me at joannaslan@aol.com. Please put "I read your book" in the subject line so I know you aren't scamming me (I'm just as gullible as Kiki). And finally, if you want to keep up with all things Kiki and receive journaling prompts to help you keep a record of your life, follow me on twitter. Go to www.twitter.com/joannaslan.

Thank you for sharing Kiki and Company with your friends!

Joanna

# ABOUT THE AUTHOR

**Joanna Campbell Slan** is the author of *Paper, Scissors, Death,* the first book in the Kiki Lowenstein Scrap-N-Craft Mystery Series, and an Agatha nominee for Best First Novel. An internationally recognized celebrity in the world of scrapbooking, she's the founder of "The Best of British Scrapbooking Contest" as well as the author of seven technique books on the subject. Joanna is a frequent contributor to the *Chicken Soup for the Soul* Series, and her work appears in a variety of other anthologies. With their son off to college, Joanna and her husband David share their home with two dogs: Victoria, a bichon, and Rafferty, a rescued bichon-poodle mix. Visit her website www.joannaslan.com for more information on writing and scrapbooking, as well as book club and trivia questions about Kiki Lowenstein and her friends. Follow Joanna on Twitter at www.twitter.com/

joannaslan and at her blog http://
joannaslan.blogspot.com.

We hope you have enjoyed this Large Print book. Other Thorndike, Wheeler, Kennebec, and Chivers Press Large Print books are available at your library or directly from the publishers.

For information about current and upcoming titles, please call or write, without obligation, to:

Publisher
Thorndike Press
295 Kennedy Memorial Drive
Waterville, ME 04901
Tel. (800) 223-1244

or visit our Web site at:

http://gale.cengage.com/thorndike

OR

Chivers Large Print
published by BBC Audiobooks Ltd
St James House, The Square
Lower Bristol Road
Bath BA2 3SB
England
Tel. +44(0) 800 136919
email: bbcaudiobooks@bbc.co.uk
www.bbcaudiobooks.co.uk

All our Large Print titles are designed for easy reading, and all our books are made to last.